THE LOST PULSE

FROM FOUND IN TIME AUTHOR

J.K. KELLY

Disclaimer

This is a work of fiction. Names, characters, scenes, and incidents either are the product of the author's imagination or are used fictitiously, and any resemblance to actual persons, living or deceased, is entirely coincidental.

ISBN: 978-0-9994099-4-7 (paperback)

ISBN: 978-0-9994099-5-4 (ebook)

Published by:

JK Kelly Consulting LLC

P.O. Box B

Media, PA USA 19063

Jk.kellyconsulting@gmail.com

JKKelly.com

The Lost Pulse is dedicated to the courageous men and women who have risked their lives to protect the innocent and continue to do so.

CHAPTER 1

MONTANA, CURRENT TIME

"You know I love it here," Michelle said. Her brother nodded and looked back to the landscape they were driving through. The beautiful aspens, the orange leaves, and the blue sky above that surrounded them. "Tommy, there's something I want to throw at you before I talk to JJ about it."

Maybe the painkillers were doing their job, numbing his senses, because he didn't respond. The raid on Camp David had taken place weeks ago, but to him it felt like yesterday. The stealth tactics used by the terrorists, who bled an odorless nerve agent into the air to neutralize the guards at one checkpoint and then another and then the next, had worked flawlessly. With the use of sound-suppressed weapons, snipers, and night vision goggles, the highly trained invaders held the advantage, this time. With amazing speed and numbers, the terrorists quickly gained ground and within minutes had silently overtaken nearly every one of the Presidential retreat's security systems and guards.

This new breed of terrorist had implemented their version of shock and awe and used it almost to perfection.

Nearly sixty invaders had gotten closer and closer to the President of the United States without detection. Luckily, there happened to be a very special group of Marines with him that night.

Inside the retreat's Aspen cabin, a joyful reunion had been taking place. Four U.S. Marines, then Major Jim "JJ" Jackson, Captain Tommy Wilson and Sergeant Christy White had recently been rescued after being stranded for three years in a Middle Eastern desert. The fourth, Sergeant Omar Sharif, had headed home to Michigan to be reunited with his own family.

An incredible life-saving mission had gone horribly wrong. Years before this, Jackson had been handpicked by then Chairman of the Joint Chiefs, Marine General Richard Stewart, to assemble two small teams and test a new, top secret technology that had been developed by the Department of Defense.

The Black Ops Time Machine program, using the acronym BOTM and nicknamed "Bottom," wasn't a machine at all. It incorporated small pulse devices worn around the necks of six participants who would form a ring. Once geographic coordinates and landing dates and times were programmed in at their secret operations hangar at Andrews AFB, the operatives were able to go back in time.

Initially Team One, T1, led by Jackson, had gone on simple missions to test the technology and themselves while the Joint Chiefs at the Pentagon, who had originally scoffed at what they thought was science fiction, discussed how best to use this new weapon or if they would use it at all. The night of that fateful journey, Jackson, Tommy's brother-in-law, had disobeyed direct orders and taken the special operators on a very risky rescue mission. He went to the

Garden of Gethsemane, to ask the most amazing man that had ever walked the earth, a man of miracles, to save his wife Michelle from the illness that was slowly but surely killing her. Learning of the insubordination while the time travelers were still in the past, Army General Robert Brooks and his aide, Army Captain Josh Scott, sabotaged the technology and left the T1 team stranded.

It took three years for the equipment to be repaired and T2 could be sent on search-and-rescue missions to find the six missing operatives. Only the four would be found alive. Roman soldiers had killed Marine Lieutenant Freddie Jones and Navy Corpsman Bennie Abrams, and left their bodies in the desert.

After Stewart became President and uncovered the details of the compromised mission, he made sure every attempt to recreate the technology was made and after many attempts, the T2 search-and-rescue mission had found the survivors and returned them home. Stewart refused Brooks and Scott a trial, declared them guilty and sentenced them to solitary confinement at Camp Delta, Guantanamo Bay, Cuba. Their sudden absence from the Pentagon was attributed to their being on a highly classified overseas assignment.

In the time Jackson and his team had been MIA, missing in Black Ops action, much had happened. Michelle's doctors had been astounded by her miraculous recovery from cancer. Stewart, once retired from the military, campaigned for the most powerful position on the planet and after his only true rival in the election died in what appeared to be a freak accident in his suite at a plush Washington hotel, he was elected in a sweep of all fifty states. Running on the pledge to eliminate domestic crime and international terrorism, using any and all means at his disposal within the law, he had surprisingly won the support of conservatives and liberals alike. Stewart was charismatic, authentic, had impeccable credentials, and was the type of real leader the tired and weary country, and the world for that matter, wanted desperately.

Within a few days of T1's rescue, after choosing to remain in modern day Jerusalem to acclimate back into the current time, the team was snapped back to reality by an attack on Stewart's motorcade in Washington. Hours later they were flying home to Andrews AFB on a military aircraft. It was time to get back to work.

Stewart had survived the bomb attack, but a concussion and three broken ribs had slowed his mind and body. While the public had been led to believe that he was resting well in the safety of the White House residence, Stewart was actually recuperating at Camp David. The size of the assault on the Camp by the terrorists had taken everyone there by surprise and the raiders had gotten so close to the President's cabin that Stewart, Jackson, and their wives had been forced to bear arms and take on their attackers alongside the T1 Marines. Only a handful of Secret Service agents survived the night, and the First Lady collapsed and died of heart failure.

After her funeral at Arlington, Stewart returned to the White House with Jackson at his side. Michelle and Tommy had both resisted doctor's orders but eventually agreed it best to return to the Wilson family ranch in Wyoming, near Yellowstone, to heal physically and mentally. It would also give them time to spend together, since they'd been separated for many years.

"Tommy, you awake over there?"

Suddenly five deer darted across the narrow road in front of their car. They left her no way around them. Michelle slammed on the brakes and slid to a stop, but the car following them swerved and slid off the road.

Michelle jumped out of her car and ran to check on the other driver. "You okay?" she called out to him. She peered through the driver's window and saw a cellphone resting in the teenage boy's lap. The screen glowed blue with text bubbles.

"You were texting?" she gasped. She was aware of Tommy moving slowly toward her, one hand pressed to the side of his body where the stitches were. "I got this, Tommy!"

Michelle opened the driver's door and pulled the frightened teenager out from behind the wheel. If the near accident hadn't scared him enough, now it looked like a crazy woman was going to give him a good beating. She grabbed the phone and threw it as far as she could into the woods. "Now go find it. You could have been killed! You could have killed us! You know that?" She blew out a breath. Was she overreacting? Maybe, but she didn't care. Next time the kid might think twice before distracting himself while driving.

Minutes later, on the road again, she continued their conversation as if nothing had happened. "Remember the time I joked that you and JJ shouldn't be having all the fun?"

Tommy shook his head. "I'm just surprised that little prick had a damn signal way out here."

"Tommy, I'm being serious. At Camp David something happened inside me. All of a sudden, I wasn't in seek-shelter mode or even protection mode. I was pissed off. In *kill* mode. Maybe that's why I'm here. Maybe Mom and Dad named me after Michael the Archangel for a reason."

Tommy, and JJ for that matter, had left her time after time to go after terrorists, she assumed. They could not talk about their missions. All she could do was watch them walk into harm's way. It was only fair now, when she felt called to action, that they respect her decision and support her.

"I think," she said, "I'm going to join the Army and become a Ranger."

Tommy turned his head and gave her a look, wondering if she was joking. He didn't ask.

"I thought we might sell the ranch, or lease it to the government. President Stewart can use it as a getaway. He did say he loved it out here." They looked at each other, and it was clear they were keeping it. "Anyway, I guess we'll need somewhere to hang out and get old once we've killed off all the bad guys." He laughed. "You do know that was sexist."

After a while, her brother looked at her again. "So, you're going to put off making me an uncle?"

"You know I can't have kids, Tommy."

"Well adoption worked for Mom and Dad otherwise I wouldn't be here."

She remained focused on the road. It was true; she had wanted to be a mother. But this…this stirred something in her that was more important than anything else.

"You haven't even hinted to JJ about any of this?" he asked.

She shook her head. "Not yet."

"But a freakin' Ranger?"

She couldn't help grinning. "Yep. You know I'm more of a mountain girl. Not into watersports all that much. I'll leave that to the Seals."

"When you tell him, I'm not sure whether I want to be there or on the other side of the world," he said as he focused back on the view. He laughed then clutched his side. "Damn stitches." And they drove on toward the Wilson Ranch.

CAMP DELTA, GUANTANAMO BAY NAVAL BASE, CUBA

News of the hurricane headed their way had caused the Navy, and the Marines guarding the Camp, to prepare for the worst. Reports of extreme high winds, heavy rain, and potential flooding meant the focus would be slightly shifted. With twenty-four hours before the projected landfall, the Marines went from protecting themselves and their prisoners to preparing for a natural disaster. Despite the warnings from NOAA, the only sign of the trouble to come were amassing heavy gray clouds. The moon was long gone, and the air grew still: the calm before the storm.

The guard towers were fully staffed and the foot patrols along the fence and shorelines continued. Suddenly, Marine guards dressed in their standard camouflage fatigues began to drop like wet rags. Those who saw it happen lost consciousness before they could muster a sound or reach for the alarm.

Employing the same tactics the enemy had used at Camp David, at least fifty highly trained, terrorist killing machines had now besieged Camp Delta, bent on destroying the infidels and freeing their comrades so they could fight another day.

Highly toxic nerve gas grenades had been fired to within a few feet of the Marines as they watched from their posts. Silenced assault rifles took out the guards. With the same timing and precision with which Jackson and his team had eliminated the SS guards at the bunker in Berlin, this enemy executed nearly sixty Americans in a matter of seconds. JJ's speech to his new White House staff had been dead on. This enemy, this animal, would be one that kept him up at night. They were like junkyard dogs on energy drinks and they were trained as effectively as the U.S. Military.

Minutes after the terrorists entered the grounds of Camp Delta, they rushed about opening all the detention cells. Most of the prisoners had been sound asleep or deep into the delirium of having been water-boarded relentlessly and kept in isolation for more than fifteen years. The assault proceeded quickly and as planned. No time for hesitation. Decisions about captives made in seconds.

"This one is gone," one operative said to another.

"Send him home," was the response.

Any prisoner unable to fight, or of no value, was shot in the head without a second thought. There was no time for baggage. The psychological effect of raiding America's controversial base at Guantanamo, freeing some of the scariest and most dangerous terrorists the U.S. had ever captured, would be immense. The jihad needed a shot of adrenaline, a boost to their recruitment drive. It would further embolden lone-wolf perpetrators bent on killing innocents. It would also show many, not just military and law enforcement men and women, but ordinary civilians around the world, a glimpse of what was to come.

"What about these two?" another attacker asked of his leader. He pointed to two white men dressed in orange jumpsuits, who sat on their beds staring at them, trying to grasp what was happening.

The sight of these two prisoners brought the leader up short. They were so different from the others they had come to free. He thought to himself perhaps they were Americans who were there for treason or some other crime against the United States.

"Do you love your President Stewart?" he asked, the words in English feeling awkward in his mouth.

"Fuck him!" the taller one shouted.

"Yeah," the other echoed.

"Free them, turn them loose," he said decisively in his own language. "If they are here they are enemies of America. Let them go so they can continue their mission."

With that, the terrorists turned and went on to the next cell and then the next. Within ten minutes they were gone.

Bodies of executed inmates, deemed to be of no use to the cause, lay in their bunks or on the floor. As the two cellmates peered down the quiet hallway they realized this was their chance at freedom.

"Let's get the hell out of here, Scott," the one called Brooks said, his voice getting stronger with every word.

His companion followed without a word but, as they stepped over fallen Marines who had kept them in isolation, he reached down and removed two side arms and a radio. Within minutes, the two prisoners, American Army officers who had been secretly sentenced to serve time at GITMO for treason, for lying to the President, and abandoning five Marines and a Navy corpsman back in time, disappeared into the night.

CHAPTER 2

ANDREWS AIR FORCE BASE, MARYLAND

Colonel Jackson's staff had been performing flawlessly. As the Director of the newly formed National Security Office with authority over all security agencies in the U.S., Jackson had access to every bit of intelligence and the ability to initiate any mission he deemed necessary to assure the security of the country. He would only answer to the President, Defense Secretary Petty, and his Maker.

His team had fully embraced their leader's mission statement and was enjoying their new freedom to seek and destroy without the restrictions they and generations before them had previously been forced to operate under. Despite their objections, after invoking elements of the War Powers Act, Congressional committees accustomed to cost and operational oversight were left without recourse. Once President Stewart had empowered Jackson's NSO to eliminate all threats to the American way of life, both foreign and domestic, they ran with it with great success. At an 0700 post-op debrief, Jackson shared his enthusiasm as he summarized their most recent BOTM mission.

"Just as planned, and thanks to the incredible intelligence the CIA and the Air Force provided us, T1 was able to appear in the center of what the shitheads, I mean our targets, thought was a safe house. Standing in their pulse ring circle, on arrival, these six were able to take aim and hit the five terrorists in two seconds. There was no time for the bastards to react; they were dead quicker than a sneeze.

Captain Buchanan, do you have anything to add? Maybe a bit more color?"

Buchanan quickly obliged. "The mission was executed perfectly. It was flawless and the expression on the only face that managed to see us was priceless. The dipshit was walking into the living room with a bottle of Diet Pepsi in each hand."

The intelligence gathered about the room, the house, and the remote location in Yemen had been spot on. The team had set up a practice house inside the hangar at Andrews. It was laid out exactly like the target, reproducing the same size, shape, and positioning of the computer desks, chairs, television, windows, front door, toilet, and kitchen entrance. In preparation for the mission T1 had used the BOTM technology to practice the entry and exit. There would be only three feet between the weapons the operators would have pointed at the terrorists' heads on arrival.

"One thing we didn't take into consideration. What if any of those assholes had rolled their chairs back to stretch, or got up to take a dump? We would have landed on them and that would have made things a bit trickier."

One of the operators joked, "Talk about shitting yourself! They would have."

Jackson and the rest enjoyed the humor. Even in the toughest of times a well-placed joke or the perfect one-liner caused them to take a breath, and that helped calm the nerves a bit.

"Anything more?" Jackson asked, wanting to hear every detail.

"Well, sir," Buchanan continued, "the dude with the sodas definitely shit himself, and the drinks left his hands at the same time my Sig put one in his forehead. The other four desk jockeys each took a close-range shot to the back of their heads and then all five received a second tap just in case there was the slightest glimmer of light left in their evil asses."

With that remark, the operators in the briefing room exchanged high fives and this mission, scoring another big one for good over evil, was a complete success.

"We spent the next three minutes grabbing their laptops or hard drives and whatever documents were left on their desks. Two of us checked the rest of the house and it was empty just as the CIA boys and girls promised. Ten seconds later we had huddled up, grabbed the ten shell casings off the floor, formed the ring and headed home."

One operator corrected Buchanan's statement. "Sir, you left out that one of the casings took a bit longer to find. Turned out my guy fell out of his chair and landed on one. Had to pull it out of his brain soufflé. Other than that, as long as the intel is as great as we think it is, I'd give the op a perfect 10, sir."

Everyone in the room was beaming with pride for the success of the tightest close-range insertion the group had ever tried.

Marine Captain Mike Buchanan was enjoying being the lead on T1. Ever since his first mission, when his group had been able to gather career-ending intel on President Stewart's only real rival in the last election, he had embraced the new time travel technology. Once he traveled to the Garden to rescue Jackson and the three others who had survived in such a strange world, he was addicted. If he and his team could travel back into time, whether it was an hour earlier or one hundred years back, they were game.

As long as the objective was black and white, cut and dried, killing bad guys, and he was safe from prosecution, Buchanan was relentless.

"Best part of that op was—we recovered all the intel those dead asses had. Hard drives, cellphones, credit cards and messages—they'll all be invaluable to us. The only things the local police or their shithead friends will find are five rotting corpses, each with double-tap headshots. Funny thing is, whoever finds them will see they were all facing the center of the room when they got their brains infiltrated. It won't make any sense to them." Buchanan was proud and so was his team.

White stood up and gave Buchanan a hard high-five. "Awesome," she said, smiling at Jackson. She turned and fist bumped or slapped the four other T1 members who had taken that trip.

This had been their method. Gain the intel, thanks to the unrestricted and relentless pursuit by all law enforcement and intelligence services, and then use it to either eliminate the enemy outright, plant bugs that could be retrieved on a later visit, or leave something behind that would cause the targets to wonder if their partners in crime were plotting against them or working with the police.

Considering how many operations needed to occur, undermining the mindsets of the terrorists and criminals would result in them doing themselves in, saving time and bullets for the BOTM teams.

They messed with a drug cartel in Mexico that, in turn, caused a civil war at every level of the cocaine business. Distribution from the Arizona border all the way through Central America to Columbia and beyond was disrupted.

The most intriguing operations, one performed by T1 and the other by T2, involved Moscow and Peking. In order to keep the leaders of those two powerful nuclear countries busy looking over their own shoulders, the Black Ops planted bugs and incriminating documents, and sent erroneous communications, all done from within the most private offices of those men. At White's suggestion, they even left the wrapper of a condom in one of the leaders' bathroom trash cans just before his wife returned home from a dinner with some of her friends. The leader might have been a tough guy and one of the most powerful men in the world, but his beautiful blonde bride wasn't a pushover. They had met at the old KGB, and over half of the country's political and military decision makers were her relatives. It was a crude ploy, but effective. With the furor behind the walls at the Kremlin, worrying about what America and terrorists were up to was left for another time.

After another twenty minutes of jokes mixed in with another review of the operation, Jackson told everyone he wanted them to take a few days off. There were some very interesting ops being planned and he wanted them rested and relaxed so they could engage again on Monday morning.

"Last thing," Jackson said, causing everyone who had headed for the door to stop dead. "My wife Michelle and Tommy Wilson, Captain Wilson, are driving in from Montana and will be here sometime tomorrow. If anyone's interested in welcoming them home let me know. We haven't all been out together for a while and we'll make Wilson buy if that helps influence your decisions."

Christy White's expression said it all. She had not seen or even heard from Wilson since the day he went on R&R after the Camp David assault. She wasn't sure if this was good news or not.

They waited for everyone to leave the briefing room and White closed the door so they could speak in private. "JJ, the one thing I would never want to do is compromise the team or complicate things," she offered. Her team leader and frequent arm-wrestling opponent listened attentively. "I let myself start to feel something for the first time in a very long while back in the desert with Tommy. I thought we would wind up running around ancient Greece and Italy after resigning myself to the thought that we would never make it home. But then we were rescued and our whole world changed in a matter of a few days. We were home, Michelle was healthy, General Stewart was now POTUS, Camp David got torn up, and Tommy got shot. The fact that I didn't hear from him while he was out west makes me think he feels the same way I do. That we can't be any closer if we're going to continue to serve on the same team." JJ stepped closer and put his arm on her shoulder.

"That's the tough part about doing what we do. Whether it's military or law enforcement it's tough to focus a hundred and ten percent on your job if you're looking out for someone even more than we normally do for your team members."

She knew what he was saying. She was a professional just like Tommy and the rest of them. If he was coming back east to rejoin the BOTM program then they'd either have to go back to arm-wrestling and busting on each other, or one of them would have to transfer out.

"I know what this all means, JJ," she said with frustration. "Maybe I need to go back to the Raiders. You told me that would be my option. We'll just chalk up what we were headed for in Israel to what it was and get back to killing bad guys."

JJ nodded that he understood what she was saying. "Smart girl. Tommy's on a personal crusade anyway so you two would have crashed and burned at some point. But don't think about moving back to Cali, at least not yet."

He laughed and said, "I did have one recreational trip laid out on the wish list that you would be very much a part of. You can take it as a reward for all you have done for the team and the Corps and the country."

Her curiosity got the best of her. "Mykonos, you're taking us to the islands!" she said, assuming she had guessed it right. JJ laughed.

"Tommy owes you that one, or at least he did." Jackson shook his head, realizing he shouldn't have said that. "Nope, more like 120 miles south and 208 years back in time." White thought for a minute and asked for another clue. "I'll bet you a nickel you won't guess it." Jackson paused for a moment. "Doing what we do is tough on relationships. Hell, I met and married Michelle and then got lost in the desert and came home only to be separated again when duty called. It's like a deployment that will never end. Sometimes I—"

Suddenly Buchanan knocked and then quickly opened the door. "Colonel, there's been an incident at GITMO!" Jackson and White tensed. "It appears terrorists used the same nerve gas and tactics like on the Camp David assault and went after Camp Delta. Of the Marine guard on watch at the time, there were no survivors. All detainees are dead or missing."

Jackson delivered a powerful martial arts kick to the

refrigerator door, virtually destroying the appliance in an instant. "Mother fuckers," he shouted. "I need to call the President, and you need to get ready to go. We have to get down there before the assault started and be ready for those assholes."

"Sir, yes, sir," Buchanan responded and left the room to prep for the mission.

"What about Brooks and Scott?" White asked.

"Oh shit," he whispered.

Within two minutes he was able to reach his friend and mentor, his Commander in Chief, in the Oval Office. Stewart put the call on speaker so Petty, the Secretary of Defense, could participate in the call.

"This is unbelievable," Stewart said in anger. "How the hell did they get the drop on us not just once but twice? That's over a hundred dead Americans as a result. On top of that, two treasonous bastards aren't accounted for. They don't deserve the term MIA."

Jackson was quiet. So much so that Stewart asked if he was still on the line. "Yes, I'm still here, sir. You don't get the drop on Marines like this. You don't get the drop on the Secret Service either. This is strange Mr. President."

There was a long pause before anyone responded.

"Meaning?" Stewart asked.

"I wonder if we have a mole. With Brooks and Scott locked up just before the Camp David assault occurred and now the raid on Camp Delta and they're nowhere to be found." Stewart let the thought sink in.

"Could be JJ," Stewart responded. "If you want to use BOTM to snoop around at the White House or anywhere else you have the authority and assets to do so. Keep us informed."

"I'll get a team on it right away," JJ replied. "Right after that I plan to send T1 and T2 down to GITMO so they arrive about twenty minutes before the attack took place and do what we can to stop it." Another long pause made Jackson wonder why there wasn't any response or comment from either of the men in the Oval Office.

"Stand down, Colonel," Petty said softly. "The President was called to the Situation Room and I need to follow him. We've got a thousand fires to work on this morning. This one complicated things exponentially."

Jackson bit his tongue. "To clarify, Mr. Secretary, stand down on trying to catch another mole or the BOTM trip to GITMO?"

Petty cleared his throat and hesitated as if searching for the right words. "You can't go to GITMO, President's orders." Jackson was exasperated but before he could say a word in protest Petty said soberly, "Believe it or not, the next of kin notifications have already begun. The media has caught wind of what's happened in Cuba. There's no changing things now."

Jackson took a moment to consider any other options, but it was clear a trip back in time to alter the outcome of the attack was not one of them.

"Permission to come to the White House for follow-up, sir," Jackson asked.

"JJ, take a breath," Petty advised. "Work this. Find out what happened. Find out if there's a connection between this and Brooks and Scott. If they, or others, are moles, find them." Petty sighed. "I know you, JJ, I know how passionate you are about your fellow Marines and about protecting people. It'll be tough, but you can't deliver shock and awe on your own, not on this one. " He paused. "Listen, we'll sort this out, JJ. But first, we'll put all embassies, consulates, government and military facilities, federal prisons, courthouses, and law enforcement agencies on high alert. These animals have been using the cover of darkness to get close enough to strike so we'll address that behavior with countermeasures immediately. We got the actors who shot things up at Camp David, but it will take some time to track these bastards."

"But, sir—"

"No arguments. When the time is right we'll make the moves needed to avenge what just happened in Cuba."

JJ knew Petty and Stewart were right. He took a breath, shaking his head as the refrigerator door finally fell to the floor with a loud crash.

Petty laughed. "Not sure what you just killed there, but let me remind you of one thing, Colonel Jackson."

"What's that, sir?"

"Absolutely, under no circumstances, are you to go rogue in any way, shape, or form. No more Garden adventures unless they're ordered by POTUS."

Jackson took a moment and thought back to that night, 2,000 years back. "Sir, yes, sir," he responded and then signed off.

He walked out into the hallway and looked at White. "Well? What now?" she asked. "I mean, if we can't stop it from happening…"

"Right. We've lost those men. And, no more gardens, he says. But I don't recall any gardens at Guantanamo, do you?"

"No, sir, I sure don't."

"Right. So I'm thinking, it might be a good idea if we get down there and at least see if we can track those bastards as they leave the compound."

CHAPTER 3

What should have been a joyful and celebratory reunion was anything but. Michelle greeted JJ with a hug that seemed to last and last, while Wilson stood behind her with fire in his eyes.

"I can't believe this happened," Michelle whispered as she backed away to look into her husband's face and try to read what he was thinking. She was still unaware of the capability of the BOTM program. She didn't even know it existed. Regardless, she knew her men were laser focused on finding those who had killed their Marines and exacting vengeance on them.

"Where's Bunker?" JJ asked, surprised he hadn't been pounced on by their black German shepherd.

As Michelle walked around their new apartment, inspecting what had been a man cave until her arrival, she laughed and reminded JJ that the dog was full grown and accustomed to the open spaces of the family ranch back in Montana.

"She loves it out there. This little box is no place for that girl," she said, hoping the news wouldn't make her husband's day any worse.

"That's cool," he responded. "We've been wide open since our world changed and what's best for her is okay with me." He thought for a few seconds. "We'll get another dog, only maybe something smaller this time."

She didn't have the heart to tell him what she had decided about serving her country. Now would be the worst time to drop that bomb.

"Let's let you and Mad Dog Wilson here go seek and destroy those assholes from Cuba," she said sternly.

The men carried the boxes from the car to the living room while Michelle looked to unpack the basic necessities. As the two Marines made trip after trip to the car their sole focus was developing a plan of attack.

"Petty might have told *you* not to go but he didn't say shit about me, now did he?" Wilson said. "I can go down there with five others. We could alert the guards at GITMO and totally overwhelm the bastards before they get off a shot."

Jackson lifted the last box from the trunk and slammed the lid down. For the next fifteen minutes the two discussed and then argued about the situation.

"We didn't go back to any of the schools to prevent those massacres, just like we didn't stop the hijacking, "JJ said with frustration.

There were certain things they couldn't do, and Wilson knew it. There weren't enough pulse devices or hours in a lifetime to go back in time and fix everything they would have liked to. "Complicated" was the political and practical reasoning behind it. That didn't mean he accepted it.

Their conversation ended as both men considered the dozens of lives lost in the GITMO assault. Rather than ha a few beers and further torment themselves over what they couldn't prevent, they turned in for the night.

Wilson stared at the ceiling from his spot on the sofa. "Complicated, my ass," he whispered and after a few restless moments finally fell asleep.

The next morning the men drove to the BOTM hangar at Andrews and left Michelle to reconnect with some of her old friends. Once Colonel Jackson finished his T1 briefing and reiterated the sole purpose of the post-assault mission to GITMO, he left for the Pentagon to meet with Secretary Petty. An hour later, while he addressed a meeting of the Joint Chiefs of Staff, Captain Wilson put his plan into action.

"Stand down," he ordered the lone Army Ranger just as the team had formed their six-operator circle and prepared to activate their pulse devices. "Stand down, Sergeant, that's an order from Colonel Jackson. I've got more hours in this program than all of you combined. He wants me to go along for this ride."

It seemed out of the ordinary, but everyone knew of the tight bond between Jackson and Wilson, and nobody had ever been given reason not to follow their orders. Plus, Wilson outranked them all.

"Dim the lights to darkness, please," Captain Buchanan called out.

Ten seconds later, counting down 3-2-1, the team of three Marines and three Navy Seals were gone.

There was no moonlight. The air was still. Only the … of the waves behind them broke the silence. In the … ow from the high-security detention center at … up the sky like a ballgame being played under … Seals headed for the beach to plant tracking devices on the Zodiac boats the terrorists had used to access the area. The rest of the small team spread out as Buchanan slid over to Wilson without either of them taking their eyes off the camp. They both flipped up their night vision goggles.

"Orders, my ass," Buchanan whispered.

Wilson smirked and was relieved to hear his friend's support. "They're coming."

A dozen men dressed in black ran toward the team, stopping every now and then to help some of the detainees who couldn't keep up. "We can't just let them go, can we?" Wilson whispered into his communication microphone.

Buchanan knew this was going to go bad. Even if Wilson could hold back his trigger finger, he had just lit up the other operators' anger. How could any of them just watch as the murderers of so many Marines ran past their position?

"Do not engage," Buchanan whispered urgently into his mic. "Repeat, do not engage! That is an order!"

One of the others responded, "I think there's something wrong with my weapon, sir. The trigger seems to have a mind of its own. Sir."

It was clear the shit was going to hit the fan. These men had never openly disobeyed an order before. Buchanan hoped they wouldn't lose sight of the big picture.

"If we do this right, we can track these assholes and find out who knows what from them. The Marines who died here tonight knew they were in harm's way. They knew what they'd signed up for and were willing to take those risks. We might be able to save thousands if the intel trail pays off. Stop fucking with me on this. I know it sucks but *do not engage*!"

As he watched the assassins continue their escape, he realized Wilson had moved away from his position.

One hundred yards to the east, Wilson had lost sight

the team and the terrorists. He was hunting for something to engage. Nothing would be lost if his prey walked toward him and he took the shot in self-defense.

"Get him back here now," Jackson yelled into the phone after BOTM control had alerted him that the mission was not going as planned. "God damn it," he said knowing there was nothing that could be done now but wait.

A time travel team could not be recalled. They could only return when all six of the pulse devices formed their tight circle and activated a return to their launch site. Andrews would serve as a homing beacon, giving the travelers the only return address they had.

Luckily, Jackson's briefing with the Joint Chiefs had ended and he was headed back to Andrews in his black government Suburban. *This isn't good,* he thought to himself. *Tommy's always been right on the edge. He might have finally gone over.*

Heightened security at the Air Force base main entrance added to his frustration. Every facility was considered a target. Anyone standing out in the open, checking identification and for weapons or devices meant to cause casualties and destruction, was also a target. Jackson got it. He was living it.

Once at the BOTM hangar, all he could do was wait. But that went against everything he'd been trained to do. He had a daunting job in front of him. The President had ked him with finding and killing all enemies of the United reign and domestic. And so, he had handpicked ll the military, law enforcement, CIA, and at rosters that had been made available to had selected weren't just the smartest or the most loyal to the country; he selected those, like him and his original T1 and T2 Black Ops teams, who would do whatever they could to achieve their objectives and would fit in.

But what he didn't need were rogue players. That had been his role to play, and it often came with deadly consequences. In the past, looking the other way to let the right things happen had been okay in his book. But putting someone else's anger or interests in front of the objective was no longer acceptable. He was managing intelligence and espionage efforts, but he was also holding the reins on what were essentially trained killers, all working for the country's safety. And that was a sensitive and tricky job.

He had often thought to himself, *how can you tell a highly trained killer it's okay to kill this bad guy but not that one*?

Luckily, ninety-nine percent of the time his people knew it was okay to take the shot. And today, once he got to the hangar, all he could do was wait.

White was there. Just as she had watched her friend Jones go after the Roman guards in Jerusalem so far and long ago, she had been forced to watch as Tommy Wilson told her he had to do this. Their reunion in one of the offices had been awkward. But jokes and the shared feeling that what they were doing was bigger than their own interests allowed them to hug it out and move forward as the closest of friends but nothing more. Despite her words to the contrary, she still hurt inside.

"They're back!" the technician shouted into the Colonel's office door.

Jackson jumped from his chair and ran down the hall. White and a dozen uniformed men and women were huddled around the T1 team as they attended to someone sprawled on the floor.

"Medic!" someone yelled. "I said, medic! *Now*, for God's sake."

Jackson stepped in closer, and saw people working feverishly to save a fallen comrade. The Marine had suffered a devastating gunshot wound to the head at close range. "Tommy," Jackson whispered. He knew immediately there was no hope of surviving it. He had seen damage like that many times before in Iraq and Afghanistan. The only thing anyone could do was follow protocol: administer CPR while others tried to stop the bleeding. They were not in a position to transport him to the trauma center. They needed to do whatever they could there on the floor.

A 911 call had been made and an ambulance siren could be heard heading their way. Jackson knew Wilson was gone. He had given Adolf Hitler a very similar wound in Berlin. There was no coming back for his best friend and brother-in-law. The solemnity of the moment, with these brave warriors standing and kneeling beside the fallen, clashed with the rushed movements and shouting of the military EMTs who were striving to get to their patient.

"Stand down," Jackson ordered. His voice was strong and direct, but the expression on his face was one of pain and intense sorrow. Realizing they had stepped into something out of the ordinary, realizing the CPR and other efforts clearly were not going to help, everyone moved back and waited for someone to give the next directive.

White had come in behind Jackson and she had known
nt from the look on her Tommy's face that his end
brant eyes had lost their luster. Quietly she
vel from the EMT's open bag, stepped in
riend and knelt to cover his face.

One of the emergency responders whispered to a T1 Marine operative, "What the hell happened here?"

Jackson locked down his emotions and snapped to attention. Everyone in the room followed and, on his orders, saluted Major Thomas Wilson, KIA.

Moments later, Jackson turned to the EMTs. "Major Wilson was shot on an anti-terrorism mission. Please transport him to the hospital. I will notify his next of kin." Jackson looked across the room at Buchanan. "Let's get everything stowed and then meet me in the briefing room in ten minutes."

Buchanan acknowledged and waited until Wilson's body was placed on the stretcher and removed before instructing the team and support staff to clean up the area and themselves and meet at 0700 the next morning in the briefing room.

"Remember this, like all of our missions, is top secret. That means no talk, no text, no nothing regarding what happened here tonight."

Jackson followed the stretcher bearing his friend out to the ambulance but didn't realize White had come along behind him. They both snapped to attention and saluted as the ambulance doors were closed. Neither moved until the flashing red lights were turned off and the vehicle slowly drove away.

"Do you want me to go with you to tell Michelle?" she asked.

It was there and then that Jackson was shaken to his core. He had seen death and destruction on every corner of the earth. He had fought for his country in the most dangerous parts of the world. His historic mission to ask Christ to help his sick wife had cost Jones and Abrams their lives. He'd lost his parents, lost Mathew and then Elizabeth Stewart, and almost lost the President, twice. He and Michelle had been apart much more than they had been together, and he feared the distance between them would eventually bring their marriage to an end. Now he would have to tell his wife, Wilson's sister, that her brother was dead.

His best friend was gone now and only two people on this earth were now close to his heart—Michelle and President Stewart. Jackson couldn't believe what had just happened but, as he stood outside the hangar, he looked up at the stars and was reminded of those thousand nights spent on the other side of the earth, so many of them alongside his buddy Tommy.

"Mother fucker," he muttered, and looked over at White.

She shook her head as tears flowed down her cheeks. They both knew Wilson was someone who would, one day, go after something that would come back to bite him. This time, disobeying a direct order had cost him his life and Jackson would need to find out exactly what happened. He turned and gave White a bear hug that lasted a long minute. It was uncharacteristic of him to make contact with one of his Marines like this, but the two of them had been through heaven and hell together. It was what they both needed before focusing on what had to be done.

"What I don't understand, JJ, is how the pulse ring worked if Tommy was," White paused, "If he was already gone."

Jackson looked back up at the stars and nodded as if he understood.

"I think his heart had just that much left in it to get him and the rest of them home." He looked away from her and shook his head in disbelief.

"It must have. He was the toughest SOB I ever met."

Ten minutes later in the briefing room, Buchanan laid it out for them.

"As reported, Wilson pulled Ranger Ley off the ring, grabbed his pulse, and stood in. The fury in his eyes told me this was going to end badly, but he outranked me, Colonel, so there was little any of us could do to stop him."

Jackson shook his head and asked the T1 team leader to continue.

"We got on the beach at the spot where the actors came ashore in Zodiacs. We placed tracking on the boat engines and on a few of the backpacks they had left behind. We were surprised the dipshits didn't leave anyone to watch their stuff. It wasn't but a few minutes later, as we spread out, that we saw them coming back to their boats. They were all in black, but the detainees were still in their bright orange jumpsuits."

Jackson appreciated the detail but wanted to cut to the chase and find out how his friend was killed. Buchanan understood Jackson's look and got to it. "As reported, one minute Wilson was right with us. Then, in a blink, he was gone. I left the other four where they could watch the escapees, and I headed off in the only direction Wilson could have gone—through the tall dunes. About a minute later I heard two gunshots. They were almost simultaneous. I stayed low and went toward the sound. I found Wilson and a detainee lying close to each other. Two of T1 came up behind me, having responded to the gunfire. The other two remained at the beach to watch the boats leave and to guard our six."

White sounded frustrated. "What the hell happened?" she demanded.

Buchanan looked at Jackson and then to White. "I know this is a tough situation, Marine, but let's remember where you are on the food chain."

Buchanan outranked her and the rebuff snapped her back to reality. She was a Marine, the first female Marine Raider, but rank was rank and she was out of place.

"Sir, yes, sir."

Buchanan continued. "I was attending to Wilson while they checked the detainee and verified he was dead. He had a 220 in his hand. It appears he and Wilson almost ran into each other in the dark. But the detainee's gun hadn't been fired. Wilson clearly had shot the jumpsuit but someone else shot Wilson. We recognized the dead escapee. It was Major Scott."

Jackson was startled. Scott and Brooks were the two who had left him and the T1 team stranded in the desert all those years ago. Wilson had wanted revenge all along. When the opportunity came and he learned that these two had escaped from GITMO, he clearly pounced on the chance to put a bullet in one of them.

"Was there any sign of General Brooks?" Jackson demanded. "Where the hell was Brooks in all of this?"

To Buchanan it was obvious. Wilson had been lucky enough to encounter Scott, but his luck had run out when Brooks saw it all happen and shot Wilson.

Yes, it all made sense now. The man who had betrayed these Marines and lied to the President of the United States was now armed and running loose somewhere in Cuba. Brooks' co-conspirator Scott was dead and being eaten by sand crabs and seagulls at this point. But they needed to find Brooks, and fast. He knew too much. And now he was a killer with nothing to lose.

"We'll formalize a plan in the morning," Jackson said. "We'll track that bastard down." He looked at White and gave her a nod. "For now, we have to go notify my wife that her brother has been killed in action."

An hour later, a grieving sister was drained of all emotion. Michelle had no more tears to shed. She went into the bedroom to hold the Bible her father had given her, the one JJ had read from and gave him the inspiration to go to Gethsemane. Her emotions ran from shock and disbelief to acceptance and sadness. She knew her brother better than anyone. She'd known that someday, somewhere, a bullet would find him.

In the kitchen, White and Jackson leaned against the countertops, drinking coffee and thinking about their friend. They had gone quiet for a long ten minutes before White offered a thought.

"We can go back and get him, JJ," she said softly to her commanding officer.

"We can pulse up, take some shithead brain dead prisoner back with us, swap the guy for Tommy and bring him back here before he ever left the beach."

Jackson had already thought of that and ten other scenarios. He was remembering all the talks he had had over the years with his general, and now President, Stewart. He'd told White that if one person was given a special chance, a special gift, like seeing their child or their mother's face one time before they died, then every parent or child should be given the same opportunity. Stewart could have gone back to see his Marine son Mathew a few days before he was killed in Afghanistan. He could have watched from afar as his son sat quietly and played a board game with his buddies. But he'd opted not to. "If I got to do that, he'd said, every parent or spouse should be given that same chance. Since they can't, I won't do it. What's done is done," Stewart used to say.

"But he let you go back to Gethsemane to save Michelle so why wouldn't he let us do this?" she asked. "If he didn't want to see his kid one last time that's on him but if we have a shot, just like we went off and disobeyed orders to meet Jesus, why not take it?"

Jackson thought for a second and the answer was very clear to him. "I disobeyed orders a few times in my life," he said sternly. "First off, Stewart didn't know we were going to Gethsemane. That's on me and always will be. Saving Michelle got Jones and Abrams killed and got us stuck in the damn desert for three years. Remember? Tommy disobeyed a direct order, and he's dead because of it. No, we aren't using the pulse to save Tommy, and that's it! We didn't kill Hitler before he went ape shit. We never went off and took out Idi Amin before he killed millions either. Certain things happen for a reason. We can't play God. We can't change everything."

"What are you saying, JJ?" Michelle shouted as she walked into the kitchen.

Her eyes were red, her face pale from all the emotion of the evening. "Are you saying you *could* save Tommy if you wanted to?"

Jackson looked at White and knew he was screwed. Their top secret mission had been exposed to his wife, and he had no idea what was going to happen next.

CHAPTER 4

Months after the funeral in Montana, where Tommy Wilson was laid to rest alongside his adoptive parents, everything in Jackson's world had changed. As he sat at the bar nursing another beer, he thought back to all that had taken place in such a short period of time. The photos and drawings of the American military's proud accomplishments decorated the walls around him, but there would never be any commemorating the Black Ops Time Machine program he led.

He thought back to the meeting in the White House between his wife and the President.

"Michelle, again I can't tell you how sorry I am that Major Wilson, Tommy, is gone."

The President's words brought her no comfort. She now understood her miraculous recovery, how the BOTM program allowed six heartbeats at a time to go back in time on missions, and how both the President and her now estranged husband refused to let her save her brother.

She debated Stewart face to face, at times nose to nose, over his refusal to send a team back to prevent his death. The President looked at Jackson as a second son and at Michelle as the daughter he and Elizabeth never had. He would give her a very wide berth. As long as she didn't threaten to go public with their top secret technology, he intended to let her vent until she was spent. He let her say anything and everything, until she was left with no words, just a sad expression of heartbreak.

Jackson thought back to the last time he'd seen Michelle. It was the day after the discussion in the Oval Office.

He stood silently in their apartment as she closed her last suitcase, threw him her keys, and slammed the door behind her. They had been physically apart and, with every twist and turn in their marriage, they had grown further and further emotionally apart. But they had never talked about it, until now.

Michelle had loved the fact that her husband and brother did everything they could to find and destroy evildoers in the world. But now her spirit was gone and any thought of joining the Army was too. No matter how they'd argued or reasoned with her, one fact remained. The two most powerful men in her world had refused to perform a simple task, to go on a mission to save her brother's life. For that, neither could ever be forgiven.

But their secret was safe with her. She had been saved as a result of one extraordinary mission. And now she was starting out fresh, on a new course, hoping to pay that gift forward somehow. There was nothing left for her in Montana other than memories and three graves. The family was all dead and buried. Her Bunker, the German shepherd brought back from World War II Berlin, was living a happy life on her cousin's ranch. Michelle needed to go nomad for a time and figure things out.

"Where do you think you'll go?" Jackson had asked her just before the door closed behind her.

"I have no idea. But it will be far away from anything political or military, I can tell you that!" She'd given him a look. "Who knows, maybe I'll go back to Jerusalem or give Italy a try. Tommy told me how much he loved it there. Maybe I'll find a new home overlooking the Mediterranean. For now, I'm not sure. Good luck saving the world, JJ," she said sadly.

The next morning, shaking off the few cobwebs the beer had left behind, Jackson looked at himself in the mirror as he prepared to leave for his office. There had been more activity from terrorists around the world in recent weeks. A cluster bomb had exploded at a public gathering of fifty or so men and women, creating panic not just in the United States but also around the world.

There were just so many who were intent on violence. Over the years they had been able to infiltrate and imbed in so many areas. It was clear to most in the intelligence sectors that individuals and families had settled into workplaces and neighborhoods in cities all around the world, dating as far back as twenty or more years ago. These imbedded terrorists raised or converted more of the same. They were instructed to lay low and wait to be called. Already there was thought to be an army of them spread across the homeland and this was just the beginning of what may come. Ready to rise up and attack from within. 9/11 had been only the first phase of what they had planned for America and the free world.

In other cases, terrorists simply walked across open borders. They had been laying low like sleeper cells but now were in full attack mode and had disrupted everyone's sense of normalcy. Every Sunday since the start of the New Year, an attack took place somewhere in the world. As a preventative measure, the Super Bowl in Miami was postponed a week and then played on a Monday night. People took note of the Sunday pattern. They stopped going to church on Sundays. Events were cancelled and eventually began to take place on any other day but Sunday.

The attacks were vicious and brutal, caught on video and streamed around the world. The horrific images continued to panic the innocents of the world while Jackson's NSO and the warriors of the U.S. Armed Forces and intelligence services, and their counterparts on other continents, planned defensive and offensive operations. Assaults overwhelmed local, state, and federal law enforcement. The military in many countries had been tasked with finding and crushing them. Governments strained to balance civil rights with an overwhelming desire to use any method available to stem the assaults and crush their perpetrators.

There was even discussion of shutting down the internet to stop the spread of speculation, rumor, violent images, panic, and outrage. But the horror was being transmitted via satellites orbiting over every hemisphere, making the images near impossible to control. Some satellites had been put into orbit by enemy countries or private corporations. Intelligence agencies knew where they were located, and consideration to strike them was still on the table. The question of bad actors gaining control of this ultimate medium was most troubling.

For all to see, terrorists had swarmed a soccer game being broadcast live in the UK. After an hour of explosive vests detonating and automatic weapons fire by the good and by the evil, forty-six terrorists were left dead in their tracks but that number paled in comparison to the eighty-two law enforcement and over three hundred civilian deaths.

The terrorists seemed to realize that while their own efforts would cause great destruction, for whatever cause they followed, it was the sheer panic of the crowds that injured or killed the most. Chaos was their real weapon of choice.

On another Sunday, this time in Beijing, tourists and locals visiting and working near the sprawling palace and grounds of the Forbidden City came under attack. The large number of Chinese military guards normally stationed in the area was irrelevant. These terrorists, willing to accept their fate, did as much damage as possible before each and every one of them was stopped.

In the United States, President Stewart encouraged people to be vigilant. People still needed to go to work, kids to school, entertainment and sporting events were encouraged to continue although under great security and greater vigilance. In an address to the nation, carried live around the world, Stewart challenged the motives of the evildoers and encouraged people to carry on. Maintaining a sense of optimism, that the terrorists had not and would not win, was crucial.

"My fellow Americans and to peaceful people all around the world," he said, "We've known for decades that there is evil in the world and living here among us. Some are foreign born, some have been born here and as such they are American citizens. Theirs is a fanaticism that encourages, no commands, that they kill what we are to them – the infidels. There are also evildoers that are just criminals, plain and simple. They've now gotten caught up in the madness or are taking advantage of it. Where the fanatics were often lone wolves, these other animals have felt a strength in numbers and have adopted a very dangerous pack mentality. They rarely seem to have a political agenda. They are just angry and have decided to lash out in a very dangerous manner. Let me assure you right here and now, that as of this moment, we will do everything in my power to take down these animals using whatever means possible."

He paused during the speech long enough for his words to sink in. The sounds of people cheering could be heard in cities all across the United States, much like the night Obama had announced the killing of Osama Bin Laden.

"My words and future actions will be regarded by some as harsh or politically incorrect but in a time of war, which we are now waging, I have little time for their concerns. We are going to put a stop to this madness and push evil as far back into the darkness as is humanly possible. Remember my friends, be vigilant and look out for one another. If you have the ability to protect yourself and others then do so. For our enemies, remember these words. We are coming for you and the gloves are coming off. Good night, and may God protect the United States of America."

People in the United States and around the world were stunned but that quickly turned to hope and inspiration. Luckily, some of the perpetrators most brazen attempts were total failures and that helped fuel the optimism that they could be defeated.

The most notable took place at the Golden Globe movie and television awards in Los Angeles. The streets in front of the Beverly Hilton Hotel were blocked off using city or county operated dump trucks filled with sand. It was thought they were impenetrable and had become the standard used at big events in the U.S. and around the world. Near the perimeter and at the checkpoint where limousines carrying famous actors, directors, writers, and producers passed through security, improperly parked cars were quickly removed. Ramp trucks dropped their thirty-foot-long aluminum ramps to a 45-degree angle. After the operator connected a massive hook and cable to the car or truck it would be slowly dragged onto the ramp and towed away to an impound area. Santa Monica and Wilshire Boulevards, and three side streets, were closed off.

The terrorists thought they had it perfectly timed. Ramp trucks, hijacked by terrorists posing as tow truck operators, set their ramps to 45 degrees and in an instant two black motocross type motorcycles, their exhausts heavily muffled, followed by a black four-wheel-drive jeep approached the ramp and in an instant were up and over the sand-laden barriers. On landing, while the intent may have been to speed between the limousines and detonate whenever they felt opportunity was at its peak, sharpshooters from the Secret Service took the bikes down in mid-air. They had been watching the area and once they noticed the tow trucks had been parked toward the security barriers rather than parallel to them, it was on.

It was like a hunter shooting skeet. These law enforcement agents had spent a good bit of time practicing hitting moving targets. In the blink of an eye it was over. The jeeps fell short of their targets, either misjudging the speed needed or failing to reach it. In all, only three bystanders were injured in the attempt and the only fatalities were the four bike riders and the two jeep drivers. From that day on, law enforcement agreed they would be in charge of operating ramp trucks or any vehicle capable of delivering a ramp of any kind.

Two hours after Jackson and Stewart, who had been

broadcast in the residence at the White House, ent, and the distance around the White House ced or buildings with bollards was set back feet. The show, despite the best attempts of the Mayor of Los Angeles, went on two hours late but it went on with one change to the schedule. The event, broadcast live around the world, began with the playing of the National Anthem and a prayer delivered by one of the celebrities who happened to also be a minister. People were scared but they showed no interest in quitting. If anything, the majority refused to become sheep and wanted to push back.

In Rome, three weeks before the customary Easter Sunday Mass at the Vatican, rumors began to spread that the Pope was considering postponing the service. Stewart was traveling to a NATO summit in Zurich that Sunday afternoon and intended to visit the Pope before returning home to the United States. Jackson and Petty accompanied him and, on the long overseas flight, the three of them sat somberly in the large conference room hoping a steak dinner and a few cigars might give them all a break from the intensity of the world below them.

A replay of the Super Bowl game was on the flat screen television but it was barely noticed. After the drinks were refilled and the shrimp cocktail plates removed, the most powerful men in America tried to keep the conversation light.

"I can remember standing beside Tommy Wilson a long time ago at Andrews and laughing that before I died I wanted to party on Air Force One, but I had no idea one day I'd be sitting on this big bird getting ready to tear into a filet mignon," Jackson said with a laugh.

Then his mood changed. He was happy to be there but

wished his buddy was sitting alongside him. He missed their friendly arguments about the merits of scotch versus beer. He missed him badly. Petty smiled, but Stewart was deep in thought and ignored the comment. It didn't take long for reality to snap them back to attention. As an aide knocked and then entered the room, she recommended they turn on CNN. The terrorists had launched another attack and this time it was in Paris.

"Breaking news," the commentator stated as the familiar notification tone sounded behind his words. "Another cluster attack by violent radicals, this time at the Louvre in Paris. Early reports as video is starting to come in are that at least one hundred tourists are dead, countless are injured, and the fifty or more bomb-wearing terrorists are all dead."

"Sons of bitches," Stewart shouted at the television screen as he stood and walked closer to see the videos as they began to play.

Petty and Jackson stood alongside him and watched. Most people, those who used to stand and take cellphone videos of car crashes and attacks, would no longer risk it. When the shots and explosions rang out people panicked, turned and ran. Only a few who felt safe from their vantage points managed to keep their wits and their cameras rolling.

People tripped over each other, stumbled over obstacles, ran screaming in hope they would find safety while others dropped dead in their tracks. As an elderly man turned to help his wife he was also killed. The videos showed the police and military stationed on-site had acted heroically in an attempt to stop the violence and capture a terrorist before the timed explosives eliminated any chance of capture.

"Turn it off!" Stewart shouted. He'd had enough.

""JJ, you need to come up with something. I've given

you every possible resource available including a goddamned time machine. You've got to figure out a way of stopping this madness or at least getting us the intelligence to combat it."

Jackson knew his friend was venting but couldn't help feeling he'd let his President, his country down.

Turning to Petty, the President launched another attack. "Damn it, Secretary Petty, you need to get those damn lab coats out in the desert to make us more pulse devices. We need hundreds, no, thousands of the damn things!" Petty began to respond but was cut off. "I know what you are going to tell me but know this—if some little old Italian woman could play with meteors and UFO garbage out in the desert and come up with the technology then you goddamned better be able to kick them in the butt and get them to find more material and put it to work for us!" Petty and Stewart had already had this discussion a dozen times before. The President was referring to Doctor Andrea Moretti, the scientist who had created the first pulse device. "And if our American scientists can't get it done then perhaps it's time we ask some of our allies to work with us on this."

Jackson walked back to his place at the table and took a long draw of his beer. "Mr. President, our people at Area 51 have been working this since the time we were lost in the desert. We've even used BOTM to go back and plant bugs in Doc Moretti's lab so we could watch and listen in on everything she did in developing the technology."

Stewart, still frustrated, wasn't looking for excuses or explanations. "JJ, if she could do it, we can do it!"

Jackson knew Stewart long and well enough to know this discussion needed to be put off for a few hours. Everyone needed a chance to breathe and come back to the table. "Mr. President, from everything we have seen and heard, she had access to tons of material that crashed to the earth. I believe there was one rock in particular that caught her attention, and she used every ounce of it to make up the twelve pulse devices we have in use today. One rock, one very special rock, and it's now been reduced to twelve small pieces."

Stewart considered the statement and nodded. "Okay, JJ, let's say there's no way we can get more operatives in action using the BOTM program. How can we put what we do have to better use?" Jackson looked at Petty and let the Secretary join in.

"Mr. President, since the cluster attacks became more frequent, we've been cycling 48 Special Ops on back-to-back missions. The pulse devices are being taken off six necks and then they're placed on six fresh ones and they're off to another mission. When they return they are switched out again. Basically the devices are on nonstop service. They just return to the hangar at Andrews long enough for a pit stop to change operators."

Stewart appeared pleased to hear his team had the technology on nonstop mode.

"But," Jackson added, "we are concerned about the devices themselves. The operators are all Marine Raiders, Army Special Forces, Navy Seals, and CIA and FBI techs who can take whatever we throw at them and ask for more. But the devices themselves—"

Petty stepped in. "The devices are showing wear. They are heating up as they are used more and more often. We're not sure what this means or if we may be at risk of losing any of them."

Stewart realized what Petty was saying. There was a chance the devices might fail. There had been no degradation of the material at that point, but they were in strange waters now. If any of the pulses failed it could leave a team stranded somewhere back in the past, under who knows what circumstances. It was a 50/50 shot that if there was a failure it would be at home at Andrews or somewhere in the midst of evil, but the military warriors and their civilian counterparts had, so far, been willing to take the risk.

"So, I am assuming you've slowed down the activity and allowed them to cool?"

Jackson acknowledged, "Yes, sir, but try telling six of our best to stand down while something's supposed to cool off. That goes over like a strip club that just ran out of dollar bills." Finally something had been said to break the tension in the room. Jackson saw the change and continued. "We haven't given up on any idea and we won't until these fuckers are all lying dead!"

Stewart nodded and as their steak dinners were placed in front of them uttered, "Oorah!"

Back at Andrews Air Force base in Maryland, where just hours ago Air Force One had taken off, for a group of six warriors things had just gone very wrong.

"What the fuck did you just do?" Marine Captain Christy White screamed at the airman. "What the fuck did you do?"

The airman grabbed for the pulse devices but White knocked past him as the rest of the team grabbed for them as well. The airman had heard about the heat buildup in the pulse devices and, without asking anyone, had taken them from each returning operator and placed them in a small bowl of water he had placed on a desk. One pulse in particular had become so hot that it had burned one of the operators as they arrived back at Andrews. As he released them into the water everyone heard ominous sounds. Quickly pulling them from the bowl, White discovered her worst fears were true. Each pulse device had shattered from the quick temperature change.

White dropped her pulse back into the water and threw the airman up against the wall. The rage in her eyes scared him and rightfully so. She was the first female Marine Raider, a trained killer with her bare hands, and for fun had beaten eighty percent of the men she challenged to arm-wrestling matches. The others on her team quickly separated her from her victim. While three Marines shuffled her to the briefing room to attempt to calm her down, another made sure the airman wasn't injured. Airman Nicholson was shaken up but okay and was ordered to return to his barracks until further notice.

The sixth Marine, Omar Sharif, the team member who had accompanied White, Jackson, Jones, Wilson, and Abrams on their extraordinary mission to Gethsemane, looked at the technicians and saw the shock on their faces. "Fix this shit if you can and get that damn water out of here!"

Within an hour, with the six devices deemed useless, White called her team leader aboard Air Force One, but the call immediately went to voicemail. She hung up and considered her options. She grabbed her cell and sent him a text.

Hours later, in the hastily arranged meeting at NATO headquarters in Brussels, the leaders of the free world and their military commanders met. The beautiful building that had been opened just recently featured walls of tall windows that let in bright sunshine and showed openness to its members and the world. The twenty-nine flags of the member nations blew straight with the winds pushing in from the east, but all of that was lost on the President and the other attendees.

They were hustled down into the depths of the building's underground bunkers, into windowless rooms that assured not just safety but focus on the only subject that mattered—terrorists, their tactics, and a winning battle plan. After a very brief exchange of pleasantries everyone took their seats and prepared to hear from the President of the United States. A travel-weary, war-torn Stewart showed he had little time for bureaucratic customs but sat patiently while the NATO President gave a rather long welcome address. Finally, it was his turn at the podium.

"Ladies and gentlemen," he began. "Rather than talk about what's happened and express our shared indignation and sadness for these inhuman acts, I want to make a few suggestions and then get back to Washington." The attendees were surprised by Stewart's directness but the room went silent and all eyes were on the President.

"Regardless of your own beliefs, whether you be right or left, Christian or atheist, pacifist or devil dog, or anywhere in between, it is safe to say that we are now bearing witness first-hand to a good versus evil battle that has been building since God and Satan went to war."

Various members of the group attempted to be recognized and be heard, but Stewart gestured for calm and sat down to finish what he had to say.

"I know that many of you, your political rivals, and your citizens were somewhat outraged at the speech I gave a short time ago. But I needed to give a very frank diagnosis of the problem and prescribe the only medicine I believe exists that can challenge this latest disease." He paused and looked around the room, making eye contact with every person sitting at the table.

"In my judgment, what we are seeing today is going to get worse before it gets better. My suggestion to all of you is that you get your sharpies and erasers out and start wiping some of the civil rights and due processes out of your constitutions so law enforcement, the military, and your intelligence services are free to wage war on these evil bastards in a manner that will eradicate them and anyone even leaning their way. You can fill your prisons and feed them forever or send them back to hell, that's for you to decide. Make it happen as part of a short-term declaration of war, if you need to but you are going to have to act quickly and your actions will have to be swift and as hard as a hammer's blow. These animals are carriers of a disease called pure evil and they need to be put down."

Jackson wanted to smile and give Petty a high-five, but both men knew to sit quietly and let their leader do his thing.

The French Prime Minister had other plans but before he could be recognized Stewart had a few more thoughts to share. "I'm going to give the floor to my dear friend André but you have to wait for my big finish."

Stewart went on to state that, in addition to what he'd just suggested, he felt the member countries should allow their citizens to purchase handguns, rifles, and shotguns to help defend their lives and property and support the cause.

Jackson got up and walked to the coffee tray. He didn't need caffeine. He wanted to be able to gauge the reactions on the dozens of faces in the room. Not the leaders' faces but their chiefs of staff and defense ministers. It was clear some were in full agreement with the President while others seemed outraged. In particular, the Prime Minister of Great Britain seemed unhappy. He had been seated beside the Frenchman and stood up to his right, in an attempt to interrupt Stewart, who wasn't having any of it.

"Most of you know me and know my country very well. In contrast, I believe some of your countrymen and women look at the United States as the Wild West they saw in movies growing up. You know we are not that way, but in reaction to the massive surge in violence I think it is prudent to encourage the people who have guns to protect themselves and the neighbors who do not."

Looking directly at his friend from Great Britain, he continued, "To this day I cannot imagine how despite all that it going on, ninety percent of the policemen and women in London go on patrol unarmed. It is a cultural difference that exists between us but remember this. During World War II, who did the European countries look to for help? Did they want us to send food and water? No, they wanted our land, sea, and air power. They wanted the armed forces of the United States. In retrospect, just like in post-war Japan, Germany and others, laws were put into effect that restricted not just guns but armies. It made sense at the time but we live in a different world now. You all know that and I would suggest that if you agree with me that you use the persuasive skills and talents that got you elected to get some sort of message across, one that works for your citizens.

"Let me tell you a quick story," Stewart said, "and then I'll shut up and hand the floor to anyone that wants it." Stewart was highly respected among his peers at the table. In some cases, they agreed with what he was now saying but would not be able to say it aloud.

"A few weeks ago, while Americans who refused to give in

to fear gathered at Lambeau Field in Wisconsin, something incredible happened. Over sixty thousand people braved the 20-degree cold. That's minus six centigrade for my European friends. They attended an American football playoff game. Wisconsin's one of our northern states and it sits in the upper central part of our country just below the Canadian border. Those people are tough, rugged, and patriotic. They love their Green Bay Packers football as much as they love their hunting and their country.

"Two men wearing what appeared to be overly large coats were walking toward the huge crowd waiting to get to the metal detectors at the stadium security checkpoint. The bombers were wearing newly purchased bulky team coats and gloves. Luckily, they walked past five tailgaters who intended to pre-game and then watch from the warmth of their RV. The tailgaters noticed the two men looked nervous and were sweating in the cold. They looked out of place.

"Two very good things happened. The bastards didn't have hold of their bomb switches because of the damn gloves. Within a minute, four heroes grabbed their guns from inside the RV and ran up behind the two as another hero went to find the police. They grabbed the two bombers from behind and after a fight the bad guys had lead in their heads and in the true spirit of what makes our country great, the game went on. Weeks later, despite an interruption, so did our Super Bowl."

Despite all the iPhones and FaceTime nonsense in play everywhere, news of this incident had been kept as quiet as possible until now. Stewart felt it was a teaching moment for the people in the room and soon for the world.

"This is what Americans do, and this is what I would encourage the rest of the world to do. Madeline Albright, you remember her, the former Secretary of State said recently "We're familiar with the 'See Something Say Something' safety campaign" But she has now added 'Do Something' to that phrase, and that's our mantra from here on – at least where I come from."

"I thought the American hero John Wayne was dead. Are you his reincarnation, Mr. President?" the Italian Prime Minister asked jokingly.

Stewart smiled and looked around the room at his peers. It was clear to everyone in attendance that under this president, the United States would return to the behavior of its earliest days. They knew America's history of citizens arming themselves against tyranny and how the cowboys of the Wild West all carried handguns to protect themselves and their property. The question they would all need to debate was whether or not that needed to be implemented globally. Could it be? Would anti-gun cultures like the United Kingdom and France not just allow but accept their citizens bearing arms? Would the Germans consider letting their people take up arms ever again?

Before the French Prime Minister could be recognized and be heard, Stewart stepped away from his chair. "My apologies to you all," he said, pausing momentarily, "I have a meeting in a few hours with the Pope and then I am flying back to the White House." He paused and looked around the room, finding Jackson and shaking his head sadly. "It's a shame, for those of you who have been to that brilliant part of American history you wouldn't recognize it now. Impenetrable walls, gun towers, sidewalks and roads blocked off for thousands of meters in all directions. It's heart-breaking to see it from either side."

He paused again but this time his anger and urgency

returned. "To all of you, André and my colleague from the United Kingdom, all I can say is this. I want to at least suggest that you get your minds wrapped around this much better than you have. This is a whole escalation and I believe we will have to fight it more aggressively and with different tactics than before. Consider getting your people armed or at least let them vote on it. In America, they say there are twenty guns for every man, woman, and child that lives there. We, under Secretary of Defense Petty and National Security Director Jackson here, are going to encourage citizens who lawfully own guns to carry them. Guns don't do anyone any good locked up in a safe at home when there's an animal shooting up a mall or a restaurant. People will have to pass a gun safety and shooting course to participate. This will agitate one hell of a lot of people back home, but so be it. We'll prod them a bit more by giving law enforcement agencies access to the medical records of every doctor, mental health institution, pharmacy, and hospital. Anyone who shouldn't possess a gun won't be able to."

The attendees immediately broke into loud conversations and protests, and many more leaders asked they be heard. Jackson walked back to his position beside the President, and Petty stood up, as if on cue.

"We will continue to share intelligence with any and all of you and we will ask that in return. But I encourage you to arm yourselves. In London, the young people with their faces in their iPhones and the people who grew up under the bombing runs of that asshole Hitler will need more than a damn cricket bat to defend themselves if you can't squash these surges." Stewart paused. "I know this means there will be bloodshed but, at the end of the day, the reality is—it is better to lose a few now than let this cancer grow and take out twenty times that later."

With that, Stewart thanked them for listening and then returned to his seat. After listening to much debate, the meeting was brought to a close with dignitaries invited to move to another room for beverages. Like many others, Stewart needed to get back to work. There was no reason to continue the debate. His counterparts from across Europe would head home to formulate their own anti-terror game plans. Within thirty minutes his entourage was in a helicopter headed for the nearby military base where Air Force One and a trip to Rome awaited.

"Damn fine speech," Jackson shouted to Stewart as they walked from the chopper to the jet.

"Thanks for choosing to leave before the debates started about how this could help enable ethnic cleansing, wars between religious factions, civil wars, coups, and all the usual suspects had the chance to get going," Petty said as he headed up the stairs.

Jackson felt empowered by his leader's words. "Mr. President, we hadn't discussed what you intended to say, but I agree a hundred and ten percent and will incorporate your directive immediately." As the three sat down in the same conference room they had just spent seven hours in, they asked for coffee and some sandwiches. Stewart asked his aide to get the Pope on the phone. Within ten minutes their call had concluded and Air Force One was wheels-up, headed for the Naval Air Station in Naples, Italy.

Security procedures and protocols were in full force, and the Secret Service had insisted the trip would take them to Naples where the 747 exterior lights would remain off to help reduce its visibility. From there they would take a 45-minute helicopter flight and land on the Vatican grounds behind the Basilica.

"You ever consider using the pulse, Mr. President? It would save a hell of a lot of time," Petty asked.

Stewart laughed and said, "No damn way. I need the downtime to be able to gather my thoughts and decompress from everything that's going on down below."

Jackson smiled. "I think he's going to give in one of these days but—"

Stewart interrupted. "Yeah, I want you to take me along to Monticello to meet Jefferson after he left office. Isn't that the joyride I heard you were considering before all hell broke loose?"

Jackson smiled. "Yes, I'd still like to meet the man, and I want to take White along with me. We wanted to try to plant seeds in his mind of what would come in two hundred years and hope he added a few things to the Constitution so maybe we wouldn't have wound up where we are today."

Stewart laughed and remarked that Jackson needed to be careful. Jefferson might take a liking to White, a beautiful and intelligent young black woman.

"Remember, JJ, you're not supposed to change history."

Jackson smiled but then his mood changed. "Yep, White would have been a planned distraction but something's happened that will kill that trip forever and is going to hamstring us in fighting these bastards."

Stewart and Petty had begun to focus on the food that was brought in, but Jackson's remark got their attention. He read them the text from White.

SIX PULSES DESTROYED. GOT HOT.
PLACED IN WATER BY ACCIDENT.

BROKE INTO PIECES. HAVE SIX LEFT.
WHAT'S YOUR ETA? WHITE

"We've lost half of our weapons, sir," he said dejectedly. "We've lost six pulses."

A few hours later Jackson accompanied Stewart and his Secret Service detail from the helicopter and walked into an entrance to the Papal residence. After exchanging greetings Stewart asked the Pontiff if they would be able to walk through the Vatican while they spoke. It was nearly nine in the evening there, and the crowds, those who felt it safe enough to visit St. Peter's Square, the Vatican Museums, and the Vatican itself, were long gone. As they discussed the grave situation that was confronting people all over the world Stewart asked the Pope to consider going ahead with the Easter Sunday outdoor Mass. They stopped within twenty feet of the front of the main altar and stood silently for what Jackson felt was an eternity.

The Pontiff said somberly, "I cannot ask believers to come to a slaughter. Easter celebrates Christ's rise from the dead. We cannot in good conscience allow any evil to ruin that celebration but we cannot risk one innocent man, woman, or child's life so the tradition can continue."

Stewart agreed but hoped something could be worked out. "Faith," he told the Pope. "People must have faith that their God won't let anything happen to them. God and Satan are at war; we are seeing that every Sunday around the world. We can't give in and I hope you won't either, my friend."

Jackson walked ahead of the two men and stopped at the top of opposing stairways, each leading from the front of the altar to crypts down below. "May I?" he asked.

The Pope nodded and gestured for him to proceed. Two

Secret Service agents and two of the Vatican's plainclothes Swiss Guard went ahead of him. At the foot of the steps Jackson stood and gazed in amazement at the ornamentally decorated gold box behind the thick security glass. He looked up and immediately felt guilty as he watched the Pope struggling, taking one gentle step after another.

At the bottom, once the president joined them, the Pope made the sign of the cross and the others, regardless of their faith, followed his lead. The gold box contained the remains of St. Peter the Apostle. Peter, who had been at Christ's side up until that night in the Garden of Gethsemane, had left Israel and traveled to Rome to spread the faith. Like Christ, Peter was eventually crucified by the Romans but at his request it was done upside down in a sign of respect for his Lord.

After a few minutes the men made their way up the opposing marble steps and continued their walk through the Basilica. It was such a different place than during the day when tens of thousands of people entered out of faith or curiosity. It was so still, so quiet. They walked the length of the church, and the Pope led them to the left and stood before Michelangelo's Pietà, the sculpture depicting a grief-stricken Mary holding her son Jesus after he had been taken down from the cross.

"I can't believe we have to look at this beautiful work through security glass," Jackson protested. Years earlier a deranged man had jumped the short gate and began to hammer away at the masterpiece. It was a new world they were living in and now it was getting much worse.

They walked along the side of the church back toward the main altar but stopped to pray before the remains of Pope John Paul II.

"That man was a rock star," Jackson uttered.

The Pope laughed and agreed with him.

They continued toward the main altar and the Pope put his hand on Stewart's arm and stopped him. He told Stewart, and the men surrounding them, that he had been weighing the strength seen from going ahead with the service, not giving in to the evildoers that might attack it, versus the impact of cancelling the event and leaving people to think Christ can't protect them. "The battle of good and evil goes on every day, everywhere. This effort might be a surge that we must all resist and push back against."

Jackson responded, "We have tremendous responsibilities. Perhaps it would be as simple as loading the side streets with military in uniforms with body armor and assault weapons. Let them come and try to interrupt the Mass. There are hundreds of thousands of events going on every Sunday, and just as many Easter celebrations on that one in particular. We can't be everywhere, but neither can the armed killers. I'd go with the odds every time."

The Pope said he had already considered this and nodded.

"If the faithful put their lives in God's hands then what will be will be, correct?" Jackson asked.

"If you go ahead with the service, I will sit in the front row to support you and the faithful," Stewart added. His security team tensed at the thought.

The Pope stopped by the main altar and bowed his head in prayer. Stewart followed his lead, but Jackson and the security detail remained vigilant and on guard. Even within the security of this holy place one could never be too careful. After a minute of meditation the Pope blessed himself and then shook the President's hands. "I will see you on Easter Sunday then, my friend," he said as the look on his guests' faces acknowledged his remark with somber smiles. The Secret Service and Swiss Guard frowned at the news.

With that, the Pope gestured for his aide to lead the American leader and his party back to the President's helicopter, Marine One, waiting for them nearby.

Jackson stopped to look one last time down below the altar at the container that held St. Peter's remains. "I saw him in person that night in the Garden," he whispered to Stewart.

The President shook his head. Jackson had been on so many incredible adventures. "For all the times you've disobeyed orders, that one time you couldn't have taken a damn camera along?"

Within an hour the Americans were back aboard Air Force One and preparing to head west toward Washington.

Stewart sank down in his leather desk chair and peeked out the window to look up at the stars. He looked down at the Mediterranean below and commented on the view. "I've always been intrigued by the moonlight's reflection on the open water. It's always reminded me that we are such a small part in such an amazingly large universe."

Jackson and Petty had settled into their seats and hoped to catch some sleep on the nine-hour flight home. Jackson thought of the sea below but his mind went back to the deadly raid at Guantanamo Bay. The tracking devices planted at GITMO and at other global assaults provided no information. At best, just as they had visited Gitmo in the moments after that attack, they could only go back in time to see where the terrorists might have come from. Whether they climbed out of parked vans near the attack venues, rode scooters, bikes, took a subway, or walked, it was impossible to trace them. At GITMO these had been professional terrorists, trained and experienced in warfare.

Not only were these murderers relentless, they were very tech savvy. They knew where the closed circuit cameras were and avoided them at all costs or used them to spread fear.

In one instance though, a particularly cocky killer looked directly into a CCT camera moments before pulling his weapon from inside his jacket. He had smiled and then gave the middle finger, using both hands, to the monitor. Since none of the killers survived the events there wasn't anyone to follow after an assault. The inability of the T1 and T2 teams to prevent the bloodshed or provide worthwhile intelligence frustrated him beyond belief.

Jackson thought of the battles to be fought. The challenges before him were as big as the Atlantic. Despite the massive power of the U.S. Armed Forces, law enforcement, and intelligence agencies, for a moment he felt as if they all fit into a small lifeboat and the evildoers were killer whales in search of food. Jackson's debates with the President were getting more and more heated. He knew it was out of frustration. Stewart knew he was doing the best he could.

Jackson had learned that all governments had formed top secret, screw all the rules task forces to go after this new type of enemy. He considered sharing BOTM with his counterparts but killed that idea as quickly as it had come to him. He realized if the time travel technology were discovered, every person, agency, and country leader would want a piece of it. That could result in even more unrest, turning neighbor on neighbor, country on country. Just like the Joint Chiefs, everyone had his or her own personal and professional agendas. People could be paranoid and suspicious. But despite all that was taking place in the world, there was one thing that continued to haunt him. Where the hell was the escaped General Brooks?

One hour before landing at Andrews, the President's aide knocked and then entered the conference room. Jackson, Petty, and Stewart were all fast asleep, exhausted from their 24-hour round trip to Europe and back. As the aide gently shook Stewart, Jackson felt his phone vibrate and pulled it from his pocket as he sat up and slid the window shade up. It was still dark. As the men slowly began to get their bearings and check their phones, two attendants entered bringing two pots of coffee, six bottles of water, a carafe of orange juice, and a bottle of Advil. Jackson wondered what else the night might bring. Would this damn day ever end?

His phone vibrated again, this time it was a Breaking News alert from CNN. His words, "Holy shit!" got everyone's attention.

CHAPTER 5

People couldn't believe what they were listening to. On television, computer and phone screens across America and around the world, the audio kept playing over and over while commentators tried to understand what they were hearing and speculated about what it all meant. CNN, and most other networks, displayed still photos of Stewart and the late Senator Maxwell side by side on their broadcast as the audio played on.

President Stewart's voice was very familiar and his words were clear. "They're saying I have a sixty percent shot at winning the nomination, winning the election and becoming President," then candidate and retired Marine General Stewart was heard to say. Ten seconds later, an audio recording of candidate Maxwell's voice could be clearly heard.

"Come in, my dear."

"Just one second, Senator, and I will be out of your way," an unfamiliar, unidentified voice responded.

"No need, Agent, I got this. You may leave now," Maxwell continued.

"We're right outside if you need us. Good night, Senator. Good night, ma'am."

After another ten seconds of silence a new voice was heard on the audiotape.

"Steam," an exasperated voice said. "We lost everything in the bathroom after the steam from the shower fogged up the video. Glad you men got out of there all right. It was too close. I'm sure the bedroom video will hurt his chances once we leak it to the media. I don't think his wife will be too happy with him either. Well done."

What was anyone to make of these tapes? Was it fake or real news? It didn't take long for people to theorize what was really being discussed on them. Then candidate Maxwell was Stewart's only roadblock to the Presidency and it seemed someone had attempted to record the late Senator's hotel room encounter with another woman. One of the recorded voices mentioned a video. Would that be the next shoe to drop or did steam make fog over a recording that may have revealed Maxwell's last moments? Had this been a covert effort to eliminate a threat to Stewart's path to the Presidency? If so, who else had been involved?

The Senator was found dead in a hotel room shower in Washington. Was this audio from that evening? Did his death come as a result of a simple slip in the shower as had been reported by authorities? Could he have been pushed? In the age of instant analysis, the breaking news looked very bad for Stewart. A statement of some sort from the White House was necessary to get ahead of it.

Within minutes, his political enemies and a relentless media demanded one. Stewart was a hero who fought for his country as a U.S. Marine. He rose through the ranks to eventually become Chairman of the Joint Chiefs of Staff. When he tired of the inadequacies of his then Commander in Chief he and many others resigned their posts at the Pentagon or were fired. Stewart, ever the patriot, threw his hat into the political ring intent on displacing the perceived weakness in the Oval Office.

People had been forced to accept the reality that terrorists intended to strike every American man, woman, and child, and they saw Stewart as the leader who had the guts and determination to stop it. The country and the world were reeling from the relentless violence and bloodshed. Maxwell may have cheated on his wife but he was liked by many and most certainly wasn't a terrorist. People now wondered if Stewart, their hero, had just been exposed as yet another dirty politician, a conspirator, if not worse.

After a quick ride on yet another Marine One helicopter, Stewart asked Jackson to accompany him to the Oval Office. They had both wanted to find some peace and quiet, some personal space to reset, but that would have to wait.

Met on arrival just inside the White House by staffers and a somewhat unsettled press secretary, Stewart waved them all off with a— "Cabinet room, fifteen minutes, coffee, and no interruptions until then." The start of a sentence by an administrative assistant was shut down with the swiftness of a guillotine. Stewart's face made it very clear he had no intention of repeating his directive.

Once inside the Oval, Stewart stopped for a moment and looked at Jackson. They had been like father and son for years and, while now circumstances dictated it would be wise to circle the wagons and stand together against any attacks, Stewart had something else in mind.

"JJ, I have a country to run and this distraction that's come up with the audiotapes..." Stewart paused, turning away from Jackson to walk behind his massive mahogany desk in the Oval and gaze out the window.

He looked out over the barriers and admired the beautiful blue sky as he considered the ramifications of this latest development. He wondered if he had let down everyone he cared about. Had the method he chose to secure the Presidency compromised not just his reputation but that of the office he now held? In recent years, the office had taken enough of a beating and he had hoped to reinstate its stature at home and abroad. Stewart kept one very important point in his mind. He did not order the execution of candidate Maxwell. From the debrief Petty had given him, Maxwell had either slipped or worse, perhaps an overzealous BOTM operative had crossed the line. Hearing that Maxwell had been a bit rough with his female guest that night meant he may have deserved a punch in the mouth, but certainly not a death sentence.

Stewart turned to face Jackson. The mood in the country had taken a sad turn dating back to the bad behavior of the Nixon White House back in the seventies. Nixon had resigned and his Vice President went to jail. Since then, other political leaders had risen and fallen amidst real and fake news stories of infidelity, nepotism, fraud, collusion and lack of backbone. But the Stewart Presidency had brought new hope to the country. In the midst of the horrific terrorist attacks around the world there was hope that this former Marine General and the brave and talented men and women who followed him would put a stop to the bloodshed and bring peace and sanity back to their homeland and help it spread around the world. Up until now, Stewart's presence and demeanor had indeed been like that of John Wayne and Clint Eastwood, an indestructible combination, all rolled into one. Now, suddenly disillusioned by the news that the once popular Stewart might be just another scheming politician, the country was hoping they would wake up from this nightmare.

"JJ, I have a country to run and a battle to fight. You were stranded in the Israeli desert in 36 AD while I was here at home in modern times making deals with the devil to get me this office." He came around to the front of the desk and leaned back against it while staring at the large portrait of George Washington that hung over the fireplace. "I can't believe you got to meet him, too." His eyes fixed to Washington's, Stewart paused for a moment. "You lucky son of a gun."

Jackson smiled and waited for him to continue.

"I'm not sure where this will take me, but I can tell you that I did not order Maxwell to be killed. Yes, I arranged for intel to be gathered and potentially leaked. In my mind, the end would justify the means but I say again, I did *not* want that man killed. Copy that, Colonel?" Jackson nodded. "Now you have a bigger mission on your plate, the most important mission you've been given to date. I want you to forget about the Maxwell mess, and focus. To keep you out of all this we will not discuss it further. Go work the mission and get me some more results. The best thing you and I can do for this country is to kill all of the bad guys. I'll work to prove to the country that I didn't order a hit on that man. He was an asshole, I'll give him that, but he didn't deserve to die in a damn bathtub."

Jackson disagreed with his mentor but acknowledged the order. He knew Stewart couldn't be swayed and was also aware that they needed to concentrate on the health and security of the nation. On the flight to the White House

Jackson had reviewed the updated domestic security report his office had emailed him and gave the President a status report.

"We have every possible asset working on two fronts. Trying to get us more pulse devices and gathering intel so we can capture or kill the enemy. Here at home your new regulations and recommendations regarding armed, law-abiding, trained citizens are taking root. There have been the immediate problems we anticipated—neighbors thinking they can settle tree trunk disputes like they're at the OK Corral—but in general 99.9 percent of the people are focused on protection and safety. Their patriotism has them lining up together rather than on opposing sides." Stewart seemed pleased but was obviously distracted by his own thoughts. Jackson shared one nugget of information he knew would bring a smile to his mentor's worried face. "One good example of citizens carrying guns was demonstrated last night in Philadelphia. Some dipshit tried to rob a Wawa convenience store. Eleven patrons drew on him and shut the event down without a shot being fired."

A smile came to the President's face. "Fuckin' A!" The two laughed for a moment but then it was time for them to both get moving.

"JJ," Stewart said firmly, "keep your eyes and your assets on the mission and leave my legal problems with me and my lawyers. I think it's probably best that you keep some distance so you don't get sucked into any of this. Run any questions you have through Petty for the foreseeable future."

It was clear to Stewart that Jackson felt he was circling the wagons without him.

"I told you a long time ago, standing right here, that some day you could be sitting in that big chair. In order to have the trust of our dazed and confused citizens, go win some wars and you'll be an American hero. Then we'll see how everything shakes out."

Jackson saluted his President with the words, "Sir, yes, sir," turned and walked from the Oval.

Petty had recently returned to the Pentagon from another trip to Area 51. The scientists who had worked tirelessly to get the late Doctor Moretti's pulse devices and control units back into operation after the Brooks-Scott sabotage had, so far, been unsuccessful. BOTM had only the remaining six devices to use and that had been cut back to once a day. The consensus was that fewer missions reduced the risk of losing a team due to pulse failure or losing the pulses through over-use. The missions that would be run would have to be of the highest priority with the best possible return on investment.

Back at the hangar at Andrews, Jackson checked in regularly with Buchanan, White and the rest of the team. He had so many daily meetings with his national security staff that he rarely had time for casual conversation, let alone a beer and some laughs. The barren grey walls of the facility were beginning to look more like a prison than a launch pad for America's Black Ops fight against terrorism.

Then from outside the briefing room, someone asked, "Know where a guy can get a good deal on a few used goats?"

Jackson tried to clear his thoughts. "Come again?"

"Not after those boys at the Naval Academy have been dating them," Army Ranger Colonel Kyle Morrison answered as he stepped into the doorway.

"Damn, I haven't seen you since that flight back from Jerusalem," Jackson said as he shook Morrison's hand and tapped at the Colonel's new braid ranks. "Not bad, Mo, congrats!"

Morrison had worked in the Pentagon for Army Intelligence and was poached by then Colonel Petty to provide internal surveillance and security for the BOTM team. It was Morrison, at Petty's direction, who posed as a diplomatic staffer who shared a State Department jet with Jackson, White, Wilson, and Sharif to Israel for their eventual rendezvous with Michelle in the Garden of Gethsemane. They were formally introduced later, outside the Ambassador's bunker at the U.S. Consulate. With suspicions about Army moles, thanks wholly to the Brooks-Scott relationship, Jackson and his team had been wary of Morrison and kept him at arm's length until Petty personally vouched for the man.

"Where the hell have they been keeping you?" Jackson asked as White and Sharif entered the room. "I'll never forget the three of you, actually the four of you including Wilson, pointing your automatic weapons at me in the bunker that day. That's something not many people have lived to talk about," he said as he shook hands with Sharif.

"Yeah, Hitler thought the same thing, and we showed that asshole a thing or two," White said under her breath but shut it down when Jackson and Morrison gave her stern looks.

"I'm so very sorry about Wilson," Morrison said to the group. There was silence.

"Permission to speak, sir," White requested of her team leader. Jackson nodded but gave her a look that let her know after yet another slip of the tongue to choose her next words carefully.

"I think we need to take all our military butts over to the bar tonight and catch up. At least one person in this group obviously needs to get laid and I know another who hasn't kicked an Army butt at arm-wrestling since I challenged the last 'Be all you can be' knucklehead to a match. I need some pocket money so let's get off base and blow off some steam."

Sharif seconded the suggestion and Jackson gave in. It had now been a month since he had been out and away from the 24/7 thinking, plotting, and planning he was tasked with. An hour later, the beers were flowing and, after a somber toast to Tommy Wilson and another to JR, Jones, and Abrams, the jokes started flying and stress was diluted away.

"Somebody bought you folks a round of shots," the waitress said as she placed the four servings of vodka down in front of them.

White wasted no time in raising her glass, chuckling out her best version of an Italian accent, "To Doc Moretti, Cent' Anni!" and the others followed. Jackson looked around the room for a familiar face but couldn't find one. This local bar was the site of his first BOTM team meeting so many years ago. It was where he'd laid out what he needed from his handpicked team and had cautioned them all that while the bar was frequented by government and military types only, they should, "watch your lips because loose ones sink ships."

Suddenly Jackson stood up, startling the others. "Bingo, it's the friggin Air Force!" he shouted as Frankie Devine, grinning from ear to ear, approached the table.

White, the other female at the table, gave the Air Force captain the once over before standing to extend a hand and thank her for the drink. Jackson introduced Devine to the group and pulled a chair from the next table and gestured for her to sit.

"I've known Frankie for as long as I've known POTUS," he offered. "We used to hang around with Matt Stewart while our dads did the same. Whenever there'd be a cook out on a holiday weekend, cousin Frankie here would show up and out throw, outrun, outlast all of the girls and just about all of the boys except maybe me."

The group clicked, despite realizing Devine was the President's niece. If she was okay with Jackson she was okay with all but one of them. White might have put up a good front but she wondered about the timing. In such a short period of time, hours, two people from the past had come out of nowhere and were now drinking heavily with them. Morrison was Army and Devine was Air Force. White preferred the company of fellow Marines, but she decided to go along while keeping her eyes and ears open. Her "something doesn't smell right," instincts were flashing and she needed to wait until morning, hours from now, to ask a more sober team leader about them.

At 0800 during their morning brief, Buchanan began to lay out plans for the next ten BOTM trips. All were focused on terrorism but Sharif respectfully interrupted to make a suggestion. "I'm starting to think we're pissing into the wind, up a tree, or whatever makes sense to describe our latest missions."

Jackson walked into the room at that moment and clearly had overheard the comment. "Listen up," he ordered. "Many of you have been through a lot, more than what a hundred average citizens experience in a lifetime." He went on, taking the time to make direct eye contact with Sharif, White, Buchanan, and each of the ten others that were attending the briefing. "We've all encountered philosophical, physical, and emotional challenges and obstacles. We all have to deal with those in the crazy world we live in today but we also have the ability to do something. We can continue to take the fight to them."

Sharif looked frustrated.

"Permission to speak candidly, sir," Sharif requested. Jackson nodded his approval. "All due respect to Major Buchanan. Yes, we've experienced a lot together, JJ, things nobody else ever will. But I think we need to re-evaluate the game plan, especially now that we are down to only six pulses."

"Okay, Marine, spit it out," Jackson said. "What would you have us do since you're so bright eyed and bushy tailed this morning?"

"JJ," Sharif responded, "late last night before I crashed I turned on CNN and saw another breaking news story. It was bad. Some crazy shithead in Honolulu took over a school bus full of kids as they left their tour of the Missouri. He shot the driver, jumped in the seat, and drove the bus into the water."

Jackson shook his head. "I got that report at 0600 this morning. Without saying another word I know what you want to do, Omar. You want to take the team to Pearl and stop that piece of shit before he got on the bus."

Sharif nodded. "They were just kids."

Jackson walked over to Sharif and placed his hand on his friend's shoulder. "We wanted to go to GITMO and stop that attack but couldn't. It was already intel and public knowledge. Same goes for Hawaii."

Sharif looked down at his boots. He knew Jackson was right. There were so many ops, so many missions but so few weapons available to save everyone.

Buchanan stepped forward and requested permission to speak. "Even if we were able to forget about terrorism, even if we were able to eradicate it from the face of the earth, there always will be bad guys doing sick shit to innocent people. There aren't enough protectors out there to stop every asshole from breaking the law and hurting people."

Jackson took over. "We've all known that, since the beginning of man, good and evil have been at war with each other. We live in that war every day, so the best we can do is what we are doing now. Our best. Trying to stop the global shitheads who are driving this over the internet, make a big statement by taking out the biggest bad guy targets, and get the country back to where we can at least catch a breath between incidents. We can't stop every bad guy or go back and fix everything that's fucked about it. We just can't. It's almost like being on the Titanic. There are so few lifeboats but there are so many people that need to be saved."

"Um, that boat sank, JJ," White said.

The room was silent. Frustration would have to give way to acceptance. Only so many people could be helped. But that was a tough pill to swallow for all of them.

Jackson thought back to how selfish he had been when he used BOTM to save Michelle. That had nagged at him from the moment they realized they were stranded in Jerusalem to when Jones and then Abrams were killed and would remain on his mind until the day he died. He'd lost everyone that had ever been close to him and in trying to save his wife, lost even more. What gave him the right to play God and save her but not those kids? His team was accustomed to risking their lives to save innocents and eliminate bad guys, but at times each had shared that they felt they were trying to put out a forest fire with a single garden hose, or kill ten bad guys with only six bullets, and so on.

Jackson knew they needed a distraction to get their minds off of it. He needed one badly too, but not the usual night at the local bar or a beach weekend at nearby Ocean City. As much as he thought about what had happened in his past he knew they had to change the future somehow. There had to be another way to go after evil. There had to be a game changer of some sort that could possibly change the course. He remembered back to one night with Tommy Wilson. They had been partying heavily, letting off a great deal of steam by trying to drown it with beer and shot after shot. It had been just the two of them.

"Why don't we just go back in time, find Satan, and kick the shit out of him," Wilson had said in a loud but slurred speech. "Maybe let a few of us Marines teach the Archangels how to take out the bad guys. Give them some Raider training." Jackson had laughed at the thought but shared Wilson's frustration.

"Would if we could, Tommy," Jackson had responded.

Then someone else was speaking and it wasn't Tommy.

"Can we at least throw the shithead who broke the other six pulses off a building?" White asked in an effort to break the tension. "Hey, JJ, you with us?" she asked.

Jackson smiled. "That's an affirmative."

Laughter filled the room finally, but White wasn't done. "Seriously?" she called out in a hopeful tone.

"Yes, I'm with you and no, you can't throw that meathead off the building," he responded. "We're not done with him yet though. Trust me on that."

On top secret operations, especially one like BOTM, everyone given access to the program had been checked and double-checked, vouched for, and then checked again before being granted access to the hangar at Andrews. The mistake by the young airman, Nicholson from San Diego, California, had been a stupid one but it had also been completely out of protocol and *that* concerned everyone. Within five minutes of learning of the incident, unbeknownst to anyone else working in the program, Jackson and Petty had put the airman under surveillance. Nicholson was written up by his superior officer, reminded of the responsibilities and penalties surrounding top secret clearances, and removed from the BOTM assignment pending further action. His emails, phone records, tweets, texts, mail, internet searches, everything, was being looked at. Rather than lock him up and interrogate him they gave the man a loose leash in hopes that if his act had been anything other than a monumental mistake, Jackson's NSO would find out.

Jackson walked over to Buchanan and the two of them huddled by the whiteboard at the front of the briefing room. "I think we need to scrub for forty-eight hours," Jackson directed. "I want everyone to get away from here and clear their heads. We've been on a nonstop fucking rampage."

"Yep, it's been a bit like speed dating but since we don't like any of them we just shoot 'em up and move on to the next one," Buchanan stated. "We'll lock the place down and await your orders, Colonel."

Still mourning the loss of Tommy Wilson, the separation from his wife Michelle, and now his inability to visit with his friend and mentor, President Stewart, Jackson felt alone again. He had joined the Marine Corps to kill bad guys and live out his life in the camaraderie of the corps but he was alone once again and was missing them all.

As he left the briefing room he waved Sharif and White into his office. "Uniforms aside, we have a bond that is more intense and deeper than most. We've been to hell and back together. We'll figure this shit out and then we'll get back after it!"

“Semper Fi,” White called out.

“Oorah,” Sharif and Jackson responded.

“I have something special in mind that I’ve wanted to do for a long time. We’re going on an intelligence-gathering mission that will be good for all of us. There’s little chance any of us will get shot or captured. Meet me back here at 1800 this afternoon. Just like in the old days, no scents of any kind, and no gum!”

“Where we going, boss?” Sharif asked with a curious smile.

Jackson felt better already. He hadn’t been called ‘boss’ since Jerusalem in 38 AD.

CHAPTER 6

Only the military guards standing duty at the pedestrian entrance to the top secret hangar and the protection detail that remained outside by their black SUVs knew who had entered the building. Marine Colonel Jim "JJ" Jackson, Director of National Security, Marine (rank) Christy White – the first female of elite Marine Raiders, (rank) Marine Omar Sharif, Buchanan, Defense Secretary Petty, Gunnery Sergeant Ley, and the two technicians operating the BOTM control device had been allowed inside.

It was just past 7:30 pm at Andrews Air Force Base in Maryland. The weather was mild and the setting sun in the cloudless sky was giving way to what would be a beautiful full moon before long. Jackson asked White to draw back the uniform curtain to reveal the wardrobe they would need to fit in to the time and place he was taking them.

"Okay, this looks exciting," White proclaimed. "You taking us to Colonial Williamsburg? I'm not going back to Valley Forge. That place was ca-ca-ca cold!"

Jackson laughed. Part of him felt guilty for giving himself and his team of trained killers time off. There were still fights to be fought. But that thought only gave way to White's joke and he moved forward.

He looked at her. "Not quite. I gave you some clues a long time ago. The last mentioned a nickel. Who's on a nickel?

"We're going to meet Thomas Jefferson?" Buchanan exclaimed. "That's awesome!"

Jackson appreciated the enthusiasm. With everything these warriors had been through, their leader was happy to see they still could get excited over something other than a successful anti-terrorism mission.

"Secretary Petty, you were instrumental in overseeing Doc Moretti and the development and the resurrection of the intelligence that allows us to travel back in time. It's an honor and a privilege to have you join us on what will be your first BOTM trip."

Petty had always thought that there would be plenty of opportunities to take a trip of some sort when more pressing matters weren't on the BOTM or his agenda. Once they lost half of their capability, half of their tickets to the past, and with the weight of a good bit of the world on his shoulders as the leader of the armed forces of the most powerful nation on earth, he too felt what was scheduled as a six-hour excursion would be good for his head and his heart.

"I'm questioning the timing of this but in all honesty, I'm curious as hell and need a few hours away from the madness. It's an honor to serve with all of you, and I thank you for giving me this opportunity. I'm going to go along for the ride and follow your leads. I've already paid for my return ticket so don't even think about getting us stranded somewhere."

They knew Petty had the authority and could have taken any number of trips to anytime anywhere in the world, but he preferred to make things happen and let others reap the glory. If it hadn't been for his persistence and dedication, T1 would never have made it home after that fateful trip. This, in part, was their thanks.

"Listen up. Our story is that we're traveling from the Pacific Northwest to Richmond, to catch a ship to Europe to work on some trading," Jackson instructed. "We're going to show up at Monticello in 1810, blend in with the crowd, eyeball the old man like we tried to do at Valley Forge with GW, and then get out of there under the cover of darkness."

Before they had been forced to focus full time on the tsunami of violent attacks, adventures like these had become so commonplace for most of them that they simply changed into their costumes, removed anything from their persons that had come after the early 1800s, and knocked back protein bars and water before forming their six-person, six-pulse ring.

"What about our hair?" Sharif asked. For the most part everyone had very short, close military cuts but that would indeed make them stand out among the people of Southern Virginia in the time.

"Bugs," Petty laughed, "We'll say we all had bugs ravage us as we crossed the country so we cut our hair short to get rid of them once and for all. As for wigs, we were forced to trade them with some insistent Indians. I'm sure that will take the attention off our hair."

"Remember Abrams with that damn chewing gum and how pissed Tommy used to get at him?" Jackson joked as they stepped into their positions. His eyes watered for a moment and then he snapped out of his emotion as the rest of them remembered and laughed rather than crying for their fallen brothers. In an homage to Tommy Wilson, Jackson called out, "Here we go, ladies."

Jackson looked around at his team. He missed his original group and thought of them often. Richard, Jones, Abrams, and Tommy were long gone but those who remained safe through all of those missions, and the two who now stood as part of T1 for this adventure, were the best of the best in his eyes.

"It is an honor to serve with each of you," he said but before anyone could give a response he continued, "3-2-1," and they were gone.

"How the hell you guys keep finding just the right spots to drop us is unbelievable," Sharif exclaimed as he stepped with the rest of them from a mound of horse manure inside a barn. Without another word, the six turned outward and formed a 360-degree circle, searching for anything or anyone that could cause them trouble. Two horses in the stable were spooked by their sudden appearance and back away quickly.

"It'll be dark soon. Let's make our way up the hill to Jefferson," directed Jackson.

Monticello's familiar white-domed cap sat atop the beautiful mansion, in clear sight. Following Jackson, the team emerged from the barn and began the hundred-yard walk to the main building.

"We put this together pretty quickly," Petty remarked. "I hope we can pull off the speech of the day."

Jefferson, now retired from the Presidency, loved his estate and he loved to entertain any and all guests every day, every season, regardless of where they were from or what it was costing his estate to run.

"Doc Moretti would have gotten a kick out of this place.

Monticello means 'little mountain' in Italian," White offered as they continued the walk.

The former President's family had their hands full managing the great expense of providing food and shelter for so many guests. But no matter how much they pushed back Jefferson insisted on continuing his way of doing things.

Within twenty minutes the six were inside Monticello and were offered water, imported wine, and whatever food was laid out for all the other invited and uninvited guests that were there that night.

"Where's the old man?" White whispered to Jackson, but before he could answer another response came from nearby.

"My dear, which old man might you be referring to?"

As White and Jackson turned they came face to face with the third president of the United States, Thomas Jefferson. At sixty-seven, over a year retired from the White House, Jefferson was showing the wear and tear of a lifetime of responsibilities for his government that dated back to his authorship of the young country's most important documents and proclamations, then the Vice Presidency, and the Presidency. He was a man who retained slaves at his Virginia property while writing the famous words, "All men are created equal" in the Declaration of Independence. He was a brilliant man, fascinated by science, and was clearly intrigued by the beautiful young black woman who was now before him.

White was stunned but before she or Jackson could offer a response Jefferson proceeded with his inquiry. "I've traveled the world, young woman, but I have never heard an accent such as yours," he said inquisitively.

Jackson extended his hand and introduced himself and White, his assistant who, according to their cover, had been freed years before in a trade with members of the Lewis and Clark expedition. For the next fifteen minutes Jackson and Jefferson spoke of the expedition, of Jefferson's desire to someday see the west, and were soon joined by Petty and Sharif. They had finished their meal and were happy to express their appreciation and enthusiasm in meeting this very famous man. They spoke and laughed for another ten minutes, while others in the room began to share their host's curiosity and fascination with these new guests.

Realizing too much attention might drag them into an awkward situation, Jackson asked their gracious host if they could have a few words in private. Petty seemed surprised by this and the look he gave Jackson made that clear. Jefferson obliged and led Jackson and Petty into his library. The remaining four members of T1 spread out, White and Sharif taking positions outside the library door while Buchanan and Ley quietly moved to outside the building to keep an eye on their surroundings and occasionally peek through the library windows.

"Mr. President," Jackson began, unsure of how to address his host, "Mr. Jefferson, I met General Washington at Valley Forge in 1778."

Jefferson seemed confused. The man standing in front of him, this traveler from the great northwest, didn't seem old enough to have been in Washington's company. Jefferson had seen and heard a lot in his life, but while the story seemed contrived he didn't sense that the men in his library were a danger to him. He'd look at them, and their friends, as a curiosity for now.

As a man of science, he studied everything and read every book he could put his hands on. He'd listen to what this young Jackson had to say. As Jackson started to speak,

Jefferson waved his hand indicating he wanted a moment to think. Moving to the large red leather upholstered chair he favored, Jefferson sat down and took a sip of wine before gesturing for his guest to continue.

Suddenly there was a knock at the door. Jefferson's adult daughter entered to inform her father that some of his guests were asking for him. Jefferson waved her off as he had Jackson. Frustrated, she retreated, closing the door behind her. White and Sharif both exhaled as they heard her say something under her breath the way daughters do of their fathers at times.

"You must have been attending his horse back then as you look to have been about seven or eight years of age there that horrible winter."

Jackson smiled. Feeling certain that it was safe to proceed, he moved closer to Jefferson and sat across from him in a matching red chair. "You are a great man, and a great student of science, I am told," Jackson went on. "I am going to share something with you that you will not believe but I will leave you with a few thoughts that you can consider over the next sixteen years before you die on July 4th, 1826."

Jefferson stared at him, looking dumbfounded.

Outside the room, White and Sharif made casual small talk to blend in with other guests. "I'm wondering if the old man's going to ask you for a date before we leave tonight, White," Sharif whispered. "He liked, pardon me, the chocolate and from the drawings I saw of his slave sweetheart Sally Hemmings you have a similar look."

White thought for a minute, not knowing whether to laugh or issue him an IOU for a punch in the crotch.

On the other side of the door, Jackson was deliberating just how much to tell his host. As he was a shaper of the constitution, and of the United States, suggesting he do things a bit differently going forward was a gutsy move by Jackson that could change the future. Since that first BOTM trip back into American history, the one to Valley Forge, Jackson had become fascinated by the men who risked it all to fight for their freedom, breaking away from the very powerful British government to form one of their own. Petty was taking it all in, unsure of just where his friend was heading but was prepared to speak up if he felt it was time to change the conversation or terminate the mission altogether.

"As a man of science, you know so many things have been considered inconceivable, unreachable, until someone proves everyone wrong," JJ said.

Jefferson nodded. "Go on, Mr. Jackson."

Jackson sat forward onto the edge of the chair. "In short, over many years medicine will evolve to a point where a beating heart can be taken from one human being and be sewn into another to replace a sick one."

Jefferson nodded again as if that thought didn't seem as extreme as it might to the average man of the time.

"In 1783, King Louis XVI of France watched as a hot air balloon was sent up into the sky and remained there for over eight minutes before safely returning to the ground. Years from now, not only will men spend much more time in the air, they will travel from place to place and also use that technology to wage wars. They will drop bombs and fire their weapons onto their enemies below them."

Jefferson nodded again, saying, "No doubt people will know to fire back at them." It was clear he understood how all of this could evolve.

"So to take this a step farther I will suggest to you that over the next two hundred years, another technology will develop and that is what has allowed us to come visit you here today. We have traveled back in time with one mission."

Jefferson listened but the expression on his face, one of disappointment, let his guests know they might have gone too far. Strangers visited Monticello daily, asking for money to feed their families or to fund an endeavor. "We are American military and we are here to suggest that you use your knowledge and influence to steer the country and its leaders to directions that will make the world, at least the United States, a better and safer place in the future."

Jefferson stood up. At six foot two inches tall he had a presence much like Washington and so many other leaders. "Gentlemen, I would like you to spend the night and allow me to think this through. We'll meet again in the morning to talk further. I must admit I am both entertained and intrigued. What you are saying makes sense but how you got here, well that's another story. We may have much to talk about."

Jackson jumped at the chance. He had been waging war, a war of good versus evil, at home and knew it was an eternal war that could never be won. Here, in this moment, he had hope and the opportunity to influence a better future for his country without firing one weapon. He hadn't planned on spending the night, or even considered having this conversation, but it had come to him somehow and he felt compelled to pursue it.

"Gentlemen," Petty stepped in as he gave Jackson a stern look, "I think it best that we allow Major Jackson to share a few more thoughts with you before excusing ourselves."

Jefferson seemed tired and looked at Petty with disappointment. Was the sales pitch coming? Jefferson sat back down into his chair, took another sip of wine, and asked Jackson to proceed.

Petty stepped to the window and saw Buchanan standing outside, gesturing to his wrist as if to say they were spending too much time in there. Petty opened his hand wide, signifying he wanted to move in five minutes. With that Buchanan and Ley left their positions outside and moved to the front entrance of the mansion.

"At some point in the future, oil will become a global currency and you will need full control over it to assure America's security. Just like you did with the Louisiana Purchase, acquiring 830,000 square miles of land from the French, you should attempt to purchase Saudi Arabia in the Middle East. It's about the same size of land that you got in that deal. More importantly, it has more oil deep under the sand than we'll ever need. It's also the center of Islam and, over time, the relationship between our people and our religions will decide whether the world lives in peace or in constant battle."

Petty was astonished at what Jackson had just presented, but Jefferson's interest had been sparked again.

"What we refer to as Muslim where we are from in the future you once referred to as Mahometan. Is this beginning to make sense, Mr. Jefferson?"

"Damn, son," Jefferson answered. "People have been fighting religious wars going on back to Christ's time both way before He walked the earth and ever since then."

The moment wasn't lost on Jackson. Standing there at Monticello, with everything he had seen and done in his life, and now a second President of the United States had spoken to him in such a way. Regardless of how this trip or his life for that matter would turn out, that moment would remain with him forever.

Another knock at the door, and this time his daughter wasn't taking no for an answer. If her father wasn't going to join the party then she was going to bring the party into his domain. Over twenty people followed her lead, and soon their host was surrounded. He looked around and realized his special guests had made their way out of the library, perhaps never to be seen again. Jefferson smiled at his guests and although he seemed to be listening to their goings on, his thoughts returned to time travel. His vast collection of books did indeed include papers written dating back to 1733 when someone had authored a story about going back in time. Jefferson wanted to find the book but the overwhelming number of guests flocking around him would force that to wait until the morning.

Ten minutes later, as Petty slowly shook his head in disbelief, the T1 team stood in the darkness, in a tight circle, and in an instant they were gone.

At Andrews, they shared their excitement and their recollections of what they had just experienced. Wishing to address the larger issue immediately, Petty asked Jackson to follow him to the briefing room and close the door behind them. The four members of T1 were surprised to see their leader and the Secretary leave so quickly.

"Oh shit, what the heck went on in that library?" Sharif asked.

Petty stood and stared at Jackson. They had been through a lot together, but this was the first time-travel op Petty had gone on, and his ride-along provided much more than he had anticipated.

"JJ," Petty said sternly, "what in the name of God was

that all about? You know the rules, we don't disclose the future to people in the past and we don't change, encourage its change, or influence the course of history. That's the charter and that's what we're all sworn to do!"

Jackson nodded and took a moment to gather his thoughts before responding. "This war that's been going on forever is between God and the devil and no matter how hard we try, no matter how many bad guys we kill there will always be more behind them. These assholes keep coming like the waves of the ocean. Sometimes they rise up in hurricanes and even tsunamis but they just keep coming."

Petty wasn't a very religious man and had never discussed God or philosophy with his friend, his subordinate, and wasn't interested in doing so now. "JJ, you and your team may have knocked off a few Roman soldiers or German SS shitheads. The Russians would have killed those bastards in Berlin and the Romans at their level were grunts and wouldn't have influenced the future anyway." Jackson tried to speak but was cut off. "But to the best of my knowledge you've never suggested to anyone that they could or should change a direction. What if Jefferson actually makes something happen and orchestrates a deal with whoever the hell owned the Saudi sand back then? All of a sudden we could all be dead. For every action there is a reaction and not necessarily a good one."

Jackson looked at Petty and from his expression knew he could respond. "I'm not trying to be a smart ass but we'd all be dead by now because that would have happened before 1826. You and I never talked about parallel universes and all that crap, but I used to talk with Doc Moretti, and a few times with the President about it. Nobody knows how it all works. Hell, I spoke to Jesus and still don't know what the hell's going on in the damn universe, but I do know this. If what I suggested would have a positive influence on a better future, what the hell. I took the shot. What we are doing is putting a band aid on one wound only to have some shithead come along and shoot us somewhere else."

Petty was frustrated. "What you suggested makes sense. It was actually a brilliant idea but through it all we now have an issue. You've disobeyed an order from the President of the United States. Regardless of your personal relationship with Stew, because of it or in spite of it, this is a problem and he's not going to be happy."

Jackson knew what he had done, but he was getting tired of fighting a war that couldn't be won. He knew their current efforts might reduce the bloodshed but never put a stop to it.

"I am concerned that if you're going to start going rogue we might not be able to contain things," Petty said somberly. "We might not be able to contain you for that matter." With that, it was clear to Jackson that this time he might have gone too far.

The next morning, two hundred years and a hundred miles away from Washington, Thomas Jefferson walked into his library at Monticello. He took a moment to take in the strong sunlight that brightened everything in the room. Sitting down at his six-legged desk, his choice for a place to read, he noticed the shine of something on it that was unfamiliar to him. Picking it up he saw that it was a round silver coin that bore the year 2017 and the profile of a face very familiar to him. "Well, I'll be damned," he uttered as he sat back in his chair, a broad smile meeting the morning sun.

In the nation's capital, current day, inside the private residence on the second floor of the White House, Jackson and

President Stewart met for the first time in nearly a year. What should have been a joyful reunion was clouded by the news Petty had relayed to Stewart. For Jackson, not only did he see the disappointment in his friend's eyes but he was surprised by how much Stewart had aged.

After a handshake that turned into a long embrace the two men stepped back and sat down on opposing sofas to talk.

"JJ, I told you that morning in the Oval that some day you could occupy this office," Stewart said in a tone Jackson had rarely heard. It was one of disappointment, spoken by a parent to a son who had been caught red-handed. Before he could respond, the President went on.

"With everything that we have going on in the world, the Brooks tapes that might take me down for good, you go off on something extraordinary and attempt to change the course of history."

Not one to sit quietly for very long, Jackson needed to respond.

"Mr. President, essentially what we are doing today is dropping lifeboats and lifejackets to all the people in harm's way, who are drowning in a sea of terrorism on steroids. My words to Jefferson were meant to help steer him toward a way to fix the structural deficiencies of the Titanic before the ship ever put to sea."

Stewart understood what he was saying. "There's validity to the concept, but you still went where we agreed we would never go."

Jackson sat there without flinching. He and Stewart had been on the same page for years, they were like father and son sharing the same blood and beliefs. But now, suddenly, things seemed different.

Stewart continued, reviewing all that had happened in Jackson's world.

"You lost your mother, then your father, joined the Marines, killed a ton of bad guys, watched us bury Mathew, got the chance of a hundred lifetimes, got to meet Jesus, got stranded in the damn desert for three years, came home to continue the fight, lost your best friend, were given the ultimate authority and assets to declare unrestricted war on foreign and domestic threats, lost your wife and your damn dog, and now after all that violated for the second or third – or is it the fourth time you violated the BOTM charter and my direct orders. Essentially with innocents getting killed every day, you took BOTM off-course and essentially went on a God-damned joy ride. Did I leave anything out?"

Jackson thought for a moment as all that was just put before him ran through his mind.

"Yes, Mr. President," he said somberly. "We buried your Elizabeth. My second mother."

Stewart's hardened eyes softened as his facial expression went from frustration to sadness. He stood up and walked to the beverage cart that had been left for them. He didn't say a word as he poured himself a scotch on the rocks and used an opener to take the cap off a cold bottle of beer. He seemed to wait for a moment and then poured the beer into a glass and as he turned to face his guest, Stewart's face assumed another expression.

"JJ, we've all been through too much these last few years. I got to enjoy my time with Elizabeth while you sat in the Israeli sand with what remained of your team for three years."

Jackson stood up and took the glass, raising it for a toast.

"To those we've lost."

The men sat back into their seats and gazed through

the large oval topped picture window that looked out onto the Executive Office Building. A full two minutes went by before another word was spoken. Jackson wasn't sure where Stewart was going to take their meeting but he was prepared for nearly every possibility.

"JJ," Stewart said softly, "I know why you did what you did but thinking about you and all that you've been through I've decided you need to take a break."

Jackson sat forward, ready to object, but the President didn't give him the chance.

"This is not up for debate. You were on kill before you got lost in time and then after your reconnect with Michelle was cut short you wound up in a gunfight with those assholes at Camp David and then you went right into command mode as Director of National Security." Jackson sat back.

"Then Tommy Wilson disobeyed orders and got himself killed. You've had absolutely no time to decompress and process everything that's happened to and around you, so effective immediately you are going to take thirty days off."

Jackson sat forward, placing his empty glass on the coffee table.

"But wait," he said, "there's too much at stake here for me to step away from the war we're fighting."

Stewart went on to assure him.

"Petty, Morrison, and their people will take care of everything while you cool down and heal. This is not up for debate. White is going to be given thirty as well. You've both been through a lot, and it's time to put on the brakes. In thirty days, come back here to the White House and we'll pop open some more beer and figure out if you're ready to get back on board."

Jackson hadn't even considered taking a day let alone a

month off but as the order to stand down began to sink in, he still had much on his mind.

"What about Brooks?"

"Not your concern. He hasn't surfaced yet but he will at some point. Then we'll deal with him. He knows if he violates his secrecy agreement there'll be a spook lining up the disgraced Army General's head in his crosshairs. Just watch your back. I don't know if he'll come to the area but he probably wants me *and* you dead."

Jackson smiled at the thought and for a moment considered asking for the assignment.

"He's a smart man but at this point a very damaged one. I wonder if he's thinking about suicide by cop, or in his case, by a black op. A man with nothing to lose is even more dangerous. But he's not stupid and he will not want to go back to any sort of jail. He may want revenge but he murdered a U.S. Marine, hell, it can be suggested that he somehow orchestrated the assault and his escape from Camp Delta." For the first time since the incident, Stewart was laying it out in his own mind and was sharing it aloud.

"We don't really know who shot that place up, let those detainees loose. He's going to find himself stuck between a rock and a hard place if he's not there already. In the end it might just mean he wants money to go away and you know how I'll respond to that. But that's not your problem right now. Get out of town for a while, son. That's an order."

Stewart was tired and walked Jackson to the elevator.

"One thing you haven't noticed since you've been shoulder deep, going after the violent. In short order, we've managed to stack the deck in the Congress and the Senate. As of today, with the appointment of retired Air Force General Shields to fill the vacant seat in his home state of Maryland, over sixty percent of those seats up in the Capitol are occupied by red-blooded former military men and women. The media's missed it and the general public never really noticed the trend, but over the last two election cycles we've made a big difference in the makeup of the Congress and the Senate. The opposition on the hill and the media will take a long time to sort through the Brooks tapes and try to get me. But when that happens, if it does, there are plenty of good people in the chain of command to fill my seat and any others that get taken down with the mess Brooks is making. Don't give him a damn thought, and don't watch CNN for thirty days. You copy that, Marine?"

Jackson snapped to attention and saluted the former Marine General.

Stewart returned the motion and then put both hands on Jackson's shoulders. "We'll get through all of this, JJ."

Jackson smiled at his president's reassuring words.

"Sir, yes, sir."

Ten minutes later, after waving off his government transportation and hoping a stroll in the night air would clear his head, Jackson found himself on Pennsylvania Avenue walking outside the White House fences, staring back at the second-floor windows. Only one light was visible and within a minute it went dark. He was sad to think of his friend, tired and alone, with the weight of the world on his shoulders. Jackson took a deep breath and looked up at the night sky.

"Okay, what's next?"

CHAPTER 7

A WEEK LATER, Jackson rolled over in the king- size bed at his apartment at Andrews Air Force Base. He had ignored Stewart's directive to leave town. He wasn't sure where to go. It was early and the morning sun was coming through the bedroom window, lighting up the pictures he had kept of Michelle and their dog Bunker on his bureau. He had spent the first few days of his forced vacation beginning with a heavy workout at the base gym, getting cleaned up and passing over a suit or Marine uniform for a plain grey t-shirt, jeans, hiking shoes and his familiar black jacket.

Long walks around Washington usually followed the short drive to a nearby Cracker Barrel for a mountain of breakfast food. He took in the sights and the fresh air, admiring the monuments and the history that came along with them. At night, he would order in pizza and binge on popular television shows he had heard everyone rave about. On a few occasions, he had Christy White over for beer, but when they found they kept talking about wanting to get back into the fight they both realized they should head their separate ways during the time off and actually relax and forget about killing for a while.

For the first time since one lonely night on the Mediterranean coast in 35 AD, when the two had sat very close to keep warm and a long embrace seemed headed for more, they had felt those same feelings and pushed each other away. Jackson wasn't over Michelle, and White was still mourning Wilson's death. They both knew there could be more to their encounter, it would be easy to fall into it, but complications were the last thing either of them had the heart for right now.

"What the hell did we drink last night?" he said to his guest.

Throwing the covers off and rolling on her side toward him, Frankie Devine responded,

"Ass beer. Yeah, that's it, Ass beer. So frikkin' hoppy it tasted more like kangaroo piss! Whoever invented IPAs should be congratulated but slapped around at the same time." The positive of a good India Pale Ale was a much higher alcohol level than conventional beer but for some, the negative was the challenging bitterness from all the hops used as ingredients.

Jackson stood up and adjusted his underwear.

Frankie chuckled.

"From the looks of things, nothing much happened right?" She got up, her wrinkled blue Air Force t-shirt smelling of spilled beer. She pulled on her jeans as Jackson walked into the kitchen to get a pot of coffee started. Joining him there, Frankie smacked his behind.

"Put some clothes on for Christ's sake, people will think we've been doing the dirty."

Jackson looked around the apartment, wondering if there were more guests he had yet to discover.

"Damn, you can drink, Frankie!" he said, rubbing his face in hopes that the cobwebs would soon depart.

"That's Air Force one, Marines zero," she laughed. "Thanks for letting me crash here, JJ. It was fun."

Devine walked around the living room looking at the photos on the wall, pulling a few CDs and DVDs from a shelf, and then dropped down onto a large recliner.

"That coffee going to get here soon?" she asked. Jackson's expression from the kitchen made her laugh. "Shhh, no yelling please," he answered.

"So where'd all the photos come from?"

Eventually Jackson walked over with two white ceramic watch mugs, ones with no handles and handed hers over.

"Guantanamo 1917 if my history is correct?" Jackson smiled.

"Aunt Liz hated when Uncle Stew would use them to serve their guests."

The two sat quietly, each lost in their thoughts of times past.

"Michelle took all of those pictures," he finally answered as he sat down on the sofa.

"That's my chair, just so you know," he continued. "When she moved out here she went nuts with her camera and I love all the ones she caught as the seasons changed around the monuments. Just like those over there from Yellowstone," he said as he pointed to a far wall.

"I see you're a movie buff just like Uncle Stew, but what's with the small and very varied CD collection?" she asked.

"Allman Brothers, Rolling Stones, Beatles, Mötley Crüe, and Bocelli give me whatever I need depending on the mood I'm in," he explained. "It's what I heard in my house growing up or I picked up somewhere along the way."

"Well at least there's no Michael Jackson in there!" she said jokingly.

"Don't laugh, Bunker ate it!" They focused on their coffee and then continued after a few quiet minutes.

"It's funny how things work out," Jackson said. "I'm remembering listening to that song 'Ramblin' Man' by the Allman Brothers and it reminds me of how much my dad was always away on Air Force duty somewhere while I was growing up."

"At least he knew the right service to be a part of," Devine said with a smile.

"After Mom died he was able to be home so much more and we finally got the chance to spend some really good time together." Jackson paused and spent a few moments deep in thought.

"He poured me my first beer on my sixteenth birthday and then another and then another," Jackson said with a laugh.

"He said – you need to know how booze will affect you – and I want you to find that out with me rather than in some car with a bunch of dipshits who are going to wind up wrapped around a tree."

"I always liked your dad," Devine added.

"We'd watch Eagles or Phillies games on TV when he was around and explore Philly and DC talking about history and warfare and tactics. He was military to the core. Boobs came up too from time to time. He was definitely a boob man!"

"So are you, JJ," Devine responded.

"Can't say about the boobs but you are a Marine to the core too. He was very proud of you. Uncle Stew has told me that plenty of times and I know he is too."

"But just as we were really getting to know each other

Dad got sick and died, so soon after Mom." Jackson's eyes began to tear and then he smiled.

"I like to think they're together now, wherever they hell they are, and that makes me feel good. I was really lost until Stew and Elizabeth took me in."

The two sat quietly and finished their coffee.

"So what'll it be young lady, Waffle House, Cracker Barrel, or back to the bar?" he asked.

"No contest, Waffle House, JJ – and then maybe the bar!" she said as she stood up, rubbed the sleep from her eyes, and headed for the bathroom to wash up.

"And by the way, that Michael Jackson CD was Michelle's!" he called out as she disappeared down the hallway.

"Thank God the dog ate it!" she called back.

Twenty minutes later, after very quick showers, they climbed into Jackson's black pickup and headed for the restaurant.

"So now you're doing the same thing your father did, JJ—always away on missions," she stated.

"Well with no wife or kids it's what I have, it's what I love." He paused.

"It's what I was born to do and I'm going to keep doing it till I find an old town out West that needs a sheriff!"

"Ha—you'd have to go way back in time to find one of those. You'll have to wait until someone invents a damn time machine!"

JJ laughed.

"Ok, I'll just keep hunting bad guys until someone does!"

A few hours later, after Frankie headed for her apartment for more much needed sleep, Jackson sat on the edge of his unmade bed thinking about the day and his state of affairs. It was time to get away from Washington and from the friends and family that were all military. He downloaded the first two seasons of *Game of Thrones* on his IPhone and packed a carry-on bag. Later that afternoon, he took a cab to Reagan National Airport and flew west to Jackson Hole, Wyoming. It was time to visit the Wilson Ranch.

Late that night he parked his rental in front of a small hotel on the outskirts of town. He knew the area well by now and looked forward to seeing the hundreds of elk in the reserve the next morning. His plan was to drive out north through Yellowstone and stop at the spot close to Little Falls where a charging buffalo had nearly killed them over a hundred years ago. From there, he'd take his time working his way to the Wilson Ranch and possibly find Michelle there. In the time they had been apart he hoped she had been able to process all that had happened. She had been stunned by her brother's death, amazed by the revelation that a top secret mission back in time had saved her, only to be devastated when her husband refused to use that same technology to spare her Tommy.

Jackson hoped they could talk. If he had a shot at reconciliation, this might be the first step. If not, this would be their final goodbye and the closure he'd need to move on.

Late the next day, admiring thousands of white alpine trees that spread throughout the region, he turned onto the dirt road that led to the ranch he had spent little time at but loved as if he'd been raised there. The SOLD sign mounted on the large wooden gate, chained and locked closed, stared him in the face. He was crushed. She had said she might sell the ranch and go back to Jerusalem to pick up where she had left off, but he'd thought she was kidding.

The soft, cool wind blew through the trees and reminded him of how different mountain life was from where he was raised in Philadelphia, surrounded by concrete and asphalt. He loved the area that Tommy, and then Michelle and her family, had introduced him to, but now that chapter seemed closed for good.

"What now," he murmured to himself. "Go east, young man," he said quietly. He thought about visiting the cemetery where Tommy was now at rest but he couldn't bring himself to it. At Arlington, where the Jacksons were buried, their son rarely came to visit.

Jackson resisted listening to the news on the car radio or on the television in the room. He thought he might be better off flying to a deserted island somewhere in the South Pacific so he could really clear his heart and mind, but he had sat around enough. He was determined to find Michelle.

Two days later, Jackson was standing face to face with the Wailing Wall in Jerusalem. He had retraced the steps he had taken so many times before. He remembered kneeling beside Michelle inside the Edicule within the Church of the Holy Sepulchre, thanking Christ for saving his wife and their rescue. Now, placing a note of prayer inside a small crack in the wall, he stepped back and headed for the guided-tour office his wife had worked at while he, Tommy, and the rest of the team were stranded.

The woman who managed the office remembered Jackson. Michelle had brought him there to introduce her husband and announce she was quitting to return with him to the United States.

"JJ, Michelle was here for a short time, but she moved away."

He shook his head in disbelief. He was the director of one of the most significant and powerful intelligence groups on the planet and he had failed to find his wife not once but twice now.

"She's in Rome," the woman offered. "She stopped there for a few days on her way here and once she arrived she turned right around and went back." Jackson smiled. He was getting something of use finally. "She was drawn to Rome," the woman continued. "She said Christ was here years ago but had moved on. She said she felt a connection to something in particular in Rome and wanted to be there. She went back and got a job giving tours to English speaking tourists. It's owned by the same company as this one so it was easy for us to help her."

Jackson grinned. "Bingo!" The next day, his flight landed at Rome's Fiumicino International Airport and after a short express train ride into the city's central station he dropped his bags off at a hotel near the Via Veneto, close to the American Embassy, and continued his quest.

That night, dining on pasta and beer under the stars at the Piazza Navona, he laughed when he noticed the name on the beer bottle. "Moretti!" He laughed out loud. *Is this a sign or just some cosmic poking?* he thought to himself. He thought of that smart little Italian scientist, that prodigy, who was responsible for it all. Without her passion and dedication, the mocking by the male scientists that drove her, despite everyone's belief that her best days were behind her, the pulse devices and time travel technology would never have been developed.

"I'll have another," he called out to the waiter. "God damned Moretti!" he said with a smile. "*Grazie*!"

The next morning Jackson opted to walk from his hotel to the Vatican but he had one stop to make along the way. He would start the search for her at the Coliseum. He loved the city and intended to lose himself in its history and remember the time he and his team had landed there, above a caged tiger, and wound up confronting one of the most savage female gladiators ancient Rome had ever seen.

Thirty minutes later he stood beneath the walls of the historic structure. It had been built in 85 AD, and he had been there then with his team, with his friends, what now felt like a lifetime ago. He knew the chance of just stumbling into her was almost zero. He could have reached out to the tour guide office she worked out of. Instead, he wanted to decompress. Until now, he hadn't considered what he would say to her if he found her.

He sat for a while and watched as tourists and tour guides from all over the world gazed at the ruins. They took selfies, came and went from the tour's main entrance, bought waters and ice cream from the sidewalk vendors lined up at their buses. A short time later he walked to the banks of the Tiber River, where his team had spent two nights before making a quick exit. White had exacted revenge on the savage gladiator for her brutality, leaving her lifeless body there as her attendants screamed out for help. Another thirty minutes, after stopping for cappuccino and Italian pastries along the way, Jackson walked into Saint Peter's Square and stood before the Vatican.

He had been there not long ago with the President and the Pope. But now, visiting as just another tourist, he soaked in the sun and admired the beauty and history of the area. "I'm amazed at how many people are here today, despite all the violent attacks around the world," he said to two city policemen.

They looked at him curiously and tensed when he reached

inside his jacket. "Just my brown passport," he assured them as he slowly pulled it from his inside pocket.

"You are a diplomat from the United States?" one said as both relaxed, the tension in their faces changing to curiosity.

"Yes, thankfully the faithful know God has not abandoned them." As the passport was returned all three men took a moment to observe their surroundings, looking for anything out of the ordinary.

"They say your President might be coming to Easter Mass," an officer suggested. "You are here as part of advance team, I would imagine?"

JJ's demeanor made it obvious to the two that if he wasn't already a part of the Secret Service he most certainly was military. Jackson nodded with a forced smile. "Be safe," he said and turned to head back to his hotel. *Easter*, he thought, *I totally had put that out of my mind. Here I am walking through Rome and I have no idea if he's coming or not.* He shook the thought from his head as he threw two euros into a beggar's cup and headed down Via della Conciliazione toward the Castle Sant' Angelo.

It had been a long day and thoughts of the classic thin pizza and a few more beers would help him wind down and get some sleep. He hadn't realized just how tired he was. He hadn't taken any time to relax, or mourn his losses, or just rest up and let his body and mind heal. Stewart had been right in giving him the mandatory leave. Whether he found Michelle or not, he intended to call the White House to thank his friend before turning in.

After downing half of his pizza and at least six bottles of his now favorite beer, he was ready to walk the last twenty minutes to the hotel but opted to wave down a cab instead. A call to the President would have to wait. Ten minutes later, the key left dangling from the hotel room door, Jackson was fast asleep, down for the count.

The next morning, three loud knocks startled him. Jackson sat up quickly, trying to clear his head as he looked for the clock and shook his head realizing he'd crashed without even taking off his coat or shoes.

"I'm still in here," he called out. "I'll be out in an hour or so."

Three loud knocks banged on the door again.

"God damn it," he yelled, "come back later."

He walked into the bathroom to get his day started, but a third group of knocks lit him up. He stormed from the bathroom and flung the hotel room door open. "What the—"

"Hi, JJ," the woman in the hallway said, looking startled to see him half-dressed and noticeably hung over.

"Michelle!"

Two hours later, after spending an hour talking over coffee, juice and pastries in the hotel bar, they were standing in the midst of hundreds of tourists at the front of the Trevi Fountain, tossing coins into the water with private wishes and hoping above all else for them to come true.

"They say once you've done that you will come back," Michelle said with a grin.

"You must come back," he responded. "What kind of a tour guide are you, giving out false information to a poor American tourist."

She laughed. It was the first time in two hours that he had seen that. It had taken some time but any initial awkwardness between them had abated. He was able to tell her as much as he could about what he and his team had been up to, but he could tell she wasn't overly interested. If they hadn't saved her brother then she didn't want to know anything more about their missions. But deep inside, if they were able to save lives although not her brother's, she could find peace with that.

"You sold the ranch?" Jackson said. Not so long ago, he had fully expected to spend the rest of his life there—with her.

"Yep," she said abruptly. "It was time for a new start. You remember that part, right?" He offered no response. She might have left, sold the family ranch, and moved 4,500 miles away but she had come to speak to him that morning so, despite her tone, he thought there might still be a glimmer of hope.

"I still can't believe you saw me at the café," he laughed. "Millions of tourists and you see me in a crowd."

She said again that she had been leading a couple on a private walking tour and based on the number of beer bottles she saw on the table she had felt it best to keep moving. "Like I said this morning, you always stay at the Stendhal so I knew I'd find you there—if I wanted to."

They sat down at the next café they came upon and ordered a spritz and a beer. The waiter, realizing they were deep in conversation, left them with bread, crushed garlic, and olive oil and told them to give him a wave if they needed anything more.

"You know, I would weigh three hundred pounds if I lived here," he said with a smile. "I've eaten more in the last twenty-four hours than I have in a week."

"I can't believe you're on holiday, JJ," she chuckled. "Let's get down to it. It's clear you're here looking for me. Jerusalem gave me a heads up just in case you meant me harm."

Jackson was accustomed to thinking on his feet and being able to react to anything in an instant. His world though had changed so drastically in recent years that he had to take a minute to formulate his choice of words. Michelle seemed to be growing tired of their time together and he knew his next words might be their last.

"First, yes, like I told you I'm on forced leave, President's orders. Turns out, as you pointed out back at Andrews, and as Stewart reminded me recently, I have been either fighting beside people I care about, been away from them for an extraordinary length of time, or burying so many of them that I haven't had time to process it all."

They sat quietly for two long minutes. "I guess what I wanted to tell you is pretty simple, Michelle." He looked into her eyes and she could see the hurt in his. "I know you might never forgive me for not going back for Tommy. I get that. But if it takes ten years for you to heal just enough to give me a second chance I'd like to begin again, like from the very start, like with a first date."

She thought it cute but then laughed. "JJ, you live in DC and I intend to live here in Rome until the day I die." He began to speak but she waved him off. "My turn to talk, Colonel." He sat back in his chair, awaiting the worst. "I fell in love with you the day I met you, and I knew what I signed up for marrying a military man. But I don't know if I can ever forget what you didn't do for Tommy. I am thankful you saved me. I just wished you had done the same for him. Like I said back at Andrews, I came over here for a new start. Every time I see you all I hear is 'We can't help him' and until the day comes that I don't hear that anymore I don't think you have a shot in hell of getting close to me again." Jackson understood and looked to the waiter for their check. "I won't ever be able to forgive you for not helping him, JJ, but…" She stopped. It was obvious she had something more to say.

"Did you know what I had intended to tell you back when Tommy and I drove in from Montana?"

He shook his head, no.

As the waiter came close to the table with the check she motioned for him to go back. "I always admired what military men and women did, and you might remember I even joked about not letting you boys have all the fun." He smiled. "So after I got healthy and I buried my mother I gave joining the service some real thought."

Jackson listened, unsure of where this was heading. "You joining the Italian navy?"

She looked to the waiter and gestured for another round. "No, I had told Tommy I wanted to join the Army to become a Ranger but I never got the chance to share that with you."

The drinks came and they spoke for another hour. From the time they first sat down until they finished their discussion the sun had moved from their table and the shadows left her with a chill.

"Meet me tomorrow at the Castle Bridge above the Tiber. I want to introduce you to someone."

Jackson had no idea at this point what would happen in the morning but for now, he knew his marriage was truly over and perhaps their next meeting would bring closure.

The next morning, around ten, she led her ex-husband into the main entrance to the Castle Sant' Angelo, up the many stairs and once entering a large courtyard she turned and said, "JJ, let me introduce you to Michael the Archangel."

JJ took a moment to regard the large statue but then stepped away to admire the panoramic view of the city beneath them. "No matter how many times I come here I still get a thrill out of seeing all of this, looking down from here at the wall that stretches to the Vatican. I always thought there would be tunnels instead of—" He stopped mid-sentence when he realized Michelle had not left the statue. He walked back to her side in front of Michael. "You okay?"

She nodded yes but kept her eyes on the statue. "JJ, the first day I arrived in Rome I spent up at the Vatican. I was hoping to see the Pope but with all the craziness going on his weekly audiences have been cancelled for some time now." JJ listened, knowing a lot more about the Pope than he let on. "I did get to see the Sistine Chapel and then walked my way here. I was in this same spot, looking out over the walls, when a tourist asked me the time. It was 11:11 and just as I read the time I felt something inside." He stood there silently, remembering the night at their apartment when he found inspiration, and a mission, in the Bible she clung to. Michelle, the love of his life, was dying of cancer until the prayers of a miracle worker saved her. Now, she seemed touched by something extraordinary.

Turning to him, taking his hand, she smiled. She was glowing.

"Wow," he remarked.

"JJ, I wasn't sure what being given a second chance meant, but the day I got here to this very spot and at that very moment, at 11:11, I knew I was saved for a reason."

The area was becoming more and more crowded with tourists, all clamoring for selfies and group pictures in front of the massive Michael. Still holding his hand, she led Jackson back down the steps, across the Castle Bridge, to the café where she had seen him earlier in the week.

"If you know what Michael the Archangel was all about and you know that 11:11 means your guardian angels are present, then I finally figured it out."

JJ sat there wondering just where this was headed.

Was she going to become a nun? Join the Army as she had declared earlier?

"Michael was a warrior, just like you and Tommy, but sent from above by the big guy."

Jackson laughed. Having met Christ, he found it incredibly strange to be having this discussion. "This is really surreal, Michelle," he said as he took a very long swig of his beer. "I'm not even sure I should be drinking a damn beer while we're sitting here talking about this."

She smiled. "I feel like I've met the wind and am now sitting in Italy as this slight, warm breeze passes over us." Michelle laughed. "Yeah, it's almost like when we were back at Andrews joking about medical marijuana. This is all way beyond trippy and then some."

They didn't speak for almost five minutes. The two sat quietly, waved off the waiter, and took it all in. The country was a wonderful place, the city was truly one of the most exciting in the world, and they were within a short walk of the center of modern Christianity, talking about angels, miracles, and the Almighty. JJ had to shake his mind free of all details and possibilities of what they were now feeling and thinking.

"Michelle, you and I both understand good and evil, vengeance and justice, sin and forgiveness." She nodded and sat forward, pushing her water and the breadbasket to the center of the table. JJ continued, "I know what I was put on this earth to do and I need to continue to do it. I am better at focusing on killing bad things than being a husband or the good boy of the Church, or God for that matter, might want me to be."

Michelle motioned for the waiter and handed him ten

euros, gesturing to JJ that it was time to leave. "*Grazie*," JJ said thanking the man. "*Prego*."

The two headed back across the bridge, crossing over the Tiber as they headed for the lighted dome of the Saint Peter's Basilica. JJ felt compelled to tell Michelle about his ancient visit to this city. How he, Tommy, and the other four had slept on its banks close to the Coliseum after a day of horror. They had watched the most vicious woman any of them had ever seen in action, slaughtering her prey before a cheering crowd of wined and well-fed Roman citizens.

"I was here with Tommy a very long time ago," he said, "right after you were diagnosed, and you pushed us off to Naples to train for our next mission."

She kept walking, gently waving off the street vendors that kept offering her deals on leather bags, wooden bowls, and imported bracelets. "JJ, how come you never brought me back a cheap wooden bowl?" He laughed.

They kept walking but were growing impatient with the vendors. The day was coming to an end and hawkers were pestering as many tourists as possible trying to get that last euro before the police would chase them from the bridge one last time before nightfall.

"JJ, right after I went back to Jerusalem I spent an entire day in prayer walking among the olive trees at Gethsemane. I spent a third of the time pissed off that you didn't save my brother. I spent another third thanking Christ for saving me." The couple stopped to watch as two vendors were arguing with two women who wanted to be left alone. Michelle turned to JJ. "Then I spent the last part of the day, until they finally chased me out of there, praying that all of my sins be forgiven and that I could understand what you did – what you didn't do – and that I could forgive you."

Distracted by the argument that was growing louder and drawing a crowd, JJ grew impatient. Was Michelle reconsidering? What did all of it mean? The statue of Michael the Archangel, the fact that in a city of over three million citizens and tourists, she stumbled across him, what did it all mean?

He turned to ask but what he saw surprised the war-hardened U.S. Marine. Without flinching, Michelle stepped into the middle of the argument and asked the vendors, in Italian, to back down. Jackson knew she could handle herself. Both he and Tommy, along with Christy White and others, had taught her self-defense and offensive maneuvers. Regardless, it was two on one, and Jackson would have none of that.

Before he had the chance to intervene in any way, Michelle went into action. She grabbed the red leather bag one of the vendors had been pushing on the tourists and threw it over the wall into the river below. JJ wasn't as fluent in Italian as Michelle but he recognized internationally infamous vulgarity and in an instant, this American firecracker exploded and threw the vendor up onto the wall, said something inaudible to the crowd, and pushed him over.

While some of the bystanders screamed others let out a cheer as others laughed. Michelle knew JJ was there but she also knew better than to turn her back on the remaining vendor. Something shiny was now in his hand and before JJ got to it Michelle had struck the man's forearm with hers, forcing the knife from his grasp. In a fluid movement, she helped the man over the wall and into the water with his friend.

The two-tone siren and blue lights of police cars slowly parted the crowd of onlookers. Within minutes the two women, JJ and Michelle were being questioned. "I know you," a policeman stated, "I met you in the square some time ago. American diplomat yes?"

JJ was relieved. He knew he hadn't done anything wrong, but Michelle might be in hot water. Throwing people off of bridges, for any reason, isn't an accepted practice in most parts of the civilized world. After they checked identification and took statements from the parties everyone was free to go. The two vendors who had taken crash courses in swimming lessons had managed to get to the riverbank and disappear into the night. With the excitement over, the crowd had dispersed and tourists went back to appreciating the view of the Vatican and the other historic buildings in the area, all lit up for everyone to enjoy. For JJ and Michelle, they had a conversation to continue.

"So are you going to finish your story of the day in the Garden?" he asked.

Michelle took his arm as they continued their walk toward the Vatican. A street vendor threw a rubbery children's toy onto the cobblestones in front of them; its squeal was something every tourist has surely heard on holiday anywhere in the world.

JJ put his hand out sternly toward the vendor. "She'll throw you into the damn Tiber if you don't piss off!" With that, the couple erupted into laughter and continued their walk at a much faster pace.

As they got to the center of the square, they stopped at the steps in front of the Vatican obelisk. "They say this was brought here from Egypt in 37 AD by Caligula," Michelle said. They both looked up to the cross at the top and noticed the stars in the sky above. When their eyes met again, they embraced and held each other for at least five minutes until he heard a voice call out, "Hey, get a room!"

The two laughed and then JJ asked her to answer his question. She smiled as they held hands and then tears began to run down her cheeks. "JJ, I was wrong. I understand why you couldn't go back and save Tommy. I get it now. It took me a long time to process it but I get it now."

It took a lot to stop Jackson in his tracks, but her words did just that. He wasn't sure where he was headed or where they, if that was to come, might be headed next. Would they continue their separate ways, stay in Italy, return to the United States? She clearly had a mission of her own in mind and he needed to sit down and figure it all out.

An hour later, they were sitting at an American football sports bar operated by a Pittsburgh Steeler fan from Toronto, Canada. "You just can't make this shit up," was all JJ could say to her. A replay of the Super Bowl was playing on all the flat screen televisions as a four-foot tall statue of Christ, wearing a Steelers helmet, stood watch over the patrons from its perch near the beer taps.

"JJ," Michelle said as she leaned in and whispered. "You Marines, and the police for that matter, can't have all the fun." JJ sat back and gave her a curious look. "I want to protect people. If that means killing bad guys, I want in!"

CHAPTER 8

THOUSANDS OF MILES to the west, in Washington, behind the high walls of the White House, life had become more like a prison to the once proud and confident former Marine General. Stewart thought back to what the Green Zone in Baghdad had looked like, bomb-resistant concrete walls topped with barbed wire. Watch towers every 100 feet, manned by Army Rangers with sniper rifles, grenade launchers, and Gatling-style machine guns capable of spraying any individual or group with a blinding shower of hollow-point bullets. The security measures were reassuring but despite the large number of warriors there to protect him, he felt as if he were stranded on the moon.

He wandered the hallways at night, taking the time each evening to stop and visit with every Presidential portrait that hung in the most famous address in the United States. It was a lonely existence now. The hours and hours of calls, briefings and meetings continued but with Stewart's insistence that from noon Saturday until 0800 Monday morning only essential personnel be at work in the building and he was to be interrupted only in the event of an extreme emergency.

Notifications of a plane being brought down over the Pacific or that a crowd had been decimated by yet another swarm of suicidal lunatics in Johannesburg had become so commonplace that only the location seemed to change while the methods and the outcomes remained the same.

He didn't want to be awakened in the middle of the night to hear that type of news anymore. It could wait until morning. Stewart knew how important it was for his staff to have downtime with their family and friends but he also yearned for it too. His life had changed so drastically though that he found himself spending more time in the residence kitchen, watching the cook prepare his dinner. He had sent JJ away for his own protection and after so many dinners with his lifelong friend Father Thomas he tired of reminiscing and of debating where their God had gone. The portraits were his companions during those quiet, sleepless nights. Jefferson, Lincoln, Grant, Eisenhower, Kennedy, and Ronald Reagan were his close friends now.

"Easter will be here soon, Mr. President," the cook reminded him one evening. "Do you have any special requests?"

Stewart, still looking fit and trim at sixty-three, towered over his newfound friend. He thought for a moment, watching her prepare his favorite lasagna with hot sausage and garlic bread. "Not sure if I'll be in town that day or not, little lady, but you're not working it regardless."

"But Mr. President," she began but he just shook his head.

"Do me a favor and stuff the freezer with some of your shepherd's pie and make sure there's plenty of my favorite beer in there, too." He walked over to the serving tray and tried to steal an early piece of bread. Hand slapped, he backed up with a laugh. "You are to spend Easter with your family and friends. I've got a big bird on stand-by to take me anywhere I want to go."

She smiled, hoping he'd go somewhere warm and sunny like Hawaii. She'd never been but wasn't too proud to ask for a ride if the opportunity ever came up.

"You do know I can have you shot for that slap, right?"

She tested his reflexes as she threw a piece to him. "And that would be the last of my cooking!" she said with a grin.

Ten minutes later, he had set a place for her at the table. He used to watch Elizabeth as she cooked and always set the table so he could say he helped out. "Join me, this way I know you're not trying to poison me," he joked as he pulled her chair from the table.

She resisted as she often did but she was hungry and enjoyed talking with him. *If my parents could see me now*, she often thought. An hour later, the dishes in the washing machine and the President off to his reading, the cook turned out the kitchen lights and called out goodnight.

"Goodnight, Emma," he responded, "Thanks for not killing me tonight!" As she closed the door behind her she smiled.

At 0800 the next day, Stewart entered the Cabinet Room in the West Wing of the White House. As everyone stood to attention, he called out, "At ease." While they took their seats, Defense Secretary Petty laughed as he smiled at his Commander In Chief. "I know, I know," Stewart responded. "Old habits. Take your seats just doesn't work for me."

Over the next hour the group gave updates from their departments. Typically the President opened the weekly meeting with some words of encouragement or a favorite quote from an American hero but today was different. He had asked them to go around the room and present while he nursed his coffee and hoped for positive news on the economy and other fronts.

"Thanks, everyone. I'll get right to it this morning. Today is Good Friday. For any heathens in the room you might not put much into it but it means a lot to the seventy-million Catholics, including me, who recognize its significance."

Secretary of State Johnson spoke up, "So much for separation of church and state."

Most of the people in the room laughed. There hadn't been much of that lately and his remark was appreciated.

Stewart went on, "It still reads In God We Trust on our currency, doesn't it?"

Joan Williams, the Vice President, agreed. "For now. I'm still waiting for some group to file suit saying taxpayer dollars shouldn't be spent on the ink."

"In the navy they used to throw folks like that off the ships at sea," Petty said with a laugh.

Stewart thought for a moment. "Ah, the good old days!" Most in the room laughed or showed their agreement with a smile. Stewart had assembled a very strong army when he chose his cabinet. With the exception of a political deal for agriculture that was needed to secure votes in the Midwest, he had hand-selected his team.

He waited for the attendants to refill coffees and replenish the waters and juices placed around the massive conference table. Once they were gone he continued. "Let's get to it then. My theme for this meeting is simple. We need hope. All of you are doing an excellent job making sure the wheels remain on the truck but our people need something more. We need to instill hope in every soul in America. The war we are fighting against terror, like all others, will pass. Life does go on, no matter what. We will win out and we need to make sure that the land we live in is in the best shape it can possibly be." Looking around the room the President read the enthusiasm in everyone's eyes.

"Consider this a directive to whatever person in your departments that can lead the charge. I ran for office on getting things fixed. While the evil that surrounds us has consumed so much of our nation's attention we have to do more than just keep the train on the tracks, the boat afloat; we need to make sure we're fixing every bit of infrastructure that's broken or worn too. We need to push optimism, volunteerism, and protecting the environment too. It won't matter if we shut down the violence and lock up all the sickos that walk our streets if the world's too damn hot and polluted to live on anymore. We also need to do whatever we can to influence the influencers."

"Meaning?" the Vice President asked.

"Meaning that the internet has been an incredible development. Heck, I can look up just about anything I can imagine on the damn thing and I'll have one hundred answers in front of me before I can blink. But—" he paused. "But there has to be a way of regulating it. Learning how to build a bomb or watching suicide bomber videos and all the other bad things that are online need to come down. That's got to stop and we need to figure out how to do that and do that now. To me, that is Job One!"

"Freedom of speech?" the Agriculture Secretary asked.

"It's no different than Facebook and YouTube and all the rest taking down child pornography or cutting off the live feeds the perpetrators were sending out from their phones while they were running around shooting people. If the content providers can shut it off when they want to, then they have the ability to shut it off when they are told to under the law," Petty responded.

"And the legal challenges could take years to work their way all the way through to the Supreme Court," offered the Attorney General.

"I'm concerned the internet ship has sailed and grown to be so large that it'd be like trying to change the orbit of the moon at this point. Impossible," the Vice President added.

"Bullshit," Stewart responded. "My apologies, Madam Vice President, but that's bullshit." Looking at Petty, he continued.

"I gave a little speech once to some folks while I was still in the military. Secretary Petty here had brought something to the table that seemed impossible but then I mentioned climbing Everest, human heart transplants, men walking on the moon, the internet, and so on. If it needs to be done, or someone really wants it to be done, anything is possible."

"Care to share what that was, Mr. Secretary?" the Vice President asked. She knew what Stewart was referring to and wanted to poke her friend Petty a bit by asking.

"Most certainly, Madam Vice President," Petty said with a grin. "But then I'd have to kill you." Laughter filled the room.

"I can just see it now on breaking news," Stewart joked, "Petty threatens Vice President's life during cabinet meeting." The laughter continued until Stewart brought the discussion back to where it had started.

"Let's make sure that everyone is on board with fixing what's broken. Get the damn infrastructure budget through all the committees and get it on my desk. I want the headlines to get away from the sensationalism of the latest attack. Bigger picture, I will be meeting with the Attorney General to discuss the internet and what we can do about it. This will not be an attempt to silence free speech. It will be a mission to take the violence and fake information from it. There are ways to influence the people who control these sort of things and we will work to that end."

A charge was passing through the room. This was a call to duty, a call to action that many across the country felt was long overdue. "People need to get back to trusting us, believing that the people who work in this building and down the street in the Capitol really do care, showing their love and faith in America, and this is the first step to rebuilding that foundation." Stewart could see that their brilliant minds were already gaming out their charges and writing down action items. It was reminiscent of the patriotic surge after the attacks on America at Pearl Harbor in 1941 and on 9/11 in 2001.

"I have one more thing to add." From his tone, he quickly had their attention. He went on to lay out what he had announced in the private NATO meeting. Objections, requests for clarification, words of approval from most of the cabinet members, and a look of consternation on the Vice President's face let Stewart know the rest of his day would now be an even busier one. He waved both hands to direct everyone's volume be lowered.

"I know this is coming at you all fast and hard, so take the rest of the day to develop a big picture action plan and then join me in the residence tonight at 1800 for a follow-up discussion over dinner. I know it's the start of the Easter weekend but I promise you'll all be out by 2000."

Petty, perhaps Stewart's closest and most loyal friend aside from Jackson, sat forward and cleared his throat. "Mr.

President, some people are going to suggest much of this is being done to take the focus off the Maxwell tapes."

To everyone's surprise, Stewart stood up and walked to the door. Everyone immediately stood up, following protocol, assuming the meeting was over, but it was clear from the looks on the faces they wanted to hear a response to Petty's observation.

Turning to face them he said, "I can assure you all, before God and on my country, that I had nothing to do with Maxwell's death. Let the FBI continue their investigation and once they deliver their findings my name will be cleared. That is all I can or will say about that subject." He stepped back from the door, nodding to an assistant to stand down. "The country was in a bit of a malaise under the last President. Hell, it was more like a coma, and once I took the oath we started to fix everything he had messed up or neglected. Things were starting to rebound until the lunatics, these sick bastards, started their enhanced attacks and the walls went up around this building."

He gestured for everyone to sit down but they remained standing. He walked from the door to the window and took a moment to stare at the top half of the Washington monument. The eight-foot-high white concrete walls that now surrounded the property obscured his full view. "They got everyone in a panic from coast to coast, and some people are running around scared to the point of being numb and in a fog again. Well, as of today, we're going to clear the storm and get things back on track. We're going to sweep across the nation with changes that are going to give people back their faith and confidence in the government and their country. Just like when we've gone to war before. People need to hold on to something, something that will bring them all together.

We're going to fix this, using whatever avenues we need to, starting right now!"

Stewart headed for the door as the Agriculture Secretary stepped from behind his chair and leaned both hands on the desk. "Mr. President, the media is going to say you took that same attitude, whatever it took, to beat Maxwell and win the Presidency."

As the aide again opened the door for him, Stewart stopped and turned to look directly at the man. "Really?" He looked around the room until he found her. "Pardon me, Madam Vice President, but they can go fuck themselves!"

With that Stewart headed off to another meeting and as the door began to close behind their leader, Petty laughed and called out "Oorah." Williams smiled, too. She liked her leader's bravado. He didn't have time for nonsense and she backed him one hundred percent.

"All of this will be nearly impossible to get past both the House *and* the Senate though," she said to the few remaining cabinet members still in the room.

As he walked into the Oval Office and pulled his chair from the desk, his secretary announced over the speaker phone, "Mr. President, there's a call for you. It's regarding General Brooks."

He sat quietly for a full thirty seconds before responding. He knew this day would come and he had prepared himself for it. "Put the call through."

"Who is this?" the President asked.

"I'm calling for a friend," a voice said. "He wants to set up a meeting with you to discuss the terms of your surrender."

Stewart laughed. "Listen, as far as I know you're some asshole reporter who's figured out a way of getting all the way through to my desk but that's as far as this goes."

There was silence on the line until a very familiar voice picked up the conversation. "Stew, this is Brooks. We need to meet."

Stewart took the phone off speaker, put the receiver to his ear.

"Bullshit," Stewart uttered.

"Ask me something then, so I can prove it's me,' Brooks replied.

"What was the name of the doctor from Italy that Petty brought to us?"

"Moretti!" Brooks answered. "Doctor Andrea Moretti from Area 51."

"I will not have any conversation with you over the phone, you've done enough already with recordings that were taken out of context and we're still trying to figure out your role in the assault at GITMO."

Stewart had been disgusted by Brooks' dishonorable behavior. He was a former Army General who had been sentenced to three years in solitary confinement at the military prison at Guantanamo, Cuba. Brooks had left six unarmed members of the BOTM Special Forces stranded in what most certainly was an extremely hostile environment. He was free now, thanks to the terrorists, and he needed to make a deal. Brooks knew if he revealed more about his partnership with Stewart to help secure the election, his own role in it all, including his treasonous acts, would erase any chances of his ever living in America again. He also knew a Black Ops team would be after him until the day he died, at their hands or someone else's.

Stewart had already touched three buttons on his phone base. At that exact moment, security would be tracing the call, a system would be recording it, and the conversation would be interfered with electronically so that no recording of it could be made.

"We're all wondering what you had to do with the raid at GITMO. We're not sure how you could have arranged it but I'd love to hear more about it. Are you anywhere near the White House?" Stewart asked.

"What happened there was unfortunate for the Marines on guard, Stew. No, I didn't have anything to do with it. The bastards that raided the camp just unlocked my door and let Scott and me go. They killed the useless trash that were vegetating in their cells but took the ones they knew were still up for killing Americans. Meet me at the BOTM hangar at Andrews at 2100 this evening. Don't make any attempts to detain or arrest me. I've left enough material with people who have been directed to release it to the Attorney General, Congress, and the media if I don't reconnect with them by midnight."

Stewart knew that he had not committed any crimes, only that Brooks and his former aid Scott had. It was a bluff but a desperate man makes mistakes and this might be his last. As long as Brooks would allow the room to be swept and his person to be checked for weapons, he would meet him. "Perfect timing. I was going to be boarding Air Force One tonight so you've saved me an extra trip on Marine One. I'll be there."

Stewart didn't let on that he knew about Scott and how Tommy Wilson had been killed. He couldn't change any of what happened. He wondered who the person was that placed the call for Brooks. They needed to find that person and soon. Hours later, after his working dinner with the cabinet had concluded, he gave Emma a hug as he wished her a happy Easter. It was the first time he had ever embraced her and, while it seemed awkward at first, it felt innocent but reassuring for them both.

Five minutes later he boarded Marine One on the South Lawn of the White House and headed for Maryland.

"The President is going to spend the Easter Weekend at Camp David. It will be the first time the newly reconstructed facility is being used since the attack. With that, the lid is on." The press secretary's announcement to the four members of the media pool still camped out late on Good Friday came as a relief. Now, at least everyone thought, the press and the politicians were free to make the most of a holiday weekend. Would evil attack on Easter? Would it be safe for families to go to church services or should they stay home? That was the question on the minds of hundreds of millions of people around the world.

Within fifteen minutes, while two diversion choppers flew off and landed at Camp David, the helicopter carrying the President had landed outside the hangar that housed the first of two massive 747s known as Air Force One whenever the President of the United States was aboard either of them. The Secret Service, in conjunction with the U.S. Air Force Military Police, had secured the nearby BOTM hangar and transported Stewart quickly under the cover of darkness in an unmarked black Suburban. BOTM's T1 and T2 teams and their support staffs had already been given a rare weekend off. Moments later, after being assured by Special Agent Hill that the unnamed person in the meeting room was alone, unarmed, and without any listening or recording devices on his person, the President entered the room and was startled to see the condition Brooks was in.

"Detainee chow just isn't what it used to be," Brooks

quipped as he read the surprised look on his Commander in Chief's face. "I've eaten more goddamned hummus and dates than I could ever imagine. No wonder those bastards are pissed off and blowing shit up all the time. Now I know why."

Stewart didn't admire his enemy's attempt at humor. He pulled a chair from the table and sat down, motioning for Brooks to do the same. "That will be all, Agent Hill." With the door closed behind them, it was time to talk.

"I have no intention of causing you harm or attempting to screw up your presidency," Brooks began. "I have some very simple demands and if they are met I can be on my way in a matter of minutes."

Stewart had nothing to say. He waited for the demands. "First, I want ten million dollars transferred to my offshore bank account. That will give me what I need to spend the rest of my life in comfort."

Stewart's face showed no emotion. He just wanted to hear the shoe drop.

"Second, I want you to resign."

The President knew Brooks wasn't stupid. He wouldn't have come here, put himself at risk of being caught, without a decent insurance policy in place with some of his old Army buddies. "And if I don't?" Stewart asked.

"Then I go public with time travel and Jesus and all the rest!"

The President stood up, opened the door, and directed Hill and his fellow agents to take Brooks into custody. "Bring him aboard the big bird. Stow him in the brig." A soundproof, 6' x 4' x 6' holding room with a bunk, toilet, and shackles, had been installed in the under belly of both 747s. Unknown to the public, an issue had arisen years before on an overseas flight and someone had needed to be detained away from the press and the guests aboard the plane. What few agents did know was that person never saw the light of day again. As the black transports carrying Stewart and his prisoner passed the open hangar doors, and the familiar blue, silver, and white 747 regarded as Air Force One, Brooks was surprised to see the vehicles hadn't pulled in.

Pulling into a much different hangar, one dimly lit but heavily guarded, Brooks could make out the silhouette of another very large airplane. This one was a 747 for sure but it was painted Air Force gray and was clearly meant to blend in with all the others at the base and around the world. Once aboard, as Stewart and his team settled into the familiar confines of a third Air Force One, the door to Brooks' special quarters for the trip was locked behind him. The media and the public might have thought the most powerful man in the world was spending time at Camp David but instead, he was headed east across the Atlantic to Rome. He was going to show up at the Easter Mass with the Pope but first, he wanted to see just what the Garden of Gethsemane was all about.

After they arrived at Ben Gurion Airport in Israel at dusk, five armored U.S. government SUVs, all with black exteriors, headed further east toward Jerusalem. Under a brightly lit night sky, thanks to the full moon above, Stewart was able to enter the Garden and spent an hour walking the paths. With him, to show him the markings T2 had left on the olive tree, were Christy White and Omar Sharif. The residents of the surrounding homes and the terrorists of Hezbollah had no idea that the President of the United States was within their reach. They also were not aware that there were over four hundred Marine Raiders and Army Rangers staged in tour buses and other vehicles and two Apache evacuation helicopters were idling nearby. This night, unlike the one he was there to relive, would be much different had the Roman Guard showed up to take anyone with them.

"It looks pretty much like it did when we first visited, Mr. President," White offered.

"Yes, all the roots are still tripping people who wander off the paths," said Sharif. "White, do you remember Benny almost falling on his face just as he realized who was standing in front of us?"

The Marines both laughed and at the President's insistence they described every moment, every step of the encounter they had nearly 2,000 years ago on this very spot. As they finished their story, White showed Stewart the spot where JJ and Michelle were reunited. He smiled and she thought she saw a tear in his eye but he walked away from her and took another moment to take it all in before signaling to his security detail that it was indeed time to go. The day before, thousands had flocked to this and many other holy sites in the area to partake in Good Friday services. As he turned to look one last time, he was pleased he had finally gotten to see this firsthand.

An hour later, they were all back aboard the gray 747. The plan was to fly directly to the air force base at Naples, Italy and then helicopter as they had just weeks before from the base to Vatican City.

Agent Hill knocked on the President's door and stepped in, closing it behind him. "All taken care of, sir," he said, smiling, "we took out the trash." Brooks was no longer aboard the plane. While the group was away taking the Garden tour, members of Israel's Mossad had approached the plane and taken custody of the disgraced Army General. Stewart had remembered that Brooks and a former Prime Minister had clashed over shared intelligence, or lack of it, and Israeli lives had been lost. With assurances that Brooks would simply fall asleep after a meal, he knew that would be the end of him.

"Now let whoever else was working with that bastard come after me. They just don't know who they're screwing with but they sure as hell will find out," Stewart said calmly.

"They got it out of him, Mr. President," Hill offered. "After his escape Brooks stole a boat in Cuba and made it to Florida. He has a nephew in Baltimore, his only surviving relative. The guy overnighted him some cash and eventually Brooks worked his way back to the area. The nephew's harmless. Brooks just used him to get some money." Stewart thought for a moment. He had never liked the idea of torture but just the threat of it was enough to get Brooks to sing. Hill had been with Stewart since Inauguration Day. He was in the Oval Office the day the Marines returned from Israel, when Brooks and Scott were led away in cuffs. He was there when the motorcade was attacked and then at Camp David when the terrorist raid almost took their lives. Stewart had developed a strong relationship with his lead agent and over time included him more and more into the inner circle of secrets.

"Nice work, young man." Hill nodded and left the room. Within a few minutes it was wheels up; next stop Naples, Italy.

CHAPTER 9

"They started it, officer, they grabbed at her," JJ told the police but they weren't buying it.

Michelle sat quietly in the back seat of the blue and white Alpha Romeo.

"She's not drunk," he assured them. "We left the bar and were walking to our hotel when the three of them purposely bumped into her on the sidewalk. They had words and the guy pulled a knife." The one officer was taking notes while the other didn't seem at all interested. He kept looking to the back of the ambulance where one man lay dead on a stretcher as the attendants did their best to clean up the faces of the other alleged criminals.

Minutes later, after spending time interviewing bystanders, the lead investigator, Chief Inspector Francisco Rizzo, interrupted JJ. "A woman threw two street merchants off the Castle Bridge earlier this evening and now this has happened. She fits the description of the woman on the bridge." JJ tried to address what had been said but the investigator put up his hand to stop him. "Do you know how many violent crimes were committed by a woman in this city since the start of the year?" he asked. JJ knew what was coming. "None. Yes, we have the beggars and the shoplifters and the purse-snatchers who harass the tourists but not one woman has been arrested for physical violence here. Not one." Turning to look at her sitting in the car, he continued. "There's more to this, and since it's almost two o'clock in the morning we're going to hold her till morning and let a few other people in our office take a look at this."

JJ gave it one last try. "How about we surrender our passports to you and promise to be at your office at 0900?"

The investigator laughed. "We already have your passports, Colonel Jackson. We checked you out the moment you handed them over to these officers. You have diplomatic immunity yes, but the woman, Michelle Jackson, does not. You can come to the police station, it's right below the U.S. Embassy in Barberini Square in a few hours. I can assure you, despite what appears to have happened on the bridge, and now this, our staff will treat her properly. She will not be put in with the drunk tourists and the prostitutes, we will treat her with the respect the wife of an American diplomat, a United States Marine, deserves."

Realizing he wasn't going to be able to talk his way out of it he thanked the officers and shook the investigator's hand. JJ stood for a moment and stared at the two men his wife had left standing. He had been so impressed with the way she had handled herself. It had been like watching Christy White or any of his special op Marines for that matter. She moved with precision and her blows were forceful and final. He had kept the two from entering the fight while she dealt with the punk who had cursed her before pulling that knife.

"It would help if someone could find that damn knife," he said to himself. In an instant, before he had the chance to say anything more to her, the police drove her away. JJ gave her a reassuring look but then turned his angry gaze back to the two at the ambulance. The police had all gone, or so he thought. He began to walk toward the two.

Their contemptuous smiles quickly changed to fearful expressions. They could tell he wanted to continue the conversation. Suddenly a car pulled up in front of him.

"Colonel Jackson," the driver called out. It was Rizzo, the Chief Inspector. "Your hotel is a much better place for you to be right now," he said from the unmarked police car. "Get in," he commanded, leaning across to flip the handle to the rider's side door.

Without a word JJ got in and, in a few minutes, they pulled up in front of the Stendhal. "Go get cleaned up and we'll see you in a few hours. That dead guy on the stretcher had a record as long as this car." JJ seemed somewhat reassured. "But since we didn't find a knife we have to go through the motions in the morning. It could have slid into the open sewer drain or someone could have picked it up. But I can tell you two things. First, your wife seems to have a slight case of vigilante in her which is okay but she needs to make her moves quietly, not in front of a crowd on a bridge or on a busy street in front of witnesses."

JJ was surprised at the investigator's candor.

"Second, if her brains are as good as her command of lethal hand combat, then perhaps we should talk over coffee after we process her out."

JJ was stunned. Was this some sort of entrapment or could Rizzo believe in getting things done legally or by whatever means necessary? As the car sped away, he stood looking down the now quiet boulevard. A trash truck and a street sweeper vehicle were the only movement on the road now. His life to this point had been an incredible one but it was Easter Weekend and that hadn't been lost on him. He thought back to that night in the Garden, to the words the man had offered.

His mind replayed the incident on the bridge and then the fight outside the sports bar that ended with the suddenness of a sniper's muffled headshot. He thought of the perpetrators that had been killing so many innocents around the world. While so many worried about raids on power grids, water supplies, and malware crippling the developed countries, the violent cancer was spreading and prayers weren't helping.

Maybe I should go back in time, tell him what's happening, and ask if turning the other cheek was what he really wanted us to do? He thought of Michelle and wondered just what the hell was going on with her. She was behaving like an executioner, eliminating anyone that behaved in an evil manner. *I was supposed to take some time off and now I'm bailing my ex out of jail, debating whether vengeance should be ours, standing in Rome at 0300 wondering if the President and the Pope are going to make an Easter appearance together here.*

Inside he hoped that the crowds of faithful would show up, whether the outside Mass was going to take place or not. Now that he had wound up a half mile from the Vatican, he would be there regardless, hopefully with Michelle out of jail and at his side. The hotel's front door opened.

"Mr. Jackson, are you okay?" The night manager had noticed him standing outside at the curb. JJ looked at him and smiled. "There is fresh coffee brewing in the kitchen." That was all he needed to hear.

CHAPTER 10

"TWO THINGS, JJ," Stewart said. There was something in the President's voice that he hadn't heard in all the years he'd been around the man. It was fear. "They've been using drones in the middle of the night to plant explosives inside stadiums and other venues all over the world. We've been able to take the drones down when we see them but it sounds like much of the damage has been done. There are too many buildings, too much infrastructure that could have been compromised. We're going to have to shut down every big event, at least in the United States, until we've been able to sweep everywhere and shut down *all* drone activity here at home."

JJ had hoped the call to Stewart would have been a much happier one, filled with enthusiasm that he would be in Rome to stand as good against the evil at Easter. This was grim. "We always knew the bastards could use drones at some point to drop weapons, guns, knives, grenades, anything once they'd got past the security screens but this takes it to another level. I'm almost afraid to ask what the second thing is, Mr. President."

Stewart laughed. "I'm in Naples right now and will be

flying to the Vatican tonight," he said. "I'm not sure where you are but if you can get to Rome perhaps you can be a part of the U.S. delegation as the leaders of the free world all walk in unity with the Pope on Sunday morning."

JJ had a smile from ear to ear. He knew Stewart well enough to know that he was going to be there to show solidarity with the leaders and the faithful. "I'm already in Rome, Mr. President. I have to bail Michelle out of jail in the morning."

Stewart paused and then laughed.

"It's a pretty good story, Mr. President, and if you're ready for me to go back to work I'd love to tell you all about, but it'll cost you two seats home on Air Force One."

The two spoke for a few more minutes. JJ poured his third cup of coffee and grabbed a Nutella croissant from the pastry tray in the hotel lounge.

Stewart was pleased to hear his dear friend's voice and that he seemed okay. "JJ, I'm going to lay low here for the day. We flew in on one of the gray 747s so we don't stand out. I'm going to try to get down to Positano for the day." Stewart's voice was cracking ever so slightly as he said the destination.

The cliff-side town on the Mediterranean coast of southern Italy was where he and his late wife had honeymooned. There was a favorite restaurant there that he desperately wanted to visit so he could watch the sunset and pray that Easter Sunday morning would start a new chapter in the fight against evil in the world.

JJ remembered the town well and the restaurant the President was referring to. "Good choice, Mr. President. I know you and Elizabeth loved it there." JJ paused, realizing he may have just driven the pain in even further. "I will get Michelle out of jail and then if it is okay with you I'd prefer to remain with her in St. Peter's Square during the service." A waiter filled Jackson's cup for the fourth time. "*Prego*," he told the young man. "Mr. President, I don't have the proper clothes to represent the United States or to be on the same stage with you and the rest. I will connect with your protective detail and get to where I need to be to fly back to Naples with you."

Stewart was tired, as was JJ. They signed off, each man looking forward to their meeting. Each hoping above all else that the violence would stay away from the Vatican, and all other holy places around the world that celebrated Easter.

Hours later, after a shower and a change into clean clothes, JJ walked to the police station. The usually bustling square was silent and the streets of Rome were still. Typically Sundays, every Sunday in the Eternal City, were fast paced mornings where tourists in taxis and tour buses made way to the attractions as the locals opened shops and hoped for a good day at the cash register. Today was different though. Much like the morning of now Saint John Paul II's funeral Mass, when everything in the city was closed and everyone stood as close to St. Peter's Square as possible to pay their respects and witness history being made.

JJ thought of that day as he watched on television. He couldn't remember where he was that day but he did remember the impressive number of world dignitaries who were in attendance. He recalled how the clouds parted as the Pope's coffin was carried toward his final resting place within St. Peter's Basilica. Seeing the sunlight shine directly on John Paul's massive wooden coffin as it disappeared through the great doors of the church, not only left a mark on JJ but on everyone who watched in person or on television around the world. For a young man who seemed lost after his parents died years before, he thought of where he was standing at that moment and all that had happened to him since then.

The fact that he had been taken in by the Stewarts as a high school senior, found his way to the U.S. Marine recruiting office late in the day on September 11, 2001, had led an exemplary career to date, had spoken to George Washington, Adolf Hitler, and then asked Jesus Christ for a miracle in the Garden nearly 2,000 years ago was so amazing that he often had to go back over those moments in his mind to make sure they weren't imagined. If it weren't for the evil actors that were raising hell all over America, JJ probably would have retired to a ranch somewhere close to Jackson Hole in Wyoming. But then, if it hadn't been for Michelle, he never would have met Christ and he wouldn't be in Rome preparing to bail her out of jail either.

"You can't make this shit up," he said aloud as he approached the building marked POLIZIA.

He stopped for a moment to consider his thoughts again. This was the stillest the city had ever been in all the times he had been there. Nearly three million people lived within the city limits but there wasn't even the sound of a scooter or bus or person walking on the cobblestones nearby. Not even the morning chirp of a bird.

This isn't good, he thought to himself. His instincts were screaming. He needed to get ready for a fight. There was one brewing and he wanted to be there to do what he could to stop it. Was he really going to take Michelle to the Easter Mass and risk the life he, his T1 BOTM team, and the special man they met in the darkness had sacrificed so much to save?

His cellphone rang, the special tone set to identify another very special woman in his life. "Christy!" he called out.

"JJ, what the hell are you doing?" He was confused. Was she reading his mind? "Michelle called me two hours ago. She said you were supposed to bail her out this morning."

JJ tried to process the information. If this was an Op he'd have sorted it already and been calling in a helo for extraction, but this was personal and it was tripping him up. He'd let that happen only twice before. A distracted Marine can get himself or someone else killed.

"She called you?" he asked. "Why the hell did she call *you*?" he said in a frustrated tone.

White made it short and sweet. She and Michelle had remained friends despite the Jackson divorce and Michelle couldn't remember JJ's cell number. "She called me. My number's easy. It ends with 1111. Now are you sleeping one off, JJ, or are you getting our girl out of jail?"

The two spent the next few minutes going over what had happened and his plan for them both. "She's going to that damn Mass, JJ," White insisted, "she told me she needs to be there so you best get her butt bailed so she can get cleaned up and headed for church. Then you two kiss and make up and get yourselves back home so we can put what's left of the band back together again."

JJ laughed. "Sir, yes, sir." He saluted to the phone.

Just then two uniformed police officers emerged from their blue and white patrol car and returned the salute, unsure if it were meant for them or not. They could tell this man was friend, not foe. He exuded confidence and capability. They knew the look. This was a warrior, a friendly one, but a warrior. Today, the city would need all the help it could get.

Inspector Rizzo was standing inside the entryway to the police station when JJ walked through the door. JJ could see Michelle had already been processed out but it was clear Rizzo wanted to offer some parting words to the two Americans.

"You wouldn't know this, but my family is from Sicily, a small beach town called Taormina on the eastern coast. It's beautiful there, except for the damn rocks on the beaches. The place would be a paradise if it weren't for those damn rocks!"

JJ laughed and thought, *isn't that what life is really like? So much beauty but there's always a rock or a weed or an asshole to mess with perfection.* "Okay, but what's that got to do with us?" Michelle asked.

Rizzo was happy to discuss this further but guided his guests through the front door of the station and out onto the sidewalk. "I don't know what you've heard of Sicilians but I can tell you this, off the record of course," he said, looking to JJ and Michelle for confirmation. "If you go back thousands of years when a man stole something from his neighbor it was settled pretty quickly and for that matter fairly. Now in these crazy days there is so much with the civil rights and criminal advocates that it is very tough to deliver swift and certain justice."

The Jacksons listened, both starting to understand where this was headed. "In the American military I know there are what you call *nero*, Black Ops, yes?" JJ nodded. "Well, here in Rome and in all of Italy we have that, too. Michelle, I commend you for doing what you did on that bridge. It's something every one of us here would like to do with any scum that harasses the locals or the visitors to this beautiful city. But!" He paused. "But whether you intend to continue down this path or not, you have to be more discreet, yes?"

Michelle looked up at JJ and then turned away from both men to gather her thoughts. She spent a long minute remembering what JJ had told her about the words her miracle worker had said in the Garden. She turned looking directly at Rizzo. "Yes, that 'whole vengeance is mine' thing meant something at one time but in the modern world, that only works so far. It's like Mike Tyson the boxer said." The expression on Rizzo's face turned curious and JJ stood silently with anticipation. "Everyone has a plan until they get punched in the face."

In an instant, everyone broke into laughter. "Yes, I know of Tyson. He's a history buff too and is very fond of the history of the Roman Empire. A killing machine in the ring."

Their laughter subsided quickly as Michelle gave Rizzo what he was hoping for. "I love this city, too, Chief Inspector, and I hear exactly what you are saying. If you can leave me to do what I believe I was brought here to do," she looked to JJ as she prepared to finish, "then I can do some good things to help protect and avenge good people."

JJ was floored. This was not the way he had imagined the morning would go at all. "Michelle, we need to get you cleaned up at the hotel and then over to Saint Peter's Square. And we need to talk!"

Rizzo knew his message was delivered very clearly and that Michelle would be a warrior for the cause. All that was needed now was to get her American husband, ex-husband, back to America and leave them to their business. He handed his card to JJ and to Michelle, pointing out that the number on the back was one that he would answer at any time of the day or night. It was obvious to him that he had recruited one very capable person to the cause of cleaning up the city. It was also obvious that JJ might try to convince her otherwise.

"I hope to hear from you again," Rizzo said, looking directly at Michelle.

JJ turned and began walking back toward his hotel. He hoped she would follow him.

"Happy Easter," Rizzo called out and JJ waved his hand in return. He could hear Michelle catching up to him and that gave him hope.

As they walked toward the Stendhal she caught JJ off guard. "Christy told me what you did for Tommy back in Montana." Startled, JJ kept walking and wondered where this might be going. "She told me you took him back to see his mother." He kept walking until Michelle pulled at his sleeve and brought him to a stop. He turned to face her and saw the tears in her eyes. "I know I called you everything in the book when you refused to go back and save my brother," she said quietly, almost in a whisper. "Christy told me everything about it. When you all came home from that one mission I knew something had happened, I knew something had touched Tommy in some special way." She paused and looked around the square. It was still incredibly peaceful for this time of day, on this special day. "I kept asking him if he'd met someone or something because he seemed at peace inside, like something he had been carrying around for such a long time was finally off his back."

JJ nodded. He saw it too in his best friend and that meant the world to him. "JJ, I said some horrible things to you and I am sorry. I know what you, what all of you did for me, and it was wrong of me to ask for anything more. I still love you but not as a wife anymore. I care for you more deeply than I could have imagined but at the same time, I feel I've been given a mission and a second chance to serve."

JJ stood there wondering what she would say next. It was clear they cared for one another but now things were different. Just as he had been driven to serve he could see it in her eyes. She had been brought back for a reason and it wasn't to sit in Maryland wondering what sort of danger her family and friends were in somewhere on the planet. Whatever she had decided, he understood and would support her decision. There was nothing greater a person could do than to protect the innocent and go after evil.

"So you're going to become a cop in Rome, I take it?" he suggested with a grin.

Michelle smiled and responded. "No way, dude. Go big or go home!" With that, she waved for an approaching taxi and within a minute they were headed to her apartment so she could change into something clean and more appropriate for attending Easter Sunday Mass at the Vatican.

An hour later, the two emerged from a second taxi and began walking along the Via di Porta Cavalleggeri alongside Vatican City. The Vatican museums, including the Sistine Chapel, are on the opposite right side of the property.

"Why are we heading away from the entrances?" Michelle asked.

JJ smiled. It was the first expression he'd had for her since he heard the word vengeance cross her lips. "I have a surprise for you, young lady," he said, "but you have to assure me you won't be going all Zorro or Wonder Woman on me when we get inside."

She laughed. The tension was cut and they both relaxed. On the other side of the walls, tensions remained high though. Dignitaries from around the world had arrived through the very same gate JJ was guiding her to. They, in solidarity with the Pope, had agreed to take a symbolic stand against terrorism by attending the open air Mass. As they reached the security checkpoint a military attaché that accompanied the President of the United States stepped forward, pointing to the Jacksons as he informed the guards that these two Americans were with the President's personal security staff and should be allowed to pass.

"He's here?" she asked JJ.

"Yep. You were there at Camp David. You know no matter what, he doesn't step down to anyone." JJ laughed and reminded her of the last time she had spoken with Stewart. "You gave the old man a pretty hard time that night in the Oval. Hopefully time has given everyone a chance to cool off just a bit. Remember that there's a much bigger picture going on here than our own personal challenges."

Michelle stopped dead. "JJ, I got this. I'll be cool." As he made the sign of the cross and smiled they continued walking. Ahead of them was President Stewart and standing to his left was a smiling Christy White.

The Secret Service detail knew the Jacksons and did nothing to stop the reunion that took place. JJ gave his President a salute and then a strong embrace while Michelle and Christy exchanged fist bumps and then an open-handed low five that Stewart noticed and asked, "Where's mine?"

Michelle stretched out her arms and gave Stewart a hug that cut the tension between them.

"Time to go, Mr. President," the lead agent whispered, and moments later Stewart was led to his seat among the rest of the dignitaries as the Jacksons, White, and the attaché took seats just over fifty feet from Stewart.

"I assume all drone and cellphone activity has been jammed?" he asked the attaché.

"10-4."

Moments later the choir began to sign an Easter season hymn and as the crowd of fifty thousand or more devoted Catholics cheered, the Pope emerged from the center front doors of the massive basilica to celebrate the Mass, to celebrate Christ's resurrection. Dozens of white doves were released from pens within the audience. Many more hymns were sung, and the sun shone brightly on the crowd. There were no visible or audible signs of any disturbances whatsoever.

"So, you forgot to tell me you accompanied POTUS on this trip?" JJ whispered to White. Leaning in, he said, "And you neglected to mention you broke all the rules and told Michelle about that trip to Montana?"

White's expression changed. She and JJ had grown very close over the years. They had been through hell and back and the only thing he had ever criticized her for was loose lips. That and allowing Jones to go after the Roman guard who had tortured Christ in His last hours on earth. She remembered the T1 team's first get together at the local hang-out near Andrews. How the commanding officer she had just met had told everyone in no uncertain terms that loose lips sink ships and insubordination would not be tolerated. Her harmless slip-up that night had given JJ and Tommy Wilson cause to wonder if it had been a one-off or would be a fatal flaw to her career and the safety of the team. That was the one and only time she had disobeyed his orders until now. She knew she might be in trouble and expected to hear much more about it in the very immediate future.

JJ knew how to play it. He'd let her sit in that hot mess of uncertainty. If anything, White was always up for a fight but when she was wrong, she knew it and it would eat at her for making such a stupid mistake. JJ would let it fester, perhaps for only a day, punishment enough. He was certain it would never happen again.

An hour later, once the Pope disappeared back into the

basilica and the President was guided from his seat to a side entrance to the church, JJ exhaled for what he felt must have been the first time in the last sixty minutes. It was over. Nothing had happened. Now if they could just reunite with the Presidential detail and get back to Air Force One and in the air over the Atlantic he'd finally be able to breathe normally.

It wasn't evident to anyone, but his mind had been racing the entire time. He couldn't have told anyone a word the Pope said during his sermon or even what color his Holiness's vestments were. Every sense had been trained on picking up the slightest of issues so he and the others working security could react. He remembered the smell of the incense the Pope had lit and had blessed the altar and the crowd with. No birds fell from the sky from nerve gas like the odorless, colorless gas that had been used at Camp David and at Guantanamo Bay.

As JJ led the way, Michelle, Christy, and the attaché followed him through the door the President and others had been led through. JJ nodded at some of the security men and women working the details of their own countries' leaders. They had gotten to know each other well in the past months, during meetings in Washington and at NATO headquarters. He smiled at one agent in particular, a former Special Forces officer with the German military who was there to guard his Prime Minister. It was clear the Major with the German KSK, the Kommando Spezialkräfte, remembered that long night at Oktoberfest too when the challenge between him and this U.S. Marine Colonel became a night for the record books in Munich. Jackson rubbed his head and smiled.

He thought back to the Hofbrauhaus they had partied in. It was in that same hall that Adolf Hitler had entertained the hungry and thirsty German citizens and convinced them they should elect him as their leader to end all of their struggles. He remembered the look on Hitler's face that night in the bunker when two shots from the Marine's German-made rifle gave the Fuhrer a headache he would not recover from. He smiled with satisfaction again, recalling how good it felt to deliver American justice and execute the man before he had time to take his own life. He wished he'd had the time that night to say to Hitler what he had said to others he had faced. "You know there's nothing like the swift administration of justice. All it takes is a grasp of your weapon, safety off, and there's already one in the chamber. No appeals, no lawyers, no nothing; just a bad guy, a bullet, and me."

After making sure the President was in good hands and watching as Michelle and White were busy reconnecting Jackson asked a member of the Swiss Guard for a favor. "It will be tight but we will make it work before you go," the Guard responded. Within fifteen minutes, as the dignitaries chatted politely while drinking orange juice or coffee and tasting Italian cookies at the reception, Stewart asked JJ and Michelle to join him in another room. White remained behind, happy to continue her trip around the tables of sweets.

As Stewart and JJ stepped aside, Michelle was stunned to see the Pope standing in the center of the small room, smiling with his hands extended to her. She remembered that she should kneel and kiss his ring. As she walked to him she took his hands, genuflected, kissed his Papal ring, and then stood directly in front of him while tears rolled down the cheeks that were smiling the entire time. She was thrilled, stunned, and in an instant confused.

The Pope also had a remarkable reaction. Holding her hands, he felt something; an energy. She clearly was a strong women and in very good shape but there was an energy that he felt that astonished him and made him even more curious about the woman Stewart had told him about.

The Pope gestured for her to take a seat beside him near the wall. As Stewart and JJ looked on, the leader of the Catholic Church spoke quietly with the woman Christ had saved when the Marines had found Him in time that night 2,000 years before in the Garden of Gethsemane. Stewart had not divulged anything about the BOTM program or Michelle to the Pontiff other than to say that she was Jackson's wife and that she had made a miraculous recovery from cancer a few years before. Normally, a guest of this kind would be respectful and in awe of the Pope and their surroundings but Michelle felt quite differently. Her confusion was turning to anger.

Ten minutes had passed, and the Pope's attendants had stepped forward at least three times to interrupt and help guide the Pope to other guests who, in their minds, were clearly more important than this unknown American woman. From the Pope's reaction, particularly after their third try, they knew they best not try to interrupt him again.

JJ and Stewart spoke briefly about the service and how the plan was to helicopter back to Naples and home to the U.S. from there. But Stewart noticed the expression on Michelle's face. It had changed from awe and excitement to confrontational and less and less respectful. He motioned to JJ that perhaps it was time for this team to try to interrupt them. As they approached, Michelle stood up abruptly, and that caught the attention of everyone in the room.

"Your Holiness," she said sternly, "as long as your Church hides their sins and protects their pedophiles I will not help you!" The Pope stood up and reached for her hand but she pulled it away. "Good is supposed to fight evil, not protect it. If you won't act then I'll have to do it myself!"

"Oh shit," Jackson muttered to himself. Taking her by the arm, Jackson stepped back, bowed to the Pope, and then guided Michelle toward the door. Two plainclothes Swiss Guards following right behind them. Jackson let go of her arm and the two walked straight to a pedestrian gate that would take them from the security of the Vatican walls. At the gate though, Jackson stopped and watched her walk away without a word.

This woman might have been his wife at one time but now she was a warrior, resurrected by a miracle to pursue the same cause he, White, her brother Tommy, and so many other men and women had followed in their lives. She was going after the bad guys, but in her own much different way and on her own terms. There was nothing to say. Perhaps they would meet again but they had closure now, and with that Jackson hoped he could go on without ever having to look back again.

A car pulled in front of him. It was the Swiss Guardsman he had spoken with earlier. Time to go for a ride.

Over the years Jackson had visited Rome and the Vatican. He'd taken the stairs to the roof and enjoyed the panoramic view of the city and was intrigued by the limited-access tour below the massive cathedral, where the bones of St. Peter were said to have been discovered. But the one place he wished to visit that had remained on his list was now available to him—the barracks of the Swiss Guard. He would have only a few minutes to break away from the reception, but the driver took him from the rear of the Vatican to an area seldom seen by the public.

After being given a brief tour and a chance to examine

uniforms and weapons that dated back hundreds of years it was time to go back and rejoin the President. As they both stepped out of the car another Swiss Guard, this one in plainclothes, approached them.

"Mr. Jackson, Colonel Jackson, you will need to keep an eye on your wife."

Jackson tensed.

"My brother's name is Rizzo, the inspector who arrested her," the guard said. "We all know that people operate under the radar, as you say, to get things done. Sometimes the dirty work is left to people willing and dedicated to do whatever it takes."

The tension in Jackson began to subside. These were men of the same mold, kindred spirits separated only by an ocean.

"But what she said to His Holiness concerned us. We worry she might view him in the same way she sees others who God may not be pleased with."

Jackson stepped closer. He knew what was coming but wanted the Guard to cut to the chase. "And so?" he asked.

The Guard smiled and put his hand on Jackson's shoulder, an awkward gesture by a young Swiss Guardsman to one of the top officials in the American government. "If your Michelle keeps cleaning up the streets of Rome like my brother told me she has been doing, that's okay with us. But if she makes any aggressive move toward the Vatican or His Holiness, she will be met by swift action, regardless of who she is or knows."

Jackson understood. It would be no different if this Guard, or even the Pope for that matter, endangered the President. Jackson would protect him no matter where the threat was coming from. Jackson extended his hand. "We are of the same mind, my friend. I will never let anyone ever hurt my President or *our* Pope. Ever."

The Guard smiled, shook Jackson's hand firmly, and ended the conversation with "*Prego*," meaning thank you. He then snapped to attention and saluted the Colonel.

Jackson smiled, snapped his heels together to attention and returned the salute. "*Ciao*."

Within minutes, Jackson had rejoined the Presidential security team as they waited for Stewart to conclude his private visit with the Pope. *It's about time to arrivederci Roma*, he thought to himself.

An hour later the Pope was resting in his papal apartment as Stewart, Jackson, and White boarded Air Force One. Michelle waived off any further discussion and remained behind in Rome. She had walked with JJ and White behind the President and watched as they climbed into one of six black armored SUVs that would follow the Beast, the Presidential limousine, to the helipad. JJ had reached for her hand to guide her into the vehicle, but she kept it at her side. The look she gave him was sincere and he felt it all to the way to his soul.

Once aboard Air Force One, Stewart sent his aide to invite the Jacksons to join him for dinner. When only JJ walked into the room it was clear she had stayed behind.

"There's much more going on with Michelle than you know, Mr. President," JJ offered in trying to explain her behavior.

While over the water on their eight-hour ride back to Andrews they would discuss what had transpired. Stewart sent his aide to see if White was interested in joining them. He had gotten to know her very well and appreciated her candor. For Stewart, he knew Michelle might have begun her own crusade against evil and if that was the case he wished her success – as long as it didn't embarrass the United States or expose the top secret nature of the BOTM program or of her extraordinary recovery. For White, she understood where her friend was coming from. She agreed with her and although she had met Christ that night in the Garden with JJ and the rest of T1, she knew this Church's behavior was not what that special man intended or wanted for His followers, for the innocents. For JJ, he knew Michelle was now completely on her own and that he might not ever see her again. He had been fighting the good fight for years and as she had once said to JJ and her brother Tommy, "Why should you boys have all the fun?"

It was time for him to go back to putting sick animals down. He would return to Washington to pick up his crusade. His time in Rome had given him the chance to develop two new strategies in dealing with the ill intentioned. First, get out of the suit and get back in the fight. Second, it was time to bring back shock and awe to anyone with evil intentions, foreign or domestic. But now, with only six fragile pulse devices left, he would need to plan missions with new techniques. He was up for the challenge.

As JJ looked out into the blue sky over the Atlantic, he thought back to the night he had headed east to reunite with Michelle in Jerusalem such a short time ago. His world, their world, was now changed forever. He sat back in the high back leather chair in the President's meeting room on the massive 747. He pictured the innocent men, women, and children lying in the rubble of so many horrendous attacks.

"Let's get it on!" he said aloud.

Stewart and White both heard him clearly and in unison responded, "Oorah!"

CHAPTER 11

It was a beautiful April morning in the nation's capital. As Jackson stepped out of the black SUV that drove him to the White House for the morning briefing, he was met by the President's Chief of Staff Bill Kennedy. They walked together to the entrance on the right side of the building and greeted the U.S. Marines who opened the twin doors for them.

"Still limping, I see," JJ joked. "I know a hundred ways to kill a person but who the hell would ever have thought that a cross pen to the thigh could screw someone up as bad as it did you."

Kennedy had been riding with President Stewart the day the massive IED erupted in Washington and tossed the extremely heavy armored limousine, the Beast, like it was a toy. Stewart had been making notations to a speech he was preparing to give and as he and Kennedy tumbled inside the flipping limo, his writing pen stuck the Chief of Staff deeply in his thigh, almost piercing his femoral artery. The ink from the pen had seeped into the surrounding tissue and caused a blood infection that nearly killed the man. Now he was back on the job full time, the only remnants from the painful incident were a distinct limp and the occasional bad joke about the pen being truly mightier that the sword.

After Jackson's mandatory spring break and closure with his ex-wife, it was time to get back to business and focus on what he wanted to do next. But first there would be two hours of catch-up briefings and staff meetings, meetings that reminded him of a fight others were fighting now. Terrorist and other violent activities were the center of attention in Washington and around the world but the extreme measures President Stewart had enacted had resulted in some surprising results. His declaration allowing all American citizens to bear arms and defend not just their own persons or property but also their schools, public gatherings, and city streets was working. The checks and balances he had put into place, mandating health care and employers report any and all questionable behaviors, and extreme penalties for abusing the right to carry arms was working. Yes there had been some problems between neighbors and co-workers who never had and never would get along but in general, people responded in the U.S. like they did right after 9/11. Patriotism was back and the protection of country and fellow citizens came first. What some feared would make the country look and feel like the old Wild West actually brought people together. With that working better than anyone could have expected, Jackson was now ready for his meeting in the Oval Office.

Pleasantries aside, the two men got right to business. "Mr. President, I want to offer my formal resignation as National Security Director, effective immediately." This was a surprise for Stewart but taking it in his stride he sat back in his leather chair and looked across the massive Resolute desk and waited for this Marine to offer more information. "Mr. President, I stood alongside Elizabeth in shock that morning on 9/11 and watched what unfolded in New York, Pennsylvania, and at the Pentagon. We thought you were dead and all of the genetics and the military environment I grew up lit up in me like an electrical current. I realized I was bred to kill bad guys. But what I've learned after all of my experiences is that I have no passion or interest in directing that from behind a desk."

Stewart understood but he also had told Jackson, not that long ago, that one day he could be sitting at the Resolute just like JFK and so many men before him. "You do know you can accomplish a tremendous amount sitting at a desk though?"

JJ realized his words might have been taken the wrong way. "Mr. President, I didn't mean to," he started, but was interrupted by the wave of a hand.

Stewart wasn't offended. He knew the man sitting across from him all too well. He stood up and walked around the desk to stand face to face with Jackson. "JJ," he began. "I love you like a son and seeing you in action and seeing what you've accomplished and what's in your heart and mind makes me prouder than anything." He placed his hands on JJ's shoulders. "But, I get it. Like me, you are a United States Marine and not a damn desk jockey. Hell, that horrible day at Camp David I felt so free when I grabbed that assault rifle and ran up the steps with you to kick some ass. I hate wearing a suit. I would much rather be wearing my Marine uniform and be surrounded by our nation's finest warriors instead of politicians. Hell, most of them are more full of shit than a Thanksgiving turkey."

JJ saw the fire in his mentor's eyes.

"But I ran for this office with the country's interests, not mine, as the driving force. I surrounded myself with the best military people the damn system would allow me to. We *will* accomplish great things and we *will* snuff out the life of every asshole that wants to harm us. So tell me what you intend to do now that you've stepped out from behind your desk?"

Smiling, JJ moved back away from the President's grasp, and snapped to attention. "Sir, I want to get back into the action on the front lines to deliver justice. Whether it's using BOTM or modern day tactics. I'm not interested in capturing bad guys and trying to squeeze intel out of them. I am only interested in capital punishment. I want to exterminate every evil animal that's walking the planet. I want to find and kill every sick motherfucker so they can't hurt anybody ever again. That's what I was put here to do and that's what I'm gonna do."

Stewart was impressed. That was the conviction he saw in the young man's eyes a few years before this but now the eyes were looking back at him from a worn face and an injured heart. "You sure you're in this for the right reasons? You sure you're just not pissed off about Michelle and Tommy? What about the discussion we had right here after you came home and I was debating what to do with Brooks and Scott?"

JJ remembered as if it were yesterday. "Yes, I said what you were planning sounded like vengeance and Christ had told me and the team that only *He* was to deal that card."

Stewart stepped forward to within a foot of his second son. "So, what you are telling me now, after you met Christ and He saved your wife and He told you to behave yourselves and leave vengeance in His hands? Are you going to ignore what He said? You trying to start something with your Maker after all that He's given you, given us?"

Jackson turned away and walked to the windows that used to overlook the Washington Monument. All that he could see now was the wall and the watchtowers. Just then an aide knocked at the door and entered the Oval Office to remind the President that he was late for his next meeting. The look both Stewart and Jackson gave him indicated they were not to be disturbed. Stewart was the most powerful man in the country, if not the world, and if he needed to make *anyone* wait a few minutes then they needed to stand down and wait for him.

After the aide retreated and closed the door, Jackson continued. "I know I met Him in a different time, but I also know he was aware of what life was like where and when we came from. He must have. But I look at evil as if it was a rampant cancer and we're bringing some radiation or maybe a mega dose of chemo to the fight. Much like Hiroshima. These people who want to cut off our heads, drive a car into a crowd, torture children, shoot up a school, beat women, kick dogs and hang cats, they aren't people. They are infected with a disease and I want to get back to being a doctor rather than an administrator. I want to deliver the cure. I'm a warrior. I want to stop bad guys. Adrenaline is my drug and I'm addicted to both. It's that simple."

Stewart moved to the matching sofas in the center of the room and asked JJ to sit for a few minutes. He poured them both coffees and then sat down across from him; quietly considering what had been said.

"Maybe we need to lay off the coffee for a while," Stewart joked. He wished the young man sitting with him had more to his life than killing but there was a war to be waged. He smiled at JJ and hoped that some day they could both return to a simpler life without the sound of gunfire and cries for help.

Stewart smiled. "I want you to go wrap things up in your

office. I assume you're okay with promoting Morrison into your role? He's Army but on the same page and he's solid. Petty works with him really well, too."

Jackson laughed and then nodded his agreement but wasn't sure where that left him.

Stewart finished his coffee and then stood up. "God damned meetings!" he complained. Turning to JJ he smiled again. "Go put your damn band back together. From here on you'll have carte blanche to act in any manner you deem necessary and I will direct Petty and Morrison to give you full unrestricted support as well as operational command of BOTM."

Jackson was elated but Stewart's expression indicated there was more.

"But, there are strings attached. You can't change history ever again and I want you to go home tonight and watch two movies. First, I want you to watch *The Kingdom* and then right after watch *The Shack*."

Jackson was surprised. He was ready to head directly to Andrews, suit up, and go after the bad guys.

"JJ, that's a direct order and not to be ignored or delayed!"

Jackson snapped to attention, "Sir, yes, sir." As he headed for the door he turned back to the President. In all the years he had known Stewart this was the strangest request he had ever made.

"I've seen *The Kingdom*. I watched it with Elizabeth a long time ago. Why watch it a second time?" Stewart gave Jackson a look that let him know his orders were clear and the meeting was over.

"Aye aye, sir," he said with a smile and left the Oval.

As Stewart prepared to leave for the cabinet meeting he slid open the upper right drawer of his desk and removed a gift the Pope had given him during their first meeting. It was a small statue of Michael the Archangel. "Separation of church and state my ass," Stewart growled. "No matter what, we will never give up the fight!"

The next night, Sharif and White joined Jackson at a table in the back of their old hangout just a short ride from the main gate at Andrews. They arrived on schedule and the waitress delivered six bottles of beer and six shots with perfect timing.

"God, I love Jennifer Garner," Jackson said.

Sharif and White looked at each other with surprise.

"What the F, JJ, you thinking about thirteen-year-olds again!" White said with a smile.

Sharif didn't get the movie reference but JJ's hoisting the first shot in one hand and his beer in the other put the focus back on their reunion.

Twenty minutes later, with another heavy round of beers and shots on the table, JJ leaned in. "Would you two be interested in going on an adventure with me?"

Sharif laughed. He had never enjoyed drinking as much as the others did and had actually managed to spill two of his shots under the table without anyone noticing. "JJ, I've made peace with my family. I've participated in some miraculous and some really fucked up outings with you. Whatever it is, wherever you want to go, as long as we don't wind up in jail, I'm in."

Both men turned to hear White's response.

She stared at Sharif. "Not until you make up for those shots, you hairy bastard," White laughed as she waved for the waitress to bring another round. Realizing he was busted, Sharif called out for vodka instead of tequila. He'd drown some brain cells like the old days but wasn't willing to puke in the parking lot like he had so many times before. Within minutes, the drink count was now even and White gave her answer.

"JJ, what do you have in mind?"

It was late, close to midnight, and there were only a few other patrons left in the bar. JJ looked around the room the way he had that first night, when Tommy Wilson, Richard, and Abrams had sat down with them for the first time as T1 to prepare for their introduction to the top secret Black Ops program. The art depicting the Marines at Iwo Jima, the Whiskey 7 over Normandy, the Enola Gay, and so many other photos and paintings reflecting America's military history sobered him quickly. He pointed to a photo of three firemen raising the flag at the ruins of the World Trade Center on 9/11.

"That day changed my life. It was the day I realized what I was here for. Earlier today I resigned my position at the White House and have been given full charge of BOTM once again."

To his surprise, White said she wanted to sleep on it and talk more in the morning. JJ smiled. He believed she'd join them but if she needed some more time he could live with that – at least until 1400 when he intended to form a circle with five other pulses and go on his first time travel mission since Monticello.

"But, JJ," White said. "Even if you want to track down and kill everyone who is an enemy of the United States there's no way we can get all of them. The intel we've been able to get from the usual intelligence sources and using BOTM has helped but there will always be some asshole that's pissed off about something and he'll learn on the internet how to make a bomb and then go blow up a bus."

Jackson thought for a minute. "You're absolutely right," he said. "But we're going to not just take out bad guys, we're going to get the bomb making stuff off the internet, we're going to encourage people who see something to not just say something but to pull out their gun and shoot. They know things aren't working the way they are, at least some of them are smart enough to realize that. So they need to put down their phones, grow a set, and stand up. The sheep need to wake up and realize the cavalry can't be everywhere and isn't coming so they need to kill the wolf that's fucking with their flock." Jackson smiled at his fellow Marines. "Christy, you know what Michelle's up to in Italy. We can't do it alone. Vigilantes can be effective if they're on the right set of rails."

"Hey look," Sharif chimed in. "Einstein said something like doing the same thing over and over again and still not getting laid, I mean, expecting a different outcome is the definition of insanity right?" His words made White and Jackson laugh.

"I hear you, Christy," Jackson stated. "We can't turn a big ship at sea on a dime. It takes time. But it also takes a wide berth and we have the technology and authority to do what we can, the best we can. That is our duty. This war between good and evil has been going forever and it will continue long after we're dead. But this fight needs to be fought. Maybe when our time comes we can hand it off with the good guys having the high ground for a change." He waited for a moment. "You in?" The look he got in return was one he had seen many times before.

"For now," she said with a smile.

Weeks later, orbiting high over the earth, the crew aboard the International Space Station had assembled in the kitchen area of one of the Russian modules. Their host,

Cosmonaut Nico Kiselva, had prepared a feast for his three American counterparts. Astronauts Brad Simmons, Frank Marvin, and Wade Burns arrived on time, floating quickly from their modules on the opposite side of the massive craft. It was a tradition aboard the ISS that the inhabitants would host dinners in their nation's modules on Friday nights after everyone's tasks had been completed for the day. Tonight's feast would be much different though. Hours later, the astronauts woke to find themselves tucked inside their sleeping bags but locked inside a storage pod that was docked opposite a Russian Soyuz capsule. Kiselva had placed them there and disconnected the power that operated the small vertical hatch. He had left it open six inches, enough, he thought, to keep his prisoners as comfortable as possible until the madness below them was sorted out.

"What the fuck are you doing, Nico?" Mission Commander Simmons shouted.

"My apologies, comrades," he replied as he floated outside the doorway. "I had orders. I was told that America had struck my country in some way and that I was to add sedatives to your banquet and then secure you until additional instructions were sent to me."

"Let us out of here, you son of a bitch!" Burns insisted.

"I have placed food and drinks inside for you and unfortunately I put diapers in there too. I can't let you come out for any reason until I receive orders to. Your modules are functioning properly but I have cut communications to the earth from all ports on your side." Kiselva paused. Tears swelled in his eyes and as he blinked, two perfect circles of moisture were expelled and then another slowly floated into the air.

"They have my daughter. Doronin has taken my daughter and if I do not follow his instructions then her head will be sent up on the next Soyuz. I hope you understand. I have no intention of harming you. I just have to keep you in there for now."

The astronauts turned their backs to him and floated away from the opening. The conversation with their captor was going nowhere and they needed to develop a plan but based on the very basic moves Kiselva had made, they did indeed seem helpless, at least for now.

CHAPTER 12

JACKSON RECEIVED A message to report to the White House immediately. *The T1 team has been busy. Nine terrorists in Dubai eliminated. A hostage situation at a high school in the American Midwest taken care of. A training camp in Syria leveled with no survivors.* And so on. When the BOTM team needed to go in and take the shots themselves they did, but when the Black Ops teams of the host country could be alerted and sent in to take out the trash, they were. He quickly changed into his Marine khakis; happy to working without a suit and tie, and within 90 minutes was greeted at the entrance to the West Wing by Secretary of Defense Petty's assistant.

"They've asked me to escort you directly to the Situation Room, sir."

Within minutes Jackson entered what is regarded as the most secure meeting room in the United States. President Stewart, Vice President Williams, Petty, and newly appointed NSO Director Morrison paused their discussion long enough to welcome Jackson as Stewart gestured for him to take a seat at the long conference table.

"JJ, Russian President Doronin called me two hours ago. He was enraged, probably more pissed off than I've ever heard him," Stewart said. "He's not sure how we could have done it but he believes we tried to sabotage his Presidency by accessing their internal email system, planting bugs in his Kremlin office, his home just west of Moscow, and his playground palace on the lake. And, get this, he said someone left a used condom wrapper in the bathroom at his home in such a way that his wife would find it. He believes we did all this to throw his government into chaos and perhaps allow us to help insert a more American-friendly leader into power."

Jackson looked around the room and wondered to himself if there was a question coming.

"JJ," Petty asked, "Did we have anything to do with this?"

Jackson thought for a moment, but an impatient Vice President asked again. "Colonel Jackson, do you know anything about this? Did BOTM have anything to do with this under your watch?" she asked.

Jackson smiled. He knew at this point he was either going to be in very deep, hot water or perhaps get a special assignment.

"Yes, Madam Vice President," Jackson stated. "And it seems to have been working in our favor until this morning."

While Director of National Security, Jackson had been operating with full Presidential authority to use any and all means available to him, including the BOTM program, to gather intel and act in the nation's best interests. It was clear Doronin had spent months fighting a war within his own political party. After putting it all together, he must have realized the United States, or some other entity, had developed something new that would enable this sort of stealth.

"Did Doronin have any demands, Mr. President?" Jackson asked.

Stewart sat back in his chair and laughed. "Well, first, he wants me to share whatever technology we used on him. And, second, he wants me to resign." There was very little chance of either happening. Stewart could never divulge the time travel capability and he would never quit. Every military and political foe he had faced in his well-decorated career had learned that; most often the hard way.

"Here's the real problem, JJ," Petty added. "Doronin has had the only cosmonaut up in space take control of the International Space Station. We have lost all contact with the three American astronauts who are on board the ISS."

Jackson's mind spun for a moment. To date he had seen some incredible things and some very horrible ones. He'd faced every challenge and always managed to find a solution, except for the time he was certain he and his T1 team had been sentenced to a solitary life 2,000 years back in time. If it hadn't been for Petty, the scientists, and the T2 team he would have remained there until the Roman guard finally found and killed him or perhaps he would have just died at peace, satisfied with the life and the adventures he had lived.

"Well, I know what we have to do," Jackson said with confidence. "I need to take T1 over to the Kremlin and force that bastard to order his flying chimpanzee to stand down. If that doesn't work then we'll have to go to Plan B."

Stewart grinned. He knew Jackson would step in and do whatever was needed to fix the problem but it wasn't going to be easy.

"JJ," Stewart said in a calm tone, "we both know there's no way at this point to get close to Doronin. He'll be so deep into secure hiding, expecting we'll use that same technology to go kick his ass."

Jackson knew his first idea wouldn't fly, but it gave him time to consider other options. "We're not done with Doronin. He'll surface at some point."

"We can't let Russia or anyone blackmail us," Petty said with confidence. "There are a dozen scenarios on how to fix this problem and we need to let them all run their course but —" he paused. "But worst case..." Jackson knew what was coming next. A never been tried rescue mission was this Marine's Plan B.

"It's never been done before but, yes, I know where this is going. We need to send T1 up into outer space, land inside the ISS, disable the cosmonaut, and return home without anyone seeing us do it, right? When can we go?" With that, the room erupted in laughter. With any thought of a diplomatic solution or even the threat of a military one dead on arrival, it became clear that Jackson's plan would be the only viable option. But despite having gone back in time nearly a hundred times, the BOTM program had never left the earth's atmosphere. It had also never tried to land on a moving target. Could it function properly? Would it?

"One thing though, Mr. President," Jackson asserted. "If we pull this off, I want to try Mars next!"

Laughter filled the room again. Humor had always been Jackson's signature response when facing the most incredible odds. "It won't be easy, and it might just get us killed, but I've seen and done enough that if I get stuck on a damn solar panel instead of inside the ISS I'll be okay one way or another."

The Vice President found the idea absurd. Stewart and Petty had briefed her about the existence of the technology after the inauguration. While she believed them she knew placing six grown men and women inside a tiny room on the ISS while it was orbiting 250 miles above the earth's surface and traveling over 17,000 miles per hour would be almost impossible. Jackson could see the look on her face.

"That's why you called a Marine, ma'am! We'll get it done." But the Vice President was still very skeptical.

"Colonel Jackson," she said, "JJ, if I may – do you have any idea how small the inside of the ISS is? I've been to Cape Kennedy and Houston and been aboard all sorts of mock-ups over the years and even if you could pinpoint target the center, the open space inside one of the modules, you'd need midgets, I'm sorry, little people, to have a better chance of someone not becoming part of the instrumentation."

"Seals, we'll send Seals, Madam Vice President," Petty suggested. "They're much smaller than Rangers and Raiders!" More laughter filled the room but after a few moments it grew silent. "That sounded patronizing, Madam Vice President, and I apologize."

Williams smiled. "It's all good, Mr. Secretary. I didn't take it that way. Besides, my skin's a lot tougher than some of the overly sensitive people we have in the country."

"All you need to do is read the book about Apollo 13 or watch the movie. Those damn scientists at NASA and our military's finest can do just about anything. We'll get up there, get the job done, and get home one way or another," Jackson stated.

Stewart listened to the exchange but his thoughts went elsewhere. He had lost his son Matt years before, and although he knew the young Marine sitting with them had inserted himself into some extremely precarious missions over the years, this might just be the one that would finally cost Jackson, and others, their lives. He had never said goodbye to Jackson before a mission and the thought of doing it this time was crushing his heart. But he wouldn't show it.

"Other than the fact that you'll need to prepare for this mission much differently than ever before, there's the possibility of a failed mission, six dead Marines stuck aboard the ISS and a Russian cosmonaut sending video of it back down to earth," Petty said.

"Not a problem, Mr. Secretary," Stewart responded. "We'll just blow the damn ISS up and people will just think that something went wrong and it fell to earth, burning itself up and all evidence to the contrary, that a military rescue mission had gone bad."

The looks on their faces were of surprise and disappointment. Seeing that, Stewart added quickly, "I hope you all understand that is not an option. Just voicing my frustration."

The four of them sat quietly, each of them considering the scenarios and ramifications of the actions they were discussing. "I might have neglected to ever tell you, JJ, but some of the satellites we have in orbit do indeed have weapons aboard them."

Jackson smiled. "Would have surprised me if we didn't, sir," he responded. "May I suggest that you give me a few hours to huddle up at Andrews with the team and come back to you by dinner time. We'll need to connect with NASA. In the event we do pull this off but for whatever reason cannot return to Andrews from the ISS we'll need to make sure there's enough oxygen and food to take care of us until we can get home. We can't possibly use the Russian's Soyuz to return since they'd have a rather hostile welcoming committee waiting for us on arrival." Jackson paused. "Emma still work here, Mr. President?"

"Yep, and you're invited to dinner, all of you are if you wish, as long as none of you make any Last Supper jokes."

"Oorah," Petty and Jackson said simultaneously.

Instead of heading back to Andrews Jackson rode with Petty to the Pentagon where a hastily arranged top secret meeting with NASA officials was set to take place. On the way, he placed a call to his counterpart at MI5 in England, the military intelligence service. Doronin might be a smart man but he was often an arrogant one prone to missteps and if that was the case here, Jackson was intended to take advantage of it.

After two hours of deliberation, Jackson had what he needed. If all six members of the T1 team crouched down, forming the smallest, tightest ring they ever had, they could indeed fit within the small corridor of an American module aboard the ISS. The Russian units were similar but also noisier and in the case of a covert op, the white noise could work to T1's advantage.

It would be a gamble as to where the cosmonaut would be holding his prisoners. When Jackson asked the NASA experts, "Where would you hold three Russians if you had to?" they provided very detailed educated guesses. Consideration was given to using BOTM to try to plant bugs at the Russian space headquarters in Moscow, Star City, or the Baikonur Cosmodrome but security had most assuredly been heightened at all three facilities. That was the only piece of the puzzle that was missing – where were the astronauts? Had they been removed from the ISS and returned under duress to Russia? NASA officials had verified that the Soyuz vessel used to take people to and from the ISS had remained docked in space. Nothing had left the station.

Four hours later, the T1 team was standing inside an ISS

training module at the Johnson Space Center in Houston. The fit would be tight, but Jackson felt it could be done. Buchanan agreed but reminded everyone of the next hurdle.

"We're gonna need to test BOTM to be sure we can land in something that's moving pretty fast, like a cargo plane circling Andrews or perhaps Dover. If we can drop six operators inside a moving tin can over Delaware, we may be able to hit that damn thing in space just right!"

It would take another four hours to fly from Texas to Andrews and assemble the team for that test. Now Jackson would have to decide who would make up the team on this most difficult mission yet.

"I'm in," and another, "I'm in," and so it went. Sharif, White, Buchanan all volunteered on going. Jackson asked for recommendations on who else should be selected to go but had pushed Buchanan to remain behind and lead the team in the event they didn't come back.

"There'll be nothing to lead, JJ," Buchanan said. "If the mission fails up there, the six remaining pulse devices, the only ones we have left, might be gone forever. Is everyone at the White House and Pentagon really sure they want to gamble this capability to rescue three space cadets?"

White burst into laughter. "We'll be up and back so quick that damn cosmonaut won't know what hit him!"

Buchanan wasn't sold on it though. He thought the risk versus reward, this time, didn't jive but all things considered, he wanted in. "You considered the fact that we're all going to be weightless, probably nauseous, and upside down on arrival," Sharif said. "I'd also like to suggest we take an astronaut or two with us on this one. Between the four of us we'll have the capability to overcome whatever we have to up there. But someone needs to make sure the ISS is operational in the event something is damaged or the hostages are unable to help us."

"Sounds like a typical Sunday morning for most of us," White responded.

This gave Jackson pause. Sharif made very good points. These were issues he hadn't considered. With NASA's help they would be taking both teams up in the gravity-free planes the astronauts train in. A simple call had one of the specially outfitted jets already on route to Dover. This would give them all a quick taste of what to expect. It would also demonstrate who could handle weightlessness and the immediate side effects better than the others.

"Weapon of choice on this one, JJ?" Buchanan asked.

With that, Jackson removed a stun gun from his inside jacket pocket. "All we'll need is a few of these and—" pulling a knife out of his pants pocket he grinned "–don't leave home without it."

This was the same pocket knife Jackson had carried on mission after mission, in Iraq and Afghanistan and then to ancient Rome, World War II Berlin, Valley Forge to see George Washington, and to the Garden of Gethsemane and many missions since then. "My father gave this to me. It's been a lucky charm. Used to piss off Tommy Wilson all the time. Even when we weren't supposed to have anything from the modern world on us, this always made it aboard."

The room became very quiet as thoughts of their missing team member, their fallen friend, tapped at their hearts and minds.

"Remember how Tommy would always yell at Abrams about his damn chewing gum?" White asked Jackson. That brought a smile to his face and the melancholy left the room as quickly as it had arrived.

"Let's go for a few more plane rides and then save some astronauts!" Jackson ordered.

"Fuckin A, JJ!" White exclaimed. "You coming, Buchanan?"

"Oorah!" the reluctant Marine exclaimed.

Within the next twenty-four hours, two astronauts had been selected to accompany T1 on this secret rescue mission. The gravity-free flying had been fun but left a few members of the T2 team looking for puke bags. Once the staffing had been determined, the roster was set and the operation a go. Jackson, Buchanan, White, Sharif, Navy Pilot and ISS specialist Colleen Johnson and Air Force Pilot and ISS specialist Susan Patrick were standing inside the BOTM hangar at Andrews, suited up, pulse devices around their necks, and ready to launch.

"We'll only have about five minutes of breathing time in these rescue helmets," Patrick reminded everyone as they formed the tight circle. On Jackson's command, they all took one knee, then the other, to form a circle that would, if all went well, wind up safely within the tight confines of the International Space Station.

"Hopefully the nut job cosmonaut hasn't cut off the oxygen and we won't have to worry about it," Johnson said in a confident voice.

"I feel like I'm in church, praying," Johnson whispered.

"We all are," Jackson responded. "Counting down, 3 – 2 – 1."

And they were gone.

CHAPTER 13

THE STRESS AND strain of the office and its massive responsibilities were taking their toll on Stewart. His face was showing the wear and tear just as Presidents before him. Sitting with him inside the White House Situation Room, the Vice President, his Chief of Staff, the Secretary of Defense, a NASA liaison, and two communications specialists waited.

"We're linked to the NASA office at the Pentagon, the BOTM hangar at Andrews, and the CIA at Langley, Mr. President," the Marine in charge of audio communications stated. "The NASA link to the ISS, should it go live, will be tied in here as well."

"Now we wait," Stewart whispered.

Two hundred and fifty miles above the earth's surface, T1 continued their mission.

"We did it," White exclaimed. Locked in their tight little circle, technology had indeed landed the team on mark. Jackson and Sharif faced the module opening that led to the rest of the craft as White and Buchanan turned to watch the opposite end of the unit. The lights were dim, but the temperature seemed comfortable. Weightlessness had been somewhat entertaining for most aboard the test flights over Delaware but with a threat within reach the team seemed able to ignore it.

"Oxygen levels are good," Johnson reported.

"We're good to lose these helmets?" Buchanan asked. A thumbs-up from the astronaut was all the Marines needed. Once they were removed and stowed, the plan was put into action.

"Okay, White," Jackson said, "go get 'em!"

Floating slowly through the first module and then the next and then another she came across a view that made her grab hold and stop fast. There it was, the cupola, the massive viewing station that guests aboard the ISS use to watch the earth pass underneath them. It was a spectacular sight with the colors of the land and sea below much more vibrant than depicted on most maps she had seen. *Oh I'm definitely hanging out here for a week*, White thought to herself. After a few moments she refocused and continued her hunt.

"Hey, hey, who the fuck are you?" White heard a whisper from her left.

Staring back at her from the small, floor-level opening were the faces of three very confused astronauts. Knowing they were all military men, she gave them a quick salute and whispered back, "The United States Marine Corps has landed." Then she placed her right index finger to her mouth, gesturing for them to keep quiet. Before they had a chance to say anything more, she moved on.

The round shape of the entry doors in the Russian modules provided ample room at the top, bottom, or either side for her to cling to a surface and maintain some degree of stealth. Progressing from one module to the next, she saw no sign of the lone cosmonaut. The visual differences between the contrasting module designs were insignificant but the change in sound, the humming sound of space station equipment, got louder and louder as she passed further into hostile territory. Suddenly, there he was, floating in his sleeping bag, attached to the right side of the module by a simple strip of Velcro material.

"Your ass is mine," she whispered and within the blink of an eye her knife was at his throat, pressed hard against it.

Kiselva's eyes widened in horror.

"Who are you?" he asked.

"Shut the fuck up, you bastard," White whispered. During their pre-op training she had been told that it was possible the Russians were maintaining audio and video feeds and could be watching everything as it transpired. She wasn't going to say or do anything to give away who she was or how she got there.

Once Kiselva was pulled from his sleeping bag, she used plastic ties to secure his hands behind him. Then his feet were bound together. She searched him and finding nothing she continued. She wrapped a gag she had brought over his mouth and before plugging his ears she whispered, "Move from here and I will kill you without hesitation, no warnings!" She covered his eyes, slid him back into the sleeping bag and zipped it up, leaving him totally helpless and unable to do anything more than float.

With her captive in tow White pushed off and headed back toward her team. Minutes later, Jackson and the rest opened the hatch to the storage pod and freed the three who were astonished to see even more strangers aboard their station. Once they had cleared the hatch White shoved Kiselva into the small space, leaving him to float aimlessly within it. With the hatch lowered and nearly closed as before, the team leader had some explaining to do but first things first.

Jackson identified himself, suggested everything was okay, and directed them to change into cleaner clothes and use a proper bathroom as soon as possible. "I had heard the air would have a metallic smell to it," Jackson joked, "but you three are pretty gamey. Meet back here in ten and we'll talk."

Hugs and fist bumps from Johnson and Patrick, both familiar faces to the men they had just rescued, were followed by assurances that these Marines and Houston were going to get the situation straightened out fast. The astronauts were a family and worked and played together on earth and in orbit. Despite a few minutes of pushback the three agreed, got changed, and were back for the briefing in less than five minutes.

After a whispered celebration and a barrage of questions the Mission Commander and the T1 Commander shook hands and agreed there was work to be done.

"You guys get reoriented as quickly as you can and make sure this bird is flying right," Jackson said. "We are all U.S. Armed Forces who have sworn an oath and all you need to know, and do know, is that there was a massive technical communications glitch on the ISS and you are in the middle of fixing that right now."

Simmons, an Air Force Captain who had flown drone missions over Iraq, Afghanistan, and parts unknown before getting his ISS assignment in space, was familiar with the look of a special operations team. They were smart, fit, fast, and not to be fucked with. Simmons' presence on the ISS, a top secret mission of its own to ensure the U.S. weaponry aboard orbiting satellites and within the ISS itself were operational, made the men kindred spirits.

"You going to stay around for dinner, or do you have a flight of some kind to catch?" Simmons asked.

"We'll double-check on our Russian friend. Then, if it's okay with you, I'll ask you and the other two to remain down there in his module for ten minutes. After that, you can carry on with whatever the hell you guys do up here," Jackson responded. "We'll let President Stewart decide how to play this out, once comms are fully back in order."

"Sounds like a plan," Simmons responded. "But we need to meet over a few beers somewhere in the future down below."

"Deal," Jackson said, "and you're buying!"

After checking on their prisoner and reorienting him so that his head was sticking out of the top of his sleeping bag, the T1 team and the crew aboard the ISS shook hands, bumped fists, high fived, and hugged with a great deal of enthusiasm. For all of them, what had taken place aboard that ship had been a monumental achievement for the BOTM program and a win for good over a Russian evil. The expression on Kiselva's face was still one of confusion and heartbreak.

"He told us they were holding his daughter, that's why he fucked us. They were threatening the only thing he cares about back on earth, his Tatiana," Burns offered.

"Yeah, he's always been a good guy," Simmons added, "until they screwed with his family and us."

Jackson glided over to Kiselva and placed one hand on the Russian's shoulder and placed his other on the ceiling. Looking back at the crew he smiled and then focused again on the Russian.

"Relax. MI6 has your daughter, in London!" Jackson assured their prisoner. "She's fine and you'll be able to talk to her soon. Right after you swear on her life that you will never let on that we were ever here. If you do, it will end badly for you. You won't be able to hide anywhere. Do you understand me clearly, Nico?"

Tears of joy floated from his eyes, into the weightlessness of space. Jackson removed the gag from over the man's mouth.

"You do know he will never be able to return to Russia?" Sharif suggested.

"I'll take England," Nico proclaimed, "or better yet, America!"

The astronauts all pushed themselves to their friend so they could embrace each other and hope that soon this nightmare would be over. They weren't quite ready to forgive him or even cut him loose, but this was great news to be celebrated by all. Turning back to thank Jackson and his team, Simmons saw that they had already retreated to the other module.

"God, I wish everything had a happy ending like that," Sharif said as they gathered to prepare for return to Earth. "There's a lot of shit that needs to get straightened out. But for now, I'm happy to say 'sayonara, space station' and head home for that damn bar you guys keep dragging me to. I need a beer!"

"Any of you ever had a happy ending in space?" White asked jokingly.

"Let's saddle up, boys and girls," Jackson ordered. Looking at the two astronauts who had joined the team on such an incredibly risky mission, he smiled and thanked them both for being part of the rescue mission.

"Before we go, I have to ask one follow-up question. Is it possible to have sex in weightlessness? I mean really, this is—"

White interrupted. "JJ, did you just ask these two fine young women you just met about sex in outer space? What would Michelle think!" White laughed.

"She's the least of my worries, Christy!" Jackson responded.

"Oh man, and he doesn't even have a beer in him yet," Sharif added.

"Must be the radiation!" Jackson said.

"Okay, okay, I'll buy first round but that's only if you all get in position and we get the heck back to Andrews."

Anticipating forming a circle in weightlessness might be difficult, they had practiced the maneuver many times in the test flights near Dover. Inside the large cargo plane it had been difficult, but in the close quarters of this American module it was very easy.

"Permission to leave the ship," Jackson said to Buchanan, but another voice answered.

"Permission granted." It was Simmons, who apparently thought he'd waited long enough before returning. He saluted the departing team.

"Okay, 3…2…1…" Buchanan counted down.

Nothing.

"Do it again, tighten up the ring, double-check the pulses, make sure they are close to your chests," Jackson ordered.

"Fuck!" White shouted. "We forgot – they'd be floating!"

Simmons saw and heard what was happening. In an instant he floated toward the circle and grabbed a roll of duct tape from a nearby storage cabinet. Handing it to Sharif he looked at Jackson while the team passed the roll from one operator to the next.

"Do me a favor and go back and check on that Russian

one more time?" Jackson said as if asking a favor instead of delivering an order.

"Safe travels, all!" Simmons said and then glided back through the end of the module and out of sight.

"Take two," Buchanan said, his voice loaded with a frustrating tone. He had been skeptical of the trip and although the ISS had been freed he wasn't confident they'd be back on earth drinking beers anytime soon.

In their circle once again, the team heard Buchanan count, "3…2…1…"

Still, no go. The pulses weren't working. The team stared at each other. What now?

Simmons gave the team another few minutes to do whatever it was they needed to do and then he returned to the module, hoping to see them gone. Surprised by what he found, he had only one thing to say. "What's it gonna take to get you freeloaders off my ship?"

There they were, floating about the module, a rapid return to earth now very much in question.

"Guess you don't have any beer on board this tin can?" Buchanan asked.

Jackson, White, and Sharif floated close together. They had spent years stranded in a desert and now, at least for a short time, they might be stranded in space.

"Well, like they say, it's not a job it's an adventure!" White laughed. "If we're going to be here for a while let's at least enjoy the view!" She extended her hand to Jackson and led the way to the cupola.

The astronauts huddled. They had work to do. They needed to make sure all systems aboard were fully functional, that communications were restored with Earth and with their families, that life sustaining systems like oxygen, water, food, and waste were addressed. For however long their passengers without boarding passes would be along for the ride they would need to take care of them and, more importantly, make sure that nobody on Earth ever saw or heard them while they were up there.

"Radiation, Mr. President," Jackson said calmly into the top secret video conference call he had with the White House. "It's the only thing we can think of at this point."

Stewart was relieved to see that Jackson was all right and that the entire group, including the compromised Russian, were okay.

"We'll get with the private companies to see what they've got flying and when. If that's not viable then we'll see how quickly we can get a ship up there to bring you all back home," Stewart said.

"If we can do a night launch from the Cape under the Department of Defense contract for shipments to the ISS and use a man-capable capsule instead of a basic cargo one, there's a chance we could bring all six of you back down in one covert shot. You just have to be sure that none of you wind up on television for God's sake while you're up there!"

So that was the plan. Wait it out. Make do with the provisions available on the ISS, and also come up with a plan to pay Doronin back for what he had done to the ISS, the Americans, and his own Kiselva.

Later that night in the private residence, Stewart scrolled through the television channels on the flat screen in his bedroom. Something in the listings caught his eye and then he switched off the television and sat back against the headboard. *Never been there*, he thought to himself. *Maybe someday, JJ.*

It would take a month for the BOTM T1 team to return to earth. Life aboard the ISS had become surprisingly mundane for the warriors. The weightlessness, rationed food and drink, cramped quarters, and extreme attention to avoiding being seen or heard on any video or audio feeds had become frustrating. Bothering them even more was the fact that this mission had taken the six pulse devices out of action for nearly thirty days. The concern over them being damaged by radiation in space left Jackson and White at odds at times.

In Russia, Doronin had slowly begun resuming his public outings and televised speeches to his country and the world. There was no mention of the actions he felt the United States, or others, might have taken against him and there was no news about the goings on in space. Doronin was anxious to get his hands on Kiselva and had ordered his immediate return on the Soyuz, which was already docked on the station.

"*Nyet*," Nico told Doronin directly on a secure communication line between the Russian module and the Kremlin. As he had in the American modules, Kiselva had shut down all feeds from the Russian areas except for the one secure line and once that short discussion with his President had concluded, it too was terminated.

"So we're floating in space, the pulses are on holiday, the only surefire way home right now is with a Soyuz capsule whose guidance system can't be overridden and would land us in hostile, remote Kazakhstan if we tried to use it to get home," White stated to Sharif.

"Don't go getting all up in it, Christy," Sharif insisted. "JJ'll use his special powers and bring that Gladiator bitch up here from the Coliseum to kick your ass if you don't chill!"

"She had something else in mind for me, Omar!" White responded as she broke out in laughter.

> "Sorry. Venting completed." Little did they know that would be their last day in space.
>
> A cargo resupply ship had been on the schedule to make the trip from Cape Kennedy in Florida to the ISS. Under the tightest security, the ship had been refitted with eight seats and the oxygen, reentry suits, helmets, and such needed to accommodate the travelers.

"So that's the drill," Jackson concluded. "The ship will arrive in eleven hours and all seven of us, including our comrade, will be able to fit aboard."

The biggest issue, one that the returning astronauts were already aware of and chose not to inform the Marines, was that this was essentially a supply vessel without consideration ever given to humans being on board. The ship's hatch could not be opened from the inside, the travelers would have absolutely no control over the flying of the vessel, and the landing would take place on hard earth rather than gliding onto a runway like the Space Shuttles had or splashing down in the ocean as the Apollo, Gemini, and Mercury flights had dating back to the early sixties.

Once the rescue vessel had docked at the ISS, and the much needed supplies were placed aboard, the T1 team wasted no time floating inside it and examining their ride home.

"If there's an issue like they had on Apollo One, we're screwed," Sharif said.

"Details, details," White said as she settled back into the seat furthest into the vessel. "No windows but we can play cards on the way down."

Jackson assembled his team and floated like the rest of them as Simmons laid it out for them in plain English. "This has never been done before," he reminded them.

"Yeah, we're kinda in that business," Jackson said as he looked at Buchanan, White, and Sharif. "Let's suit up and get the hell out of here. It's time to get back to work."

Ninety minutes later seven people were harnessed tight into their seats, helmets on, all systems go.

"Edwards, fuck Edwards," White exclaimed.

"I agree, we're that close," Buchanan joined in. "If you can't drop us at Nellis then I'm calling an Uber!"

Johnson and Patrick, the two mission specialists, didn't partake in the banter. They were busy going over checklists, but with limited instrumentation on the barren supply ship the list consisted of making sure everyone was buckled in, oxygen flowing, and a perfect seal once the hatch was latched closed from the outside.

"I'll bite, Marine," Johnson finally said, "Why Nellis?"

"Vegas, baby!" Kiselva shouted. "Even this dumb Russian knows it is close to Las Vegas!"

With farewell salutes exchanged at the ISS, the hatch secured and an air-tight seal verified, operational command of the vessel was taken over by scientists and technicians in Houston. Twenty-eight days after departing Andrews, T1 and its Russian detainee were coming down fast in the middle of the night over Edwards Air Force Base in Southern California. Concerns had been raised about the extraordinary weight the ship would be carrying as it hurled back to earth. Typically one massive parachute would have been enough to slow the ride and land with a gentle thump. A back-up chute had always been in place if needed but NASA added a third unit they hoped would adequately handle the mission and opted to deploy all three. Despite the technology that went into the effort, T1's rescue mission ended with a very unceremonious thud.

"Damn," Jackson uttered as he and the rest of the crew recovered from the hard hit at touchdown. The others offered more colorful comments or descriptions of the landing.

"What the fuck," White said angrily. "I paid for first class."

"This feels like a Workman's Comp claim," Buchanan joked in a whispered voice. The wind had been knocked out of him but he wasn't about to let on.

"Welcome to America," Sharif said as he looked to Kiselva and reached for his gloved hand. "I hope you brought your passport."

It took five minutes for the heat and vapors coming off the rescue ship to fade enough for the recovery teams to open the hatch and welcome the travelers back to the United States. The T2 team and members of their support group had flown out to Edwards from Andrews to secure their arrival and identities, and quickly ushered the seven into a large passenger van and drove directly to a remote barracks that had been secured at the order of the Commander in Chief for their top secret return, rest and recuperation. Most chose to grab a beer and pizza that had been prepared for them as part of a welcome home buffet. Reacquainting themselves with earth's gravity would take a short time but the medical team cleared them and suggested they eat, drink and be merry, but a shower and some sleep was highly recommended too.

For Kiselva, NSO Director Morrison welcomed him to America and escorted him to another location on base. He would not be allowed to leave the building or communicate with anyone on the outside, but there was someone waiting for him. With his daughter back safe in his arms, nothing else mattered.

When the news reached Stewart in the Situation Room his heart slowed to a normal beat. After a quick telephone conversation, Stewart headed up to the residence for some much needed sleep. Happy that they had all made it home safely, he had two things on his mind that would keep him up a bit longer. "Will the damn pulses work now that they're back on earth?" was one he asked himself. The other: "What do we do about Doronin?"

A day later, Stewart got an answer to at least one of his questions as Jackson walked into the Oval Office. "How'd you get back here so fast?" Stewart exclaimed as he stepped from around his desk and gave the Marine an uncharacteristic hug. Stepping back to look at him, Stewart asked again, "Well, boy, you're supposed to be getting your sea legs and resting up. What are you doing here?"

Jackson had been surprised by the embrace but was caught up in the moment as well. "Pleased to inform you that the BOTM program appears to be fully operational again, Mr. President. We opted to forgo some time off out West and tested the pulses first thing this morning. Got from California to Maryland in an instant. We left Kiselva and the two astronauts back at Edwards and grabbed some help from T2 to complete the ring and get us home AOK."

CHAPTER 14

Stewart's speech at NATO headquarters had taken place two years earlier and he took great pride in the fact that terrorism and crime overall in the United States had been reduced dramatically. His "Wild West" policy, where more and more citizens raised their awareness, their vigilance, and their action, was paying the dividends he had hoped for.

In the rest of the world things were improving as well. Not all countries embraced Stewart's call to arms, but peace-loving people had banded together and began following the mantra he had suggested. "See something, say something, do something," was working. For a 4th of July speech the President was to give at a World War II Warbird museum event in Virginia, he asked Jackson and Emma to accompany him. As the three military helicopters circled the field, two being decoys and the third carrying the President and his party, Stewart sat forward in his seat to peer out the windows of Marine One and urged his guests to do the same.

"Look at those beautiful birds," he exclaimed. A few thousand feet beneath them, the restored Memphis Belle B-17 bomber and the Whiskey 7, a C-47 military transport plane, heroes of the past, sat parked on either side of the podium where he would deliver his address.

"We've come a long way since then," Jackson said. "B-52s, and drones and B-2 stealth bombers, but those men that flew missions in them, and jumped out of those C-47s, were some bad asses."

Stewart nodded as he kept his eyes on the planes.

"It's one thing to operate a joystick from five thousand miles away and drop bombs but it was a whole other thing to jump out of the Whiskey 7 over Normandy on D-Day. Those men jumped from low altitude into the night sky, with Germans spread out across the countryside below them." Stewart paused. "Our fighting men and women are the best of the best, but I still have to admire and be amazed at the stories that came from that invasion."

Jackson was ready to continue the conversation but he noticed tears had filled Stewart's eyes. He decided to let the moment be and wait for the landing to take place so they could get up and get moving.

Emma had noticed the tears as well. Her family was from the UK and had endured the bombings and threats from Hitler's Germany. She remembered the stories her grandfather had told of how frightening it was for an entire country to expect to be bombed every night during the war.

Once the helicopter landed it was time for Stewart to greet the crowd and make his way to the podium. Agent Hill had been riding with them and began to lead the President directly to the stage. But, as Stewart shook hands and stopped to pose for a picture every ten feet or so, Hill noticed Stewart was pointing at something.

"Grizzly wants to go over to the plane," Hill spoke into his wrist-mounted microphone. Grizzly was the Secret Service's code name for this President and with good cause. Stewart carried a presence that showed confidence and capability and he knew it. He was a warrior himself having spent a lifetime in the Marines. Nobody wanted to get in the crosshairs of this man.

Both planes had been open to the public until an hour before Marine One was scheduled to land. Once they were cleared, the areas were cordoned off and the Secret Service's advance team inspected them again for people and weapons. The machine guns that were mounted in the nose, tail, belly, top, and side gun ports had been inspected. With the firing mechanisms disabled they could render no harm but were checked again before the okay to proceed was given.

Hill had expected Stewart would bypass the podium area and head straight for the Memphis Belle but instead he walked directly to the rear, pilot's side, of the Whiskey 7. He turned and waved to the crowd, gestured for Hill, Jackson, and Emma to wait for him outside, and then stepped onto the aluminum stairs that led into the aircraft. Hill followed him to the doorway but waited and watched as the President took a seat on the pilot's side of the plane. During missions, up to twenty-eight paratroopers would sit down either side of the plane, flying to their missions, waiting for the red jump light at the doorway to change to green for go.

Patriotic music was being played over the facilities loudspeaker system while Stewart sat quietly with his thoughts. Hill watched as the President slowly inspected the plane. The walls were painted a drab military green with not a shred of sound or temperature insulation to be seen. This was the most bare-bones personnel aircraft he had ever seen.

"Sir," Hill said. "You okay, Mr. President?"

Stewart took a deep breath, stood up, and took three

steps toward the doorway. "Can you imagine jumping out of this door in the middle of the night in the dark and floating down into harm's way?"

"I've seen all the movies, Mr. President, but no, for most of the young men who went through these doors, I can't imagine what they were feeling."

"I've never been inside one of these before. I'm glad I came aboard. Now let's do this speech. Then I want to go home. That's more than so many of them would live to do."

Stepping back down onto the ground Stewart gave the crowd a big wave and then followed Hill to the podium and delivered a powerful speech carried live on CNN and other networks. When it was over, he spent a great deal of time shaking hands and exchanging greetings with well-wishers. An hour later, Marine One was back at the White House but Stewart's mood had turned somber.

At his request, Emma got dinner started in the residence kitchen while Jackson poured them both a beer and sat down in the massive living room. They sat quietly for a time, listening to their Scottish cook as she spoke to herself while she prepared the cheeseburgers, hot dogs, and potato salad that had been requested.

Normally the three television screens would have been turned on, but Jackson sensed the President wanted to talk instead.

After nearly five minutes, Stewart began to tell a story.

"JJ, I know you've never heard this before because I have never discussed it with anyone other than my mother. World War II touched everyone who was alive back then in one way or another, but for her something happened that crushed her soul and took her from me long before she ever died. I'll give you the short version."

Jackson put his beer down on the coffee table and sat forward on the chair. Stewart went on to tell how his uncle, his mother's only brother, had been a young paratrooper during that war and was stationed in England prior to the Allied invasion of Normandy in June of 1944. He was on one of those C-47s that took off for France that night, but he never came home. The worst of it was that he was never found. Word coming back from the men he flew with that night was that he chickened out and never jumped. He was the last man in the line. He let all of them go out that door into the night but stayed aboard.

"So, when they landed back in England he was probably arrested?" Jackson suggested.

"Nope, there is no record of him ever arriving back at the airfield. There is no record of him from the point he put on his chute and climbed aboard one of those transports that night. Believe me, with the assets at my disposal at the Pentagon and everywhere else, I checked."

Jackson sat back in his chair. "And your mother?"

Stewart shook his head slowly. "She couldn't bear to think she had lost her baby brother. Worse yet, that he had been yellow and didn't jump." Stewart's expression changed from sadness to anger. "It broke her heart and her mind, and depression whittled away at her spirit until there wasn't much left."

Jackson was amazed that he had never heard this story. Not from Stewart or Elizabeth.

"That's one of the million reasons Elizabeth and I took you in when you were lost. I had lived a bit of your journey myself and wasn't ever going to let anyone else feel that alone ever again if I could help it."

Emma called out that the dinner was now ready and as

the two men walked into the kitchen, Jackson's mind was already fast at work.

Meanwhile, five thousand miles south southeast of Washington, Michelle Jackson was on a mission of her own.

"I've never seen so much meat for breakfast, lunch, dinner, snacks – it's like pizza and pasta in Italy- it's everywhere," she said to the waiter. Argentina is known for its cattle, music, and the fading tales of members of Hitler's Third Reich, including Adolf himself, who was said to have fled to this South American country at the end of World War II. She had never been to Buenos Aires before, but in a town on the outskirts of that metropolitan city a predator of children, one who wore a priest's collar, was rumored to be still on the loose. Michelle intended to turn the tables on the sinner and turn him into her prey.

She had been doing this around the world for some time now. She often used press credentials issued to her by an American news magazine, a favor repaid to a powerful Cardinal in the U.S. When they met to discuss her next assignment, their next target, Inspector Rizzo passed her a satchel full of twenty and hundred euro bills, for travel and expenses.

Michelle had arrived in Argentina three days prior. She had flown on an eleven-hour nonstop from Rome to Miami, took a day in South Florida to take out some trash, and then took the nine-hour flight from Miami to Buenos Aires. She opted to acclimate to the weather and the five-hour time zone change between Italy and Argentina relying on wine and sleeping aids to ensure each night's rest. She had little time for sightseeing but was intrigued by the tango dancers who performed in her hotel lounge each night. Now well rested, she was ready for the hunt.

"This animal is connected and that means he is also protected," Rizzo had briefed her before she left Rome. "His family is in politics and cattle ranches and once the local police, the ones that weren't on the family payroll, started to investigate the complaints of the children and their families, the bastard left the local church and began serving the sacraments in the private chapel at his parents' home. It's much more than a home though," Rizzo had cautioned her. "It's more of a European style villa, I was told, much like you would find in Germany or the north of Italy. We have been told that it has perimeter walls, security gates, guards, dogs, and motion sensors."

"Piece of cake," Michelle had said with a laugh. "I'll do my own recon and then decide how to proceed," she continued. "From what I read in his file, this bastard needs to feel something very uncomfortable just like his victims have."

"*Quello che temevo*!" Rizzo said as he shook his head. "I was afraid you would say that—but you must remember, His Holiness said they should just be eliminated, nothing else done to them in any other way."

"*Prego*," Michelle responded. It was an acknowledgement she struggled with but would follow orders nonetheless. At least that is what she always led Rizzo to believe.

Michelle had driven past the family compound a few times and said quietly to herself, "If I can't get him here I will in Montevideo, but I want his death to be the talk of the conference. I want to put the fear of God and me in any of those attendees that prey on children or protect those who do. They might think their heavenly God will deal with them at the Pearly Gates, but they must also know this unseen guardian angel is delivering earthly justice beforehand!"

Posing as she often did as a journalist, she met at a café with the local police detective who had been pursuing the arrest of the suspected priest. He had been taken off the case by the police chief who was a close friend of the priest and his protective family. Frustrated, he was of little help, offering only that it would take an army to raid the estate. It was time for her to implement Plan B and she was ready to go.

Months earlier, the Pope had directed that a special conference was to be held in Montevideo, Uruguay where priests, bishops and two cardinals would assemble at a four-star hotel, there to pray and to discuss how to increase attendance at weekly Masses. In an attempt to appease the locals and the media, addressing the sinners of pedophilia would also be on the agenda. Attendance would be mandatory. His Holiness would open the conference and address that congregation by live videoconference by satellite feed from the Vatican.

Michelle left the small Argentine town and the local detective, and drove back to Buenos Aires and took a flight to Montevideo. She checked into a hotel that was located near where the conference would take place and now she would wait, impatiently, while sitting at the hotel pool and reading her homework. She hated to wait for anything. She remembered how JJ and the other Special Ops would seem to act with such swiftness. They'd plan a mission and then execute it. "Get in, get off, get out," was an informal motto she and her Special Ops friends had said jokingly in happier times.

While other vacationers around her were drinking beer or clerico, a mix of wine and fruit juice, reading their Kindles or just enjoying the sun, Michelle was studying the files

Rizzo had given her. Most missions were one-offs and then on to the next assignment. For her, this was an opportunity to make a statement right there in front of the priests and the world media. Now, her target—the most elusive one so far—just needed to show up.

The morning before the conference was to begin, Michelle took a long walk through the neighborhood surrounding what was regarded as hotel row. As she passed a Catholic church at just before eleven, with church bells calling the believers to prayer, a woman stopped her.

"Are you coming in, my child?" she asked.

"No, no thank you," Michelle replied. "I am a sinner and there is no forgiveness for what I have done." Startled by the response, the woman took Michelle's hand and held it for a moment.

"Christ forgives all sinners who repent, who are sorry and remorseful."

"That's the problem," Michelle said softly. With that, she slowly withdrew her hand, bade the woman a good morning, and continued on her excursion.

The morning of the conference, Michelle sailed through the metal detectors and the security staffers who rooted through her handbag and then collected her media credentials in one of the smaller conference rooms located adjacent to the lobby. She took a spot on the stairway that led up to the main ballroom so she would have an unrestricted vantage point as the clerics arrived and headed for the elevators. The crowd outside had grown, filled mostly with sign-bearing protesters demanding justice for the innocent, and a large number of photographers and video camera operators. Not much happened in the largest city in Uruguay and so this event drew quite a crowd.

"Is he coming?" Michelle murmured to herself. She had been accustomed to easily locating and accessing her previous targets but this one was different. He had been operating under a veil of security in his homeland but here, in another country, he might not be as familiar. But, if he came, she was sure to see him.

Amidst all the black suits of the security and the black robes of the clergy, one man stood out, his red skullcap signifying his rank as Cardinal. "Bingo!" she uttered when she recognized him. One of the most powerful men in the Church hierarchy had also been the target of lawsuits and public denunciations by victims of abuse. He was never thought to have committed crimes against children. His sin, at least to many, had been looking the other way. "Él *sabía!* Él *sabía*!—He knew, he knew!" she had heard the huge crowd chant as the elderly high priest walked from his car and through the massive doors to the hotel.

It was clear after she waited throughout the day that the Argentine priest would not show, at least not through the front door, but for Michelle, the focus had changed. In her mind, Cardinal Falso was like the man who let his untrained dogs wander the neighborhood terrorizing people. To her, that was a more vile sin and she was not going to leave without another sinner being expedited to their judgment day.

She caught herself remembering the words President George Bush delivered after the 9/11 attacks. "You're either with us or against us," she recalled his saying, "You're either friend or foe."

She attended Falso's press conference, held after the day's first session concluded, and with some help from within the Vatican she managed to secure five minutes of his busy schedule for a brief interview. Freshening up first in the lobby's ladies room, she rode the elevator to the top floor and was escorted down the long hall and into his suite. Falso was just finishing a glass of what looked like orange juice and sat back in a large chair that overlooked the Montevideo skyline. A member of his security team searched her handbag while another examined her credentials and then she was introduced to the man with the red cap and reminded she had but five minutes to sit and talk. That was all she would need.

She bowed her head ever so slightly as she reached to shake the Cardinal's extended right hand. It had been a long day and his grasp felt somewhat frail. She held it gently with both hands for a moment as they exchanged greetings. Agreeing to speak in English, they began the interview, but Michelle wasn't paying much attention to what the Cardinal had to say in response to any of her probing questions. The rage in her was trying to take over but she maintained her composure and continued.

Maybe I should just throw him through the window, she thought to herself.

"Do you think, Your Excellency, that the day will ever come that the Church publicly identifies its sinners and the conspirators who protected them?" she asked.

His candor surprised her. "It is all about the lawyers and the accountants and the consultants now, my child," he said. "If the Catholic Church began to publicly identify not just those who have sinned but also those who ignored it or who covered it up then it would open the Church to a culpability that would destroy her financially and worse than that, emotionally."

Michelle listened but her rage grew even more. *My child?* he had said. *How dare he*, she thought as the Cardinal continued to speak.

"Not only that," he continued, "it would betray the vow of silence in the confessional. Sins confessed to a priest, regardless of who is admitting them, are protected. If people do not feel what they confess to a priest will remain private then contrite confessions, absolution, and forgiveness of sins, is no longer a part of our world. Christ started this sacrament and so to compromise it could end the Church as we know it and could further challenge a belief in God that would make this earth a very different place."

Michelle had heard enough. His answers, his excuses might have had merit, but it didn't matter. The Cardinal's timing had been near perfect. Their short interview had come to end, and she could see the next journalist waiting at the door for their turn. As she stood up and thanked him, this time he extended both hands to hers.

"Forgive me for I do know what I do," she whispered.

Seemingly confused at what he thought he heard, the Cardinal grasped her hands even tighter and then bade her goodbye. From there, Michelle casually walked to the elevator and pushed the call button with a knuckle. Minutes later she was in the lobby and headed toward the ladies' room where she washed her hands vigorously with soap and hot water. She then squirted a glob of hand sanitizer from a small bottle she had taken from her purse and scrubbed her hands a second time before checking her make-up and exiting the hotel. The crowds had diminished and the night sky was rolling in.

An hour later at her hotel, a white t-shirt, blue jeans, and sandals replaced her smart business suit and heels. A red Phillies baseball cap sat atop her short blonde hair.

Red looks better on me, she thought to herself as she looked in the mirror one last time before heading out for a meal. But first, she went online and booked a return ticket to Buenos Aires. Her target there had been elusive but she was up for the challenge. The next morning her cellphone's ring woke her from a very deep sleep.

"Michelle," Rizzo said in an angry tone. "The Pope wants you to return to Rome immediately."

She listened but didn't respond.

"Did you hear what I said?" He waited for an answer but still nothing. "Cardinal Falso is dead but the Argentinian is still alive. They are saying it looks like he died of a heart attack in his sleep. The Pope asked me if you might have gotten confused. I told him you wouldn't have."

"What the fuck," Michelle said in an angry tone.

"Michelle, are you okay?" Rizzo asked.

"I need to wake up and get some coffee in me. I don't know what you are talking about, especially on an international call like this, Inspector Rizzo. Falso was a very old man. I interviewed him late yesterday and he seemed frail. His heart finally gave out so now he is facing his Maker."

There was silence on the phone. This was the first time the two had ever spoken about business over a phone.

"Rizzo, you there?"

"They don't know for sure what killed Falso yet," Rizzo continued, maintaining his calm tone. "Perhaps someone poisoned his food. He did have quite a few enemies and the South Americans are a very passionate people. Come home and we will sort this out with His Holiness."

"Still not sure what you are saying," Michelle responded. "Sounds like you've been watching too many spy movies. It's not like anyone could deliver a nerve agent in a handshake – at least not like they did in that movie *The Interview*. That's all Hollywood shit."

Hours later, Michelle boarded a flight that would take her fifteen hours, with a stop in São Paulo, Brazil, back to Rome and a meeting with the Pope. *I'll have a few things to say to him as well,* she thought as the flight attendant gave instructions on the use of seat belts and floatation devices.

"*Ciao*, South America," she whispered as she watched the land grow further from her after takeoff. "I'll be back!" she said with conviction.

CHAPTER 15

For Jackson and the rest of the team, it felt like old times. Years before, their Hollywood producer and war memorabilia collector Bill Griffiths had supplied their missions with the proper clothing and weaponry to return to just about any time in the past. He supplied them for the wintry Valley Forge of 1778, the Japanese surrender aboard the U.S.S. Missouri in 1945, and so much more. With him long gone, others had been taken into the veil of Black Ops secrecy with the promise that someday they too would be rewarded for their patriotism and their confidentiality.

Jackson, Buchanan, Morrison, and Petty would make up T1 for this adventure, taking the President of the United States on a top secret BOTM mission that fascinated and intrigued every one of them. Unfortunately Sharif and White, due to their ethnicity, would have to remain behind and watch as frustrated bystanders. There weren't many men of Arab skin tone and appearance or black women walking about military installations in England in June of 1944 during World War II and there was no need to draw any additional attention to T1's movements or personnel. It wasn't unheard of but this mission, especially with their VIP along, couldn't bring any more attention to itself than was absolutely necessary.

Morrison and Petty had both been on missions before, Morrison going along to plant bugs in the Kremlin and other Russian offices, and Petty had gone on a similar one to China. Both had careers full of military service and specialized in intelligence and counter intelligence before assuming their national roles at the White House and the Pentagon. Stewart had wanted both to experience BOTM first hand. Plus, it was Petty who brought Moretti and her remarkable time travel technology to Stewart and the other leaders at the Pentagon so it was a fitting reward, Stewart and Jackson felt. Petty also felt China was the biggest threat to U.S. security and he wanted to do whatever he could to subvert them.

But who would they select to wear the sixth pulse around their neck on this next mission? Based on his service and relationships with most members of the team, Stewart's Lead Secret Service Agent Jason Hill got the call. Once all the research had been conducted, checked, and double-checked, and uniforms, side arms, and light gear were acquired, the team met in the Situation Room many levels below the White House.

Back at Andrews though, Sharif and White weren't happy. "We've gone from meeting our Maker to setting up a suicide by cop in the Vatican. I think I may have seen and done about all I can take of this. Other than our mission to Gethsemane, when did BOTM become a thrill ride for the rich and powerful?" White said after she finished her beer and placed the glass down somewhat forcefully.

"Yeah, we've gone from twenty-four-seven missions to kill bad guys to episodes on the Travel Channel," Sharif responded. "But you seem to have enjoyed meeting Jefferson, and don't tell me you knew what JJ was really up to that night."

The expression on White's face changed from frustrated and angry to one of guilt and remorse.

"Christy," Sharif said. "We all need a break now and then. All of us do, even you, the badass from the Bay Area." That line made White laugh.

The waitress brought them four more beers, White's standard order when there were two drinkers. "We do have two hands, don't we?" she would often joke.

"And that bullshit in outer space, what the fuck was that all about?" she went on. "If we had been lost, or just the pulses been damaged, think of everything that could have been done that we wouldn't have been able to. With only six left, we need to use them wisely."

"JJ had said that we couldn't go on the way we were, that eventually the pulses or the people would fail or fuck up, so it was time to slow things down and really make sure that whatever missions any of us went on going forward, they needed to have a bigger picture value," added Sharif. "I guess the ISS needed saving and even more so, Russia needed to be shown they still can't fuck with the USA!"

"Well, I've said it before, I was ready to quit and just teach self-defense classes at the damn Y if I ever got bored or frustrated with whatever the fuck this is—politics, boys clubs, whatever." White was an exceptional Marine and after the hard life she'd grown up in back in Oakland, once she found her place in the Corps, she was on a mission to seek and destroy. Deviating from that wasn't of much interest to her.

They sat quietly. The lives they had lived, all that they had seen and done so far, both still only in their early thirties, left them wonder from time to time what they could possibly do to top where their lives had taken them so far.

"I'm not ready to become a beach bum quite yet like JJ jokes he might be," Sharif said. "But I think JJ's right, we need to slow it down and smell some roses now and then."

"Remember all the rules back in the day about not changing anything, not taking or leaving anything?" White asked him.

Sharif looked at her, his expression indicating he wanted her to go on.

"Forget I ever said that. I guess I'm just trying to say, for a while our lives were like we were binging on war movies and terrorist plots and we were the main characters, but it was crazy. If it weren't for BOTM, and Michelle, and all that, we never would have been stranded in the desert, Tommy would be alive today, and so on. We didn't leave things or take things but the act itself had repercussions."

"Yeah, but think of the thousands of lives we've saved by using it against the shit heads," Sharif added. "This all started out as a test program, testing us and the technology. It's just a shame we had to lose some of the team along the way. But remember, except for Bennie Abrams, it was mostly people's own fuck ups that cost them their lives."

"Okay, when you meet JR in heaven make sure you tell him that hole in his head was his fault. That's bullshit!"

The waitress stopped by the table to see if they wanted anything else. Last call.

"Tell me something," White asked her. "You've worked here a long time and you know we're all military right?" The waitress nodded but seemed impatient. Last call discussions with patrons that had been drinking all night typically were a waste of time, at least for her.

"Did you ever want to change places with any of us so you could shoot bad guys and we could just sit here and serve drinks, flirt with customers, and go home safe every night?"

The waitress laughed. "Fuck that! Those assholes shoot back!"

White nodded while Sharif finished his beer.

"Not always," Sharif whispered.

A few miles away, in the BOTM hangar at Andrews, Stewart walked from Marine One into the hangar that housed one of the two Air Force One 747 jets. He passed through an entry door into a garage that contained twelve black SUV support vehicles and rode from that hangar down to the BOTM one. With Hill walking alongside him, they were soon in the changing room dressing as World War II Army journalists covering Operation Overlord, the D-Day invasion.

Just as they always had during the early days of testing, the T1 operatives joked back and forth as they watched the transformation from modern day Marines to whatever the costume of the day might be. Once they checked and double-checked that they had the proper forged identification documents, 1944-era United States currency, and nothing from the current day along with them, Jackson had the team huddle up in the transport room.

"It just occurred to me," Jackson said, "do any of you know how to operate a typewriter?" None of the team answered.

"You're all too damn young," Stewart said with a laugh. "Just keep your notepads and pens and pencils flying, boys. If anyone needs to do any typing I think I can handle that chore."

"Remember our ranks, ladies," Jackson said one last time. Pointing at the President, he continued. "That man there is

Major Dick Stewart, United States Army War Correspondent and our team leader. He's not POTUS on this run!"

Forming their circle, they reached underneath their uniform ties and through their shirts to make sure the pulse device was centered, close to their beating hearts.

They were all looking at Stewart. He had never done this before, but he was a U.S. Marine, a career badass who had seen more action than any of them. The look on his face was one of confidence and conviction. He was on a mission and nothing was going to stand in his way. Counting down from three to one, in an instant, they were gone.

On arrival, the sound was deafening. More than thirty of the massive C-47s, painted brown in color and with three distinctive white stripes on the fuselage and wings, roared to life. Their twin engine, propeller-driven power plants roared with life as they lined up outside. That night, June 6 1944, hundreds of these same scenes were taking place at countless airfields located across England. Aboard each plane U.S. paratroopers, carrying nearly one hundred pounds of weaponry and gear, were sitting against the wall on benches that ran the length of the inside of each transport.

Soon, they would be flying over the English Channel toward the French coast and the area known as Normandy. There, along with a massive attack from the sea, the Allies would launch their famous campaign that would push the Germans to their graves or back to Berlin in defeat. On one of those planes, this one taking off from Cottesmore Airfield in the East Midlands of England, was carrying Stewart's uncle, a very young U.S. Army man named Roy.

"Wow!" Buchanan said as he regarded the sound of the massive engines. The team had landed perfectly as planned within an empty hangar on the base. The C-47s were taking off for their first paratrooper air drop and then would turn back to England, at least those that survived the onslaught of enemy flak, and begin waves of supply drops. The paratroopers attacking from the air and the troops coming ashore at the beaches were loaded down already with essentials they needed to defend themselves, attack the enemy, and survive until those drops would occur.

"Best thing to do now is look like we know what we are doing," Jackson said. "Ask some of the grunts how things are going, avoid officers, and wait for the planes to return. It's then that we'll have our only chance to find out what happened to Roy Stewart."

As the last of the planes left the ground the sound of so many others just like them, flying high above, gave the area a relentless hum that lasted for ten minutes. After that, ground crews began to move supplies and refueling equipment into place. Then and only then would there be time for coffee or a smoke.

"How's it going so far, soldier?" Stewart asked one of the hundreds of men that were moving about the area.

Saluting, the man had only one thing to say. "God be with them!" Now everyone, including T1, would wait. High over France, things were much different.

"Did you see that?" Roy Stewart shouted to the man sitting on the bench beside him. "Look, down there in the sea, you can see our ships!"

Below them, just as the sky was filled with planes, the Channel between England and France was full of war ships. Within minutes, the roar of the planes' engines was interrupted by the sound of enemy fire. As the flights continued on course, first one and then another, and then another was hit by the barrage of flak that cut into their flight paths.

Sitting at the front end of the left side bench, directly behind the pilot, Roy turned his attention back inside the fuselage and the twenty young men he had trained with in jump school in Georgia before heading overseas on a troop carrier that cut across the North Atlantic. They had survived the training and their gray Navy transport had managed to avoid the German torpedoes that sank many of the American ships that were bringing men, machinery, and supplies to England. How much of his luck, their luck, remained was only a guess. If they could get to the jump zone in one piece and survive the German gunfire aimed at them from the enemy soldiers waiting on the ground, they just might make it to daylight, he prayed.

Back at Cottesmore, to his surprise, Stewart was having trouble managing his emotions.

"Any thought to slapping on a parachute and going for a ride?" he asked the rest of the team. They had managed to grab some coffee in the mess hall and returned to wait with him outside and had been discussing cigarettes and how everyone seemed to smoke back then compared to nobody in their group today.

"Wait, what, Major?" Hill asked. He appeared to have acclimated very well to the journey; like Stewart it was his first. In his career on the Protective Detail of the U.S. Secret Service he had been trained to stay cool, calm and collected no matter the circumstance and he looked the part. If he was excited or nervous it certainly didn't show.

But Stewart's remark set off alarm bells. Hill was sworn to stand at the President's side, no matter what, and despite the incredible journey they were on, and the honor of being in the presence of those brave men as they flew off into history, he wasn't sure how to take what his protectee had just suggested.

"Part of me wants to suit up and go kill some Germans!" the President stated.

Jackson had seen the expression on Hill's face change ever so slightly and approached the two men.

"We good?" he asked.

"Thinking about a change of plans, JJ," Stewart declared and then proceeded to share his thoughts on being able-bodied men standing there drinking coffee while so many Americans, all much younger than them, were flying off into the darkness and harm's way.

Jackson waved to his team to follow him and Stewart back into the hangar where they might be able to talk more openly. Once inside, Jackson and Stewart engaged in a discussion that challenged them to their cores. But Jackson had been in this place before, being faced with an enemy within striking distance, and returning home to fight another day. The BOTM program had rules for very good reasons. Every time, except at Monticello, that Jackson or a member of the team had deviated from the rules, something bad happened.

"What about Elizabeth?" Jackson asked Stewart. "What about Matt?" he continued. "What about the America you cared so deeply for that you resigned your position at the Pentagon to run for President so that you could fix things?"

Stewart was listening but the warrior in him still wanted in on the fight.

"Remember what you told me a long time ago," Jackson continued. "If you were going to take a shot then everyone else should have gotten to take one too. If we go off and jump over Normandy and we save some young men and kill some asshole Germans, what guarantee do any of us have that we will make it back alive? How would that affect the future?"

Stewart still wasn't swayed. "I'm of the mind that if

that house is on fire, we put it out and let the cards fall as they may."

"What about Roy and your mother?" Jackson asked. "Did you forget why we came?"

That was enough for Stewart to hear. He was angry and his facial expression showed it very clearly.

"You chaps all right back here?" a man with an English accent asked from doorway.

All six of the team turned to face whoever it was that had interrupted the discussion.

Nearest the door, Buchanan tensed and considered what might have to come next. If this man was in a position to alert anyone that something about these men in the hangar just wasn't right, they would have a real problem on their hands. Worst of all, the last thing Buchanan or any of the team wanted to do was hurt an ally or take time or manpower away from the effort to come.

"Yes, indeed," Stewart responded as the highest-ranking officer in the group. "Just a bunch of American war correspondents debating which one of us is going to get aboard the next transport and go help the boys that just left here."

"You must know Ernie Pyle then, old chap? He was just here a few days ago," the Brit added.

Buchanan stepped closer to the man. His uniform was that of a British Army Lieutenant. The man identified himself as their British counterpart, "Lieutenant William Woods at your service." After salutes and casual introductions, Woods went on. "Was on the *Daily Telegraph* before the war. Worked with Clare Hollingworth, you heard of her over in America yet? She's the reporter who spotted the tanks staged on the Polish border with Germany before the invasion in '39. What a scoop. Dying to have one of those these days. What papers are you boys with back home?"

This guy's had too much coffee, Jackson thought to himself.

"I've never met Ernie, but I know who he is. He had an aviation column in one of the papers if I remember correctly and he's running around Europe these days," Stewart offered. "Amelia Earhart said any pilot who didn't know Ernie didn't know aviation. I never met her either, but it's a shame about her disappearance."

"This man never fails to impress me!" Hill whispered to Buchanan. "Talk about doing your homework."

"So here's the deal, Lieutenant," Stewart said in a firm voice. "There's a lot of serious business going on here tonight and we have a lot of work to do. Once the pilots get back, we have to be ready to interview as many as we can while they're sucking down a coffee and a smoke and a sandwich before flying back into the madness again and then again. We need to prepare to do the best job that we can, so let me suggest that once we get through the night perhaps later tomorrow we can get together in the mess hall and talk about typewriter shortages and whatever else you wish."

"Brilliant!" Woods responded. "I imagine you've got the same problem back in the States. All the typewriter companies were forced into making planes and weapons but the government needs thousands of typewriters too. What a mess."

With that, Buchanan shook the man's hand and told him they looked forward to sitting down after this night was over. Guiding him back toward the mess hall, he returned to find Stewart and Jackson had picked up where they left off.

"You're right, JJ," Stewart said. "I'm always ready for a fight but you are right. I need to do what we came here to do and then go home to fight the battles of our day."

Relieved that the detour had been averted, the rest of the team checked their watches. The first plane should be returning in a few hours. Whether this mission would be a success or not was unknown but for one curious newsman, he was on a mission of his own.

"There's something just not right about those Yanks over there," Woods indicated with a head bob to the left as he related his story to four U.S. Army Military Policemen, the MPs, who were standing guard close to a vehicle entry gate.

"Yanks?" the one said in response. "What's not right about them?"

"They're much bigger than most Yanks, no offense intended. Most of the boys here for the operation weigh about ten or eleven stone. Those men over there must be twelve or thirteen stone."

"That's what we weigh, Lieutenant, about 185 pounds. What's your point?" one MP asked.

"They're supposed to be war correspondents, chum. How many reporters do you know back home that are built like you boys and not a one of 'em smoking a cigarette?"

Those last two sentences caught the MP's attention. The Brit was right. Even at a distance the war correspondents did look bulkier than most in their Army uniforms and nearly everyone smoked, especially preparing for D-Day. After thanking him for his diligence they directed Woods to head back inside the mess hall and leave this matter to them.

"Don't say anything more to anyone. If there *is* something going on here, we don't know how extensive it is." Watching Woods head inside, two of the MPs turned their backs to the T1 team and resumed their watch.

"Dumb Brit. If these guys were spies, they would have let

Hitler know the assault had begun hours ago or they would have already blown up the fuel depot," one proclaimed to the others.

Considering all that had been said, and that flights still needed to be flown and the fuel supplies could be at risk, the other two MPs checked .45 caliber side arms and their Thompson machine guns and then headed for the hangar. Having watched what was happening, Stewart moved into action and walked directly toward the oncoming MPs.

"Top of the morning to ya," Stewart called out as he continued walking toward them. "Oh wait, this isn't Ireland now is it, boys?"

One MP raised his Thompson slightly as he stopped in mid stride. The other continued on saying, "You must be lost, this isn't Kansas, Auntie Em!" and then raised his Thompson and pointed it straight at the oncoming man in the Major's uniform. Stewart stopped abruptly.

"They modeled that wicked witch of the west after my mother-in-law," Stewart said, "Now if only a house would fall on the old bird!" Realizing this could only come from a friend, not foe, the lead MP lowered his Thompson and began to laugh.

"Someone thinks you might not be who you say you are, Major," he called out. "Let's see some ID before we start talking about flying monkeys and the yellow brick road."

Moving slowly, Stewart reached inside his uniform jacket pocket, pulled out two documents and began walking slowly to the MP. Back at the hangar, Jackson and the rest stood quietly and watched. This was much different than their excursion at Valley Forge. The weapons trained on Stewart and the rest of them could terminate their lives in one or two short bursts. Able to fire at over seven hundred rounds per minute, eleven per second, those weapons rivaled what the U.S. Army, Marines, and Special Forces carried in the modern world. After reviewing the documents, the MP began his questioning as his partner moved twenty feet to the left of him where he had a direct line of sight on the rest of the T1.

"State your business, Major Stewart," the MP ordered.

"Sure thing. But what's your first name?" he asked.

"Frank, Frank Devine from Philadelphia, Pennsylvania, USA," the MP responded.

"Nice to meet you, Frank," Stewart added. "Can I bum a cigarette? These boys are all in training and don't smoke. They drink like fish though so go figure."

Jackson and the rest continued to listen but didn't move an inch.

"Did he just say Devine – Frank Devine from Philadelphia?" Jackson asked aloud.

Stewart's niece was named Frankie Devine, actually Frances Devine, and was Jackson's drinking buddy after Michelle moved away and Stewart put him on mandatory R&R back at Andrews. They had met as teenagers at family barbeques when a young Matt Stewart and the rest would play tag football while the adults drank beer and flipped steaks and burgers.

"Dude, if this is Frankie's grandfather I'm going to lose my mind," Jackson whispered. "I wonder if Stewart has thought this through, too. This guy could be related to Elizabeth somehow." He paused to consider it all. "This is a little too trippy."

After another ten minutes of small talk, Devine waved to the three MPs at the gate that all was okay and told the MP standing to his left to come forward. Stewart turned to his team and asked them to come up, slowly. He had explained to Devine that they were indeed war correspondents but were military men first. All had played football or wrestled in college and were journalism majors before signing up to fight. That explained their more massive size than most correspondents. As for not smoking, they had all noticed that cigarettes affected their athletic performance but had opted to keep that to themselves. If someone headed off to war needed a smoke to relax, so be it.

"I say it's all a bunch of bologna," Stewart said as he bummed another cigarette and a light from Devine.

After introductions the entire group walked back to the other MPs at the entry gate. Jackson had suggested they'd be helping the cause if they stood watch there until the planes began to return. Stewart continued the charade.

"So, we're here to interview the pilots as they return from Normandy and then once we're given the word we're supposed to suit up and jump in a day or two if our gear ever arrives. They want us to jump with our typewriters and Thompsons! Of course, we aren't going anywhere until someone shows up with our stuff."

An hour later, all six members of T1 were inside the mess hall and grabbed a sandwich and cup of coffee while they waited for the first planes to return. Stewart bought four packs of Camel cigarettes. The lighter he had with him, one that he hadn't shown Jackson or the rest that he was taking, had belonged to another of Stewart's uncles. Captain Stewart had served proudly in the U.S. Navy and was killed during an aerial attack by the Japanese. His body, after months, had been returned to the U.S. for burial. The lighter and other personal effects were delivered to the Stewart family and over time made their way to him.

Taking a seat across from Lieutenant Woods, Stewart smiled and then blew a large billow of cigarette smoke toward him. Sitting down on either side of the Brit, Buchanan and Jackson each nudged the thin man with their elbows.

"You did the right thing, old chap," Buchanan said in a forced British accent. "The Americans have landed to help save you and the Queen. Cigarettes or not, we're here to save the day, mate!"

Woods gave them an uncomfortable smile in return.

"Thanks for coming," Woods responded in a fervent tone.

"Any of you chaps from Philadelphia?"

The roar was returning as the C-47 engines could be heard coming closer and closer to home. One by one they landed and taxied back to the spots they were directed to. A sense of pride and exhilaration had spread through the ground staff but when it was clear so many planes were not coming back, and these same men and planes would have to fly right back into it again, the mood sobered. Leaving the half-finished coffees, sandwiches, and cigarette butts behind, everyone left the mess hall and got back to the supplies and fuel trucks that had been staged for their arrival.

For Stewart and the rest, they knew which plane they were hoping to find. It had been easy to acquire that information. Now they could only wait to see if it made it back. The eleventh plane to return, its fuselage bearing gaping wounds from the relentless flak assault the Germans had fired into the sky, W-99 rolled to a stop and within a few minutes the pilot and co-pilot hopped down from the open doorway the paratroopers had jumped from into the darkness and the unknown hours earlier.

Stewart saluted the pilot and was shocked to see the expression on the man's face. He looked like he had flown to hell and back. Returning the salute, the pilot said he needed to take a leak and get some food in him. Just as Jackson had felt in the Garden that night years before, like an intruder bothering someone who had much more important things on their mind, Stewart felt a selfish guilt come over him that he had never felt before. But this was his only chance and he had to take it.

"Mind if I walk with you then, Captain?" Stewart asked.

"As long as you can keep up, Major, I'm on a tight schedule," the Captain responded.

"How was it out there?" Stewart said in a softened tone. He already knew the answer but had to start somewhere.

The Captain didn't wait to get to the toilets. He couldn't. He simply stopped alongside a parked Army jeep and watered the lawn. From there he stormed through the mess hall doors, Stewart following close behind. Jackson had gone ahead and had a plate of food and two coffees waiting for the pilot as they entered the hall. They sat down and it was then that the tension in the pilot's shoulders seemed to abate. Stewart knew now was the time.

"Captain, I only have a few questions and then we'll leave you to your thoughts," Stewart suggested. A moment later, the plane's co-pilot joined them, and Buchanan brought the flyer a plate of sandwiches, a coffee, and two bottles of Coca Cola.

"She's shot up but checked out AOK, skipper," the co-pilot reported as he gulped down the food.

"Can I bum a smoke, Major?" the Captain asked.

Stewart handed them each two packs and then flicked his lighter to Jackson's surprise. Lighting Camels for both men, Stewart continued. "We're asking about a young paratrooper named Roy Stewart. He was supposed to be on the 99 with you. Know him?"

The pilot and co-pilot looked at each other.

"What's it to you, all due respect, Major?" the pilot asked and then drew long and hard on his cigarette.

The British war correspondent Woods had noticed the Americans walk to the mess hall and followed out of curiosity. Taking a seat alongside Buchanan he was preparing to ask a few questions of his own until a few very distinct words were spoken.

"Fuck off!" Buchanan and Jackson both said in unison. The expressions on their faces matched the words and Woods quickly excused himself.

"Good luck, boys," he said as he walked away.

The airmen had filled themselves with food and drink and knew it was time to head back to their plane. Surely the holes had been patched, the fuel loaded, and the supplies to be air dropped had been showed inside. As they stood up to leave, Stewart rose with them.

"Roy Stewart – did you know him?" he asked again. Turning to his co-pilot and waving him to go ahead, the pilot came around the table and stood face to face with the Major.

"That boy, whoever the hell he is to you, is a God damned hero! We thought everyone had made the jump but as we turned to head back to England the kid scared the crap out of us when he shoved his head in between me and my co-pilot. Said his chute had some sort of a malfunction on the line so he unhooked and took it off. Said he still wanted to jump using his back-up chute so he wanted us to slow it down a bit so he could still make the jump. We offered him ours but he said we might need them. I told him he was crazy, but he insisted."

Stewart, Jackson, and Buchanan were stunned. Hill and the others had been asking around outside but had come up empty. They entered the mess hall, their rallying point, just in time to hear the story for themselves.

"We had already moved up and away from the drop zones, but we hadn't made it over the water yet. I told him we'd do what he wanted but I warned him he'd probably be landing right onto a damn German convoy and there wouldn't be another American within miles of him."

Just then the co-pilot came back into the hall. "We're loaded and waiting on ya," he shouted.

"Gotta go, boys," the pilot said as he noticed the name embroidered on Stewart's uniform. "You related?"

Stewart was beaming already and nodded with pride.

"Whoever that boy was to you, he had guts. He jumped out of a C-47 over enemy territory with nothing but a machine gun, his .45, my .45, and some ammo. He took off the rest of his gear. He said he was gonna make up the weight in weapons and ammo and then jumped somewhere over northern France near the coast is my best guess."

With that, the pilot saluted and with tears in his eyes, Stewart returned the salute. T1 followed the pilot through the doors and then watched as he ran to his plane and climbed aboard. Stewart went back inside for a minute and returned with a carton of cigarettes. As they walked toward the hangar they had arrived in, Stewart threw the carton to the MPs still guarding the entry gate and then followed Jackson and the team inside.

Woods had kept his eye on the Americans and followed from a distance. As he entered the hangar, the sunlight streaming in through the half open doors, it was empty. The men he had followed behind by a mere twenty yards had disappeared. Waving to the MPs he shouted, "They're gone.

They're bloody gone!" but the roar of the C-47 engines had come alive again and they couldn't hear what he was saying.

Back at Andrews, Stewart stepped back from the pulse formation and walked quietly to the changing room. Alone with his thoughts, he couldn't believe what he had just done and what he had learned. Hill had followed as standard operating procedure and Jackson came along a minute later. Looking in on the President, Jackson smiled.

"Know where a guy can get a beer around here?' Stewart asked.

"Well, there's this bar we frequent but it might not be open yet," Jackson responded.

"Then load your team into Marine One, all of you, and we'll head back to 1600 Pennsylvania Avenue and see what Emma can cook up for some hungry Marines – and my friend Agent Hill here."

"I feel a Semper Fi coming," Buchanan said as he stuck his head into the doorway.

"Oorah!" Stewart and Jackson said proudly.

An hour later, without letting on anything about where they had been or what they had seen, Emma served up a full Scottish breakfast of sausage, eggs, baked beans, mushrooms, tomatoes, toast, and pots of hot coffee.

"What've you boys been up to?" she asked with a grin.

"Love to, ma'am," Buchanan responded, "but then we'd have to kill ya!"

"If I had a dollar for every time Mr. President there or Colonel Jackson had said that to me I'd be back in Edinburg living the life!' she quipped.

"All in good time, Miss Emma," Stewart said through a proud smile. "All in good time."

CHAPTER 16

THE WOMAN HAD visited the Pope in his private study dozens of times over the last few years. Despite objections from the Swiss Guard, the most important man in the Roman Catholic Church, its leader, insisted that she be given direct access to him without reservation or interference by anyone. Not even the Pope's deputy or the head of his security detail dared overrule the directive. Tonight, that order might cost him his life.

At the White House another young woman was meeting with the leader of the United States of America.

"I still can't believe there is nothing they can do for you, Mr. President," Emma said as tears streamed down her cheeks.

"Now there, little lady," Stewart responded. "There's plenty I can do. I can go plant my butt on a beach chair somewhere tropical and for the first time in decades forget about phones and briefings, and drink beer until the big guy up above shows me my last sunset."

His attempt at humor got her to laugh if just for a second but then his young friend, the Scottish cook who had endeared herself to Stewart and his late wife, changed the subject.

"So the Surgeon General says I should be serving up a special dinner for you of cottage cheese, fresh fruit, and perhaps some sugar free apple juice. What's it going to be then?"

The quiet of the small private kitchen in the residence at the White House had been the location of hundreds of hearty meals over the last three years. The Stewarts had lost their only son and after Elizabeth's death the President had begun to look fondly on the young woman first as a fun loving staffer then as a niece and now in more recent months as a platonic companion. He'd insist she come along on overseas trips so that he was always assured of not just his favorite foods aboard Air Force One but the company he wanted to keep while enjoying the rare times he had to sit and enjoy a quiet meal.

While there had been public and private rumors about a romantic relationship between the two, he in his mid-sixties and she in her early thirties, they had been just that. Friends. Anyone who worked at the White House caught fanning the flames of gossip was stripped of their credentials, regardless of who they were or where they were from, and escorted off the White House grounds.

"I'd say it's time for some lasagna and garlic bread but to keep the doctor appeased I'll only have a light beer this time to wash it down."

Jackson smiled. He'd been quietly standing there in the kitchen, listening to their exchange and enjoyed seeing his dear friend at peace with where he was in his life.

"And you, JJ, what'll you have?" Emma asked.

"I'll have what he's having," he responded in a funny sounding tone and the three of them burst into laughter.

"Movie lines!" Stewart laughed. "Rather than napalm in the morning I'll take the smell of lasagna in the evening. Now *that* smells like victory!"

Two hours later, as Emma had cleaned up and Stewart and Jackson sat quietly in the residence watching the film that launched that line about napalm, *Apocalypse Now*, for perhaps the twentieth time, Stewart reminded her it was time to go as he and the man he looked on as his second son needed to talk in private.

"Good light, luvs," she called out in her distinctive Scottish accent as she closed the door behind her. For the men, it was time to go over the exit strategy one more time.

The only people in the world who knew of the President's health issues were his Chief of Staff Kennedy, Emma, Jackson, Petty, and Stewart's personal physician. They had managed to keep Stewart's diagnosis a secret. Alzheimer's disease had struck another President, Ronald Reagan, but that was in retirement where he had been allowed to quietly fade into his final years in privacy. Stewart had been feeling confused and unfamiliar for months but had hid it well until his doctor saw past the diversions and identified the problem. This rare form of dementia would develop much quicker than most and in short order it was certain Stewart would forget his name and the faces he was so fond of.

"You sure you don't want Bill Kennedy in on this?" Jackson asked.

"Yep, he's a dedicated friend and excellent at what he does but this will be my call, our call, and once we have it all thought through we will present it to him and the Vice President. He needs to be focusing on keeping the wheels greased."

Visibly frustrated, the President leaned forward and used the remote to stop the movie and shut off the television.

"That scene pisses me off the most," he declared. "They let an Asian woman run through their loose security and toss a grenade satchel into the rescue chopper. Their fuck up cost a dozen lives."

Jackson nodded but chose to argue the point. "That abortion in *Zero Dark Thirty* was worse, a lot worse, because about twenty security people should have overruled her."

"Maybe someone will learn from her mistake, their mistakes," Stewart added.

In the film, non-fiction, an overzealous State Department official in Afghanistan ordered her security team to essentially stand down and allow a car with a purported snitch aboard to pass through the gates and waive off a full inspection of the vehicle and its occupants before it was allowed to get closer to the official and a group of her staffers. In all, when the alleged snitch activated his suicide bomb, the terrorist taught everyone a lesson and reinforced the point to security teams around the world that you do not break protocol. Ever.

Jackson sat quietly. He had been responsible for the loss of many lives since he was first given the task of testing the BOTM technology. Some were deserving of their sentence, others a result of mistakes or a failure to follow orders. He wondered if his missteps would some day be illustrated in a book or a film where others would point to his selfishness and tainted judgment. If it would save innocent lives then he was at peace with it.

"You with me, JJ?" Stewart asked.

"Yes, sir, just got lost in the moment," he responded.

"So, we agree that there is no way I can actively campaign

through to rest of the primaries and the convention and the general election," Stewart stated.

"Yep, so that means you have to simply decide how you want to go out – out of the White House I mean, not your last days on the planet," Jackson added. "Not yet."

This had been their tenth discussion on the matter and while the first few private dinner meetings in the residence had been filled more with anger, denial, tears, and frustration, Stewart had come to terms with his Maker's decision and he had managed to persuade Jackson to do the same.

"My biggest challenge is this," Stewart said in a slow and very serious tone. "I want a woman to be President of the United States. It's long overdue. But I want that woman to win the election on her own merits and claim the office as hers without an asterisk. If I resign and Williams gets sworn in then she's got the asterisk for the rest of time. I don't want that for her."

Jackson hopped up from his end of the massive brown leather sofa that faced the media center. Typically the three flat screen monitors would be broadcasting the CNN and BBC live news feeds and the massive center screen would be filled with a favorite film or perhaps a football game or an auto race. Stewart had turned all three of them off this time for their discussion.

"Sugar-free apple juice, Mr. President?" Jackson said with a laugh. Stewart didn't respond. The look he gave his friend was enough. A moment later, Jackson returned from the kitchen, light beers in hand.

"We've kicked this back and forth already but so I am clear," Jackson stated, "you want the VP to win the election and be sworn in so in order for her to do that you would have to pull out of the election. If you do that, with your approval ratings as high as they are right now, people will know there's something wrong with you and that could influence her getting the votes. With or without your endorsement, she'd get some of the pity vote and neither of you would want that."

Stewart smiled. Jackson had summarized exactly what Stewart had been thinking.

"We have to figure this out, JJ," Stewart said softly. "Hey, maybe I need to come out and say that despite my previous claims I had Maxwell killed and am not deserving of this office. Then you whisk me away in your damn time machine."

Jackson looked at Stewart with great surprise. That was not true as far as he was concerned and that was no way to go out. Not this man, not this hero, not on a lie.

"Not an option Mr. President," Jackson said in a determined voice. "If Maxwell was killed it was not on *your* order!"

"No matter what, JJ, I want to go out fighting. No wheelchairs for me. Not unless it's got a .50 Cal mounted on it. I know I've always said I look forward to sitting on a beach and watching sunsets but I'm not anywhere near ready for that, especially sitting around watching my own."

The two sat back to their own thoughts while the smell of Emma's cooking began to reach them from the kitchen. Stewart had another topic on his mind though.

"JJ," he said leaning forward, "It hasn't been lost on me that at some point in the near future you're going to be sitting in your apartment over at Andrews without your parents, Tommy, Michelle, Elizabeth, or even this old man." Jackson leaned in and assured his friend that he would be just fine.

"The way I figure it, you come into the world alone and go out the same way. Nobody rides tandem on any of those adventures." Stewart tried to interrupt him but he continued.

"I consider myself one of the luckiest men to have ever

walked the planet. Loving parents handed me off to two more as far as I'm concerned. Michelle and I didn't work out for a variety of reasons but those relationships and the ones I've had in the Corps will keep my heart and mind company until the day I die. I've made some mistakes, some very serious ones, and I'll have to live with those as well. But whether someone special ever comes along again, or never does, I am at peace with where I am in this world."

"What about Christy White?" Stewart asked.

"I always thought you two might have something."

"Hell no, sir," Jackson responded quickly.

"Rule #55 is Never Date Someone That Can Kick Your Ass!"

Stewart wanted to discuss the matter further but he could tell there was no use, at least not tonight.

"Maybe the way this has all played out was meant to be," Jackson offered.

"Perhaps for the mistakes I've made this has all been a penance of some kind for me. If I hadn't lost focus in Berlin and then disobeyed orders and gone to Gethsemane maybe things would have turned out different."

"Don't be too hard on yourself JJ," Stewart said in a confident and reassuring tone. "Things happen for a reason. Hopefully someday we'll all get the chance to ask the big guy about it. " Stewart paused.

"We've all made mistakes but to totally change the subject and the mood, are you ever going to start dating again? I'd like to see at least one grandchild before I go!"

Jackson laughed.

"Well, I've had my eyes on a certain cook you've been keeping way too busy," Jackson continued.

"Maybe someday she and I can do something normal like dinner and a movie – that's not upstairs in the White House."

"Are you calling me a damn cock blocker, Colonel?" Stewart asked jokingly.

"Sir, yes, sir," Jackson replied and then both men laughed for quite some time.

"One other thing I will say, JJ, is how damn proud I am of our people, our fellow Americans," Stewart said as he sat forward.

"Many people thought I had lost my mind. Little did they know that was actually in the cards. But charging our citizens with stepping up and taking care of themselves rather than waiting for someone else to do it was a challenge they really met."

Jackson smiled. In a time where the world seemed it had lost its way, people did step up as they always had in tough times.

"Yep, just like a neighborhood would band together to oust the troublemaker in one way or another or dispose of a dog that chases the kids, everyone stepped up and reclaimed what was theirs," Jackson answered.

"It got a little messy a few times and the founding of this country took time and shed some blood, but in the end people were standing united and proud, just as they are today."

"Just like our enemies have always said, JJ," Stewart continued. "They will never invade the United States. There are just too many guns and too many people ready to fight to defend it."

"Yep, and luckily the guys and girls with the guns and good hearts here greatly outnumber the bad ones that are here."

"Semper Fi," Jackson stated in a proud tone.

"Oorah," Emma answered before the President could. "Now, gentlemen, dinner is served!"

Just then Jackson's phone began to vibrate. It had been set on ring on 911 emergencies so that only a call from a dozen or so people would wake the phone. This time the caller ID read Rizzo—Rome.

The President's phone on the end table also began to ring as a knock at the door let them know something big was going on.

The knock at the door was from Stewart's security team leader. Hill noticed the televisions were all off, which was very rare for Stewart.

"Mr. President, there's been an incident at the Vatican!"

"Colonel Jackson," Inspector Rizzo said in a very calm voice. "It appears that your Michelle, our Michelle, has decided to have a very private, very troublesome audience with His Holiness this evening. She has secured the entries to his residence and has told the Swiss Guard and his papal assistants that they are not to be disturbed."

Jackson remembered Rizzo very well, the police official who released Michelle from the local jail in Rome without charges being filed. He and the Italian hadn't spoken since that Easter Sunday morning but he remembered his voice and that weekend very clearly.

"You've got to be kidding me!" was the best response he could muster.

"No, this is no joke. I can go into more detail but not over the phone. Let me just say that she has been working at the Pope's direction on Black Ops as you call them and apparently somehow it seems to have come full circle and back to the Pope himself. The problem here is that the federal police, our country's special forces, and the Swiss Guard are planning to do, with great aggression, anything they need to protect His Holiness."

Jackson couldn't believe what he was hearing. This was incredible.

"Are you able to communicate with her by phone?" he asked.

"Not at all. To demonstrate that His Holiness is okay she has sent me a, what do you call it in America, a Face Time and I saw they were sitting in the papal residence, face to face, perhaps two meters apart. She had a handgun, an automatic weapon in her right hand resting on her lap."

Rizzo went into greater detail, relaying how the security camera feeds and the audio mics in the hallways that approached the residence and inside that modest apartment had been cut. The Swiss Guard had been able to confirm through the use of infrared heat tracking that there were only the two people in the entire apartment.

"Let me work this for a few minutes on my end and then I will call you back," Jackson said calmly.

"But do me a favor. Send me a floor plan of the apartment and the area immediately surrounding it."

Rizzo agreed but expressed his reservations.

"Colonel, you must remember that there is very little a Roman police officer can do at this point as far as an intervention. Vatican City is its own principality and there are at least five law enforcement and military organizations involved here."

Jackson understood but he knew something Rizzo and the others there on scene did not.

After briefing Stewart on the situation, Jackson tapped

Michelle's number on his phone. He hadn't seen or spoken to her since that Sunday at the Papal reception where she and the Pope had a private conversation that escalated and had to be interrupted.

"Thought about deleting this number a hundred times," Jackson said to Stewart, "but I just couldn't for some reason. Now I'm glad I didn't."

No answer.

Jackson then tried FaceTime and still no answer. At least with the incoming caller being identified, Michelle might now know that Jackson and his T1 Marines were aware of the situation.

"You'll need to go for a ride, JJ," Stewart said. "You and I know that needs to happen right away or this will end badly for Michelle and quite possibly the Pope." He sat quietly staring at the blank monitors. "Should I come too, perhaps offer myself in place of the Pope?" Stewart suggested. "I can't imagine what's gotten into her. But if she's going to hurt the Pope, given my situation, I'd take a bullet for the man if need be."

Jackson shook his head. "No need, Mr. President, I know exactly what we can do to resolve this. We'll be in and out of there in minutes."

An hour later, at the BOTM hangar at Andrews, Jackson briefed his team. Buchanan, White, and Sharif had traveled with Jackson on numerous missions. Before coming to the top secret program they had all seen action in Afghanistan and Iraq or Syria and were highly trained experts in various special fields. But they all shared one competency in particular, the ability to disable a person by hand or by weapon in an instant. Jackson had thought long and hard during the ride from the White House to the base in Maryland.

God, I wish Tommy was here for this one, he kept thinking. *If anyone could walk Michelle off whatever ledge she's gotten onto now, he'd be the one.*

To fill the fifth and sixth slots on the T1 team he selected Army Rangers Dixon and Redd from T2. They had performed flawlessly on their own missions and had very similar credentials and abilities on their CV's. Meeting as they had so many times before this, Jackson explained the issue and the mission. In addition to the standard Sig 220s the group carried as side arms, they each added Tasers, stun grenades, night vision goggles, and suited up in body armor and Kevlar helmets before forming their circle. All they needed now was for Jackson to finish his overseas call and join them to complete the ring.

"Inspector Rizzo," Jackson said calmly. "All I can tell you is that we have developed a stealth technology that will allow us to form a protective barrier in front of the Pope and persuade Michelle with voice or force, to stand down almost instantly."

Rizzo sounded doubtful. "I know American military and intelligence services are second to none in technological developments but how you intend to pull this off seems impossible."

"What I have to ask, what I insist on, Inspector Rizzo, is that your reaction teams do not move until you hear back from me. President Stewart has already spoken with your Prime Minister and your President, offering our assistance. And our Secretary of Defense has spoken with his peer in Rome. We are all systems go here. We just need you to all stand still and let us do what we do best."

Rizzo laughed. "I will stand here in St. Peter's Square and watch the sky to see how you are going to pull this off,

Colonel. I must caution you though. Michelle has changed since you last saw her. She has become hard, cold. She is like a dog with a bone and you best not try to take it unless you wish to get bit."

"Got it," Jackson responded. "The dog catchers are on the way."

Inside the papal apartment, the Pope was confused by Michelle's behavior. They had been working together secretly for some time, cleaning up some of the sensitive issues and problems the Catholic Church had been facing. In all, eighty-nine priests and bishops from around the world that an internal, secret investigation had found guilty of pedophilia, had been found dead in their residences or their cars, a bullet to the back of the head. No clues, no witnesses, plenty of motives, but no suspects found or detained by the law enforcement.

"I took out the trash for you, just as we agreed, Your Holiness," Michelle said for the fourth time. Her eyes fixed on her prisoner, her intentions unclear to him.

She and the Pope had spent hours over the last few years discussing and debating the Church's role in protecting the children.

"Yes, I agreed to deliver a painless euthanasia to the sinners," she said, "and it could be said that their demise has served as an unspoken warning to anyone else who wears the collar that hurting a child will be met with an earthly punishment long before they had to face God."

The Pope recalled one discussion in particular they had a few months earlier when he had asked her what she intended to do when his list of names ran out.

"There are sinners everywhere," she had said. "I was told

once that Christ said 'Vengeance is mine' and that it was not up to any man to take another's life. But I also remember the story of Him yelling in one of the temples as He upended tables that merchants were selling goods from inside the place meant for prayer."

She had paused and seemed to take a minute to fully process the next thought.

"So with that, what would Christ say if He walked into this fancy apartment right now, facing you knowing that you let priests commit crimes against children for years and did nothing and that once you did act, it was delegating murder?"

The Pope had told her then and reminded her now. "We are all sinners, my child. I will serve my sentence, whatever that may be, when God decides what I should do or where I should go once my time on earth has ended. Our world is a much different, a more complicated one than the time Christ walked the earth. Hopefully that will be taken into consideration, but if it is not, I guess you and I both will be seeing much more of each other in hell."

Michelle sat quietly looking at the Pontiff. He appeared to have aged greatly since she first met him, much like Presidents of the United States always seemed to. The weight of their offices was great and serving in them would cost them.

"Here's all I need for you to do now," she said. "I want you to confess your sins, that you looked the other way and then, only when bowing to public pressure, decided to act. That act, of course, was murder and in order for you to ave this room alive tonight you will have to do it live on nternet feed from my phone."

e six more heat signatures in the apartment," the elled from his station inside the remote command center in St. Peter's Square. "There are now eight people in the apartment!"

Jackson and the others stood still and listened. The Pope enjoyed listening to Pavarotti CDs after his evening meal and prayers. The sound of the tenor's voice flowed through the rooms.

Thank God we can do something about that bullshit right now, Jackson thought to himself. As quietly as possible, Jackson typed a text to his team back at Andrews.

MONITOR ALL FEEDS FROM 1.407.555.1212

RESTRICT ALL VIDEO AND AUDIO FEEDS IT SENDS.

On his signal, the T1 team spread out. Jackson and White looked to the open doorway that led from the Pope's dressing room where they had landed. Just six feet past that entry were the Pope and the woman holding him at gunpoint. Buchanan and Sharif lined up behind them, the two Rangers facing their six, watching the hall that led to the front door of the apartment.

In the remote command center, the technician watched as the six new heat signatures moved from their circle to more strategic positions.

"Squadra Uno, team one, there is activity in the apartment. Two individuals at the end of the hallway, four more moving toward the Pope," the Italian Special Forces commander radioed to his team.

"How the hell did they get in there?" the commander whispered.

The Pope smiled at Michelle. "If I say this, I must implicate you as well, my child."

"No, I have much more work to do," she responded.

"You'll do this and then deal with whatever the world decides to do with you."

"It would seem we are still at a stand-off then."

A second later, Michelle's phone received a text. It was from Christy White.

MICHELLE. PUT THE GUN DOWN.

CHAPTER 17

SHE SAW THE look in the Pope's eyes change ever so slightly. Despite having been trained by some of the best special operators the U.S. Armed Forces, the lack of sleep and her false sense of security in his private residence left her vulnerable for just a moment and that was all it took.

An electrical charge surged through Michelle's neck and immediately sent her limp body crashing to the hardwood floor. The gun she had set on her lap fell away and landed with a thud. As Jackson and Buchanan jumped past her as she fell, they grabbed the Pope under both arms and moved him quickly into the kitchen area. Sharif reached down and grabbed her gun as it slid a few feet from them. White knelt and within fifteen seconds had the kidnapper secured; Michelle's arms now wrapped behind her with plastic wire ties.

"Are you okay, Your Holiness?" Jackson asked as he pulled the black ski mask off his head, revealing a familiar face to the Pontiff.

"I know you, I know you," the Pope responded. "You

are a friend of the President. You have been here many times before."

Buchanan pulled a kitchen chair from the table and asked the Pope to sit down so he could check his pulse. The Pope may have appeared to be in good shape for a man in his eighties but the excitement of this event could have put his heart and mind into a tailspin.

"I'm okay. I'm okay," the Pope insisted. Buchanan continued to hold the man's wrist for another thirty seconds while Jackson grabbed a glass and filled it with water for him.

"Not bad, Your Holiness," Buchanan said as he let go of the wrist. "Your pulse is already back to normal."

Jackson stepped back into the room where Michelle was being held. She was regaining consciousness and protesting angrily through the gag White had placed over her mouth.

"Looks like even angels fall from grace," Jackson said to their captive.

Standing there with weapons drawn in the Vatican, considering everything they had seen and done in their battle for good over evil, their team leader's words made the moment even more surreal.

The technician monitoring the heat signatures inside the Papal apartment was stunned. He had watched the encounter unfold. To him, and the superiors that were watching the computer monitor from over his shoulder, they were amazed first by the appearance of six individuals and then as the rescue attempt took place.

"How the hell did they get in there?" the Italian commander insisted. "There is something very wrong here!"

As that commander discussed the next move with his team, Jackson had a decision to make of his own and he needed to act quickly. First he assured the Pope that this would all be over very quickly and then he had to decide what to do with his fallen angel. They had issues to address and time was critical. The Pope and the local security forces would have questions that would have to be left unanswered. What to do with Michelle? Leave her for the authorities? If she had gone as rogue as this, would she continue to maintain silence over the existence of a time travel program or of the miracle that saved her?

Then there was the question of how the T1 team would leave the apartment. Could they insist to everyone that they used the same stealth technology that American airplanes began using years earlier? Had U.S. Special Forces developed a way to drop into areas undetected? The heat signatures appeared out of nowhere to the technicians. They just appeared in an instant without detection while entering through a door or window. He needed more time, and Jackson wished they had thought this through a bit further. But there just hadn't been time.

"Not the first time you took us on a spur of the moment joyride, JJ," White cracked with a smile.

After placing a secure satellite call to Stewart and Petty at the White House, Jackson was assured he had only ten minutes left to finalize the mission one way or another. The Italian Special Forces had stood down at America's request but with the Pope appearing to be in safe hands now there was little reason, at least to the locals, to wait another minute to enter the apartment.

White and Sharif had helped Michelle up and sat her down on the same chair she had fallen from. With her promise that she would talk in a calm tone, White removed the gag as she stared sadly at her friend's eyes. After a pause, White cut the restraints from her hands.

"Michelle, I can't even imagine how you got to this point. But considering what you have done you've left us with very few options," Jackson said, his voice strong but reflecting a sad tone.

The Pope pushed past Buchanan. He wanted to be a part of whatever was going to happen next.

"JJ," Michelle said as she looked at the Pope. "You and Special Ops teams, Black Ops teams, from all over the world have been doing the same shit I've done for this man."

He wasn't debating with an ex-wife or an old friend anymore. She was different, colder, harder than he had ever seen her. "I cleaned up the streets of Rome. Crime is down. Crime against women is down dramatically. Crime by priests is now down, too."

"Rizzo related those figures to me, Michelle," Jackson said. "I guess we should assume that you had something to do with that?" He knew the answer already but wanted her to say it, confess it, to the others in the room.

Michelle hadn't taken her eyes off the Pope since he entered the room. "Yep! At *his* request, the leader of the Church had me take out his global trash in a discreet way so that the internal message to everyone else that wore a collar was clear. The wrath of God is upon them!"

"Oh fuck," White said somberly.

"So what was the plan here, to force the Pope to go public and admit his sins?" Jackson asked.

Michelle didn't respond but her smile conceded her intention.

"Bingo!" Sharif whispered as he stepped to the hallway to check on the two operators who were watching the main entry.

Michelle took a moment to gather her thoughts and then presented her point.

"I remember the story of Christ walking into the temple and upon seeing merchants doing trade there instead of worship He threw a fit, upended the tables, and yelled at everyone to get out."

She had everyone's attention but took a moment before continuing.

"So, Your Holiness, and you too for that matter, JJ," she went on. "What do you think Christ would say of all of this – the murder, the vengeance we are all guilty of, if He walked into this room?"

"I can hear them warming up that flaming chariot headed to hell right now," Sharif said. He had used that same line years earlier when he felt their trip to meet Christ in the Garden had a potential for pyrotechnics.

"Oh fuck," White uttered again.

"You do know that's the Pope, standing right there, Christy – the Pope, right there!" Jackson said pointing at the holy man.

"My child," the Pope said to Michelle. "You said He had saved you. So now, how do you think He would feel about the miraculous gift He gave you being used to do the devil's work?"

"This is fucked up," Buchanan whispered under his breath. "Well I never got to meet the man, Christ that is," Buchanan added. "Let's mount up and take the Pope and Michelle back to the damn Garden and present their sins and let Him decide. I had been prepared to meet my Maker once He told me to come home but this trip could be worth the ride!"

Jackson looked at his watch. They had five minutes left

before the Italians were going to kick down the door and save their Pope from whatever armed force was not allowing him to leave his apartment.

"Nope, not going on that adventure ever again," Jackson insisted. "I said back then that it was a once in a lifetime miracle mission, standing before Christ and asking Him for a favor. It's one that I now regret. It'll be over my dead body that anyone else gets to bother Him like that ever again," he said looking at Michelle.

Disappointment and then a sense of anger flowed in his eyes. He had shed tears for her while she lay on her death bed but now, remembering again that his selfishness not only cost Jones and Abrams their lives but also dozens of men of the cloth… "I'd throw these six pulses into a damn volcano before I'd ever let anyone do that again."

"You're being shortsighted, JJ," Michelle said in response. "Think of all the young boys and girls that will now be able to grow up and lead normal lives rather than ones corrupted and destroyed by the devils that wore the collar."

"Okay, we can't debate this all night, JJ. I just hope you weren't eliminating some of the Pope's enemies as part of this. Whatever happened to innocent until proven guilty anyway?" Buchanan asked. He didn't know Michelle but the question he asked seemed to make her wonder suddenly if she had been played.

"I love the smell of zealots in the morning," Sharif smirked.

Jackson looked at Buchanan and their eyes met. It had been Buchanan who led the team to find and rescue them from Gethsemane, but it was Buchanan who entered Maxwell's bathroom that night in the suite.

"Yep," Jackson muttered and then looked away.

Minutes later and with little time to spare, the T1 team

walked back into the room they arrived in and formed their circle. In an instant the room was empty. The countdown reached zero and the order to forcefully enter the Papal apartment was given. As quickly as the six heat signatures had shown up on the monitor they were now gone. Only two were left. As the Italian Special Forces stormed in through doorways and windows and the lone skylight in the kitchen ceiling, standing alongside the Pope, Michelle raised her gun toward the first operative that entered the room. The Pope reached for the gun and yelled, "*non è caricato*!"

Three muffled shots rang out and Michelle fell to the floor.

The assault team immediately surrounded the Pope and began to rush him from the room but he insisted on going back to her.

"*Non è caricato*—it wasn't loaded," the Pope said in a hushed tone. "It wasn't loaded."

There, a few feet from where Michelle had fallen, the empty clip from her 9mm Beretta automatic weapon lay in the open. Members of the team searched the entire apartment looking for people, weapons, explosives, listening devices, anything that should not be there, or the intruders may have left behind, but they found nothing.

Taking a knee beside the Pope, the team leader asked, "Where are the six people who were here with you, Your Holiness?"

The team medic checked the woman lying on the floor and acknowledged that she was dead. The Pope placed his hand over Michelle's face to close her still eyes and then blessed her.

"God forgive me, and her, our sins," he said as he made the sign of the cross.

"Your Holiness, where are the six people that were here with you, who were they?" the team leader asked again.

The Pope stood, never taking his eyes from Michelle's now peaceful face.

"They were *my* guardian angels. God sent them to protect me, and they did," the Pontiff stated. "And now they are off to continue His work."

CHAPTER 18

"Well that was fucked up," White said somberly as tears ran down her cheeks.

They stood quietly in formation without breaking their circle for close to five minutes. Finally, one by one, the T1 team members stepped away and without anyone saying another word walked from the landing area at the BOTM hangar to their changing room down the hall. Jackson kept going though, turning into his office and slowly closing the door behind him.

After a call to the White House to brief the President, Jackson sat back in his desk chair and stared at the walls around him. His eyes swelled with tears. In all the times he had sat there planning missions and then recounting them he had never sat still long enough to notice much about the space. Much like his life, the focus had always been on the mission. On his gray metal government-issued desk sat a group photo of his T1 team, the original bunch that had confronted Hitler moments before young JR from Lake Havasu was killed in action. Alongside that was a photo that had been taken of him with Doctor Moretti at her birthday party at the local Olive Garden. He thought of how far she had come and what she had accomplished after being sent as a child from Italy by her father in hopes of finding a better life, of opportunity, in America. She found that and then some. A knock at the door interrupted his thoughts. He wiped his tears but the redness would remain.

"JJ, it's me," White said from the hallway.

"Come aboard," he responded in a softened tone.

In came White, then Sharif, and then Buchanan. The Rangers from T2 who had gone along for the rescue mission to Rome knew their place. Out of respect, and with Buchanan's permission, they had already left the hangar to find a beer or solace of some other kind and consider what they had just been a part of.

As the three poured into the small office space they too began to look around at the items that decorated the walls. For all the years they had been working together at Andrews, they had spent most of their time in the briefing room next door or out on missions but hardly any in Jackson's space. A photo of Jackson at his high school graduation posing with Elizabeth and Dick Stewart hung on the wall facing the desk. Another photo, this one of Tommy Wilson throwing a ball to their infamous German shepherd, the seventy-four-year-old, Bunker.

"Michelle took that one," Jackson said somberly. "God, she used to have so much love for them, for all of us."

The four of them continued to gaze at the various photos.

"That one there, of the Missouri in Tokyo Bay, is something special. Standing on those decks with old man Griffiths and watching as the beaten bastards bowed in defeat was incredible."

The tension and confusion in Rome had been overwhelming, at least for the three who had saved Michelle years before. There before them was the smiling face of their dear friend whom they had seen evolve from being the life of the party to near death, and then to survive only to become an assassin for a spiritual leader of millions.

"You just can't make this shit up," Sharif said.

"So we call this episode Suicide by Swiss Guard?" White uttered.

The room fell silent as the four continued to look at the photos, but it was clear emotions were numbed by this latest excursion. There was no reason to debate the decisions that were made at the scene. They could have left one person behind and transported Michelle back to Andrews but what would they have done with her then? How would they have explained the Marine left in her place?

Jackson jumped up from his chair, grabbed Michelle's photo from the desk, and threw it against the wall.

"Fuck!"

The others stood silent until Sharif said,

"JJ, you're going to have to pay for that frame, it's Air Force property."

Another time, the line should have brought laughter back into the room. It didn't but it was time to move forward.

"JJ, have you given any thought to anyone claiming her body?" White asked.

Jackson thought for a moment and then nodded.

"All taken care of, Christy," he responded.

"Before we left the Pope promised me that he would allow us to have her body flown home, back out West, where I'll have her buried with Tommy and her parents." Jackson paused.

"He's a man of his word and I know he'll make it happen,

especially if POTUS adds a little help from the United States Air Force."

Jackson thought for a moment.

"I told the Pope that his secret was safe with us and I would sit down with him again some day to tell him what I could about our missions. But he is sworn to secrecy and I think he knows that this is one group he, and nobody else, would want to break a promise to."

Considering all that they had done, who they had met, and where they had traveled, not just as part of the extraordinary Black Ops Time Machine program, but as some of the American military's finest even before their top secret assignment, their lives were nearly complete. They all chose the Marine Corps and service to their country over everything else. No children, one failed marriage, and few regrets left the four of them; the question everyone was considering but not addressing was brought up with two simple words.

"What's next?" Jackson asked. "Considering it all, I think it might be time to go on one last adventure."

"JJ, fuck that, you're not thinking about that trip to hell on a chariot of fire are you?" Sharif asked, only half joking.

"I was kidding about going straight after Satan!"

"Hell no!" Jackson said as he sat back down in his chair.

"I have something better in mind. We're going to do something special. We're going to help someone."

Over the next twenty minutes he laid it out for them. Without hesitating, they all signed on with a great deal of enthusiasm. It would be the medicine they needed to begin the healing from Rome.

Declining White's invitation to go commiserate over a few beers, Jackson suggested they all go unwind however they needed but asked Buchanan to remain behind to talk a bit more. Closing the door as White and Sharif said their goodbyes, Jackson invited Buchanan to take a seat.

"You know, we never discussed what happened that night in Maxwell's suite," Jackson began.

"Technically that was a top secret op that I am not permitted to discuss, sir," Buchanan responded. He had been wary of repercussions to his military career, or even criminal prosecution if details of the mission Brooks had assigned him ever became public and was reluctant to discuss them now, even with his commanding officer.

Jackson smiled.

"Our little band of brothers, *and sister*, has always had and always will have each other's backs. I can assure you, with everything I've done in my career since taking over BOTM, what happens in here stays in here," Jackson assured him.

Buchanan looked deeply into Jackson's eyes. They were brothers in arms and had always done what they believed was best for their country and for their fellow Marines. They had worked well together, fought, partied, laughed, and cried together since Jackson and Tommy Wilson handpicked him to replace JR on the T1 team.

"He slipped on the soap, JJ," Buchanan said, and then raised his right hand ever so slightly as if to show more was coming. "I admit I went in there to very discreetly knock him on his ass but he must have seen my shadow and turned toward me. It was obvious I scared the shit out of him and when he jerked in surprise his feet went out from under him and his head hit the wall hard and he was gone."

Jackson wanted more and the look on his face showed it.

"That's it, JJ," Buchanan said. "I checked him, he was gone. I left the bathroom and joined the circle and we were out of there in seconds."

"What would you have done if the Secret Service had stormed in and saw you all standing there?" Jackson asked. His tone had softened.

"Not sure, JJ," he responded. "Guess I could ask the same thing of you. What would you have done if the Roman soldiers showed up in the Garden while you there that first night?"

"Not sure either. I guess we both would have had to make a split second decision but that's why we get the big bucks right?" Jackson joked.

"So you know, JJ, my dad used to rough up my mother while me and my brother lay in our beds and listened to it night after night," Buchanan muttered. "We've all done things we may have regretted in life but one thing for sure, and I know this about you, and Tommy, and the President and the rest of our little band – none of us will tolerate bullies, especially those taking their shit out on the innocent!"

"Damn straight," Jackson said as he stood up. "Now let's go. I need a beer."

CHAPTER 19

THE BREAKING NEWS appeared on every medium around the world;

STEWART RESIGNS; WILLIAMS BECOMES FIRST WOMAN AMERICAN PRESIDENT

Once the decision had been made by Stewart to resign without advance notice, the President spent five minutes in the residence running through his farewell address to the nation before heading down to the Oval Office. Jackson and Kennedy accompanied him. Emma opted to remain behind in the residence, making sure the last minute packing of the President's most personal belongings and a week's worth of casual shirts, blue jeans, walking shoes and hiking boots were complete. She would accompany them downstairs and across to the south exit where the arrival of Marine One was due very shortly.

Sitting behind his desk for perhaps the last time, President Richard Stewart waited for the director to count down to start the recording and then begin to deliver what he intended to be the last speech or address he would ever make.

With only Jackson, COS, Williams, her husband Rob, and Chief Justice Katharine Malone, Agent Hill, the director, a still photographer, and two camera operators, Stewart watched the director as she counted down with her fingers, 3, 2, 1 and pointed to the President.

"My fellow Americans," Stewart began. "It has been the greatest honor to serve my country as a United States Marine, Chairman of the Joint Chiefs of Staff, and now as your President. A very short time ago, I was diagnosed with Alzheimer's disease. As many of you may be aware, this disease is incurable and the particular type of dementia that I have been diagnosed with is very fast in its development and will render me unable to fulfill my duties as your President. Therefore, here in the Oval Office I have signed my formal resignation papers and they are being delivered to the leaders up at the Capitol as I speak. I have decided that my final mission is to be a private one. After this evening you shouldn't expect to see much of me and I ask that you respect my request for privacy."

Jackson stood proudly as he watched his mentor, the man who had saved him from the brink so many years before, speak with the class and dignity that was emblematic of the man's character and demeanor. Listening to each word, he gazed around the room and caught himself remembering the day they were reunited. He had wondered how this would all end, when it would come, but smiled knowing what was planned for Stewart's immediate future.

"So, I want to thank you all for your trust and support in the good times and in the bad. Don't worry about me. I'll be in good hands, in the Lord's. I ask you to pray for each other, pray for our country and the world, and pray for your next President of the United States, Vice President Joan Williams."

With that, Stewart pushed his chair back, stood, and then walked around to the front of the desk. There, with cameras recording their every move, Williams took the oath of office. Once congratulations, hugs, and handshakes were exchanged Stewart looked to Jackson and it was clear it was time to proceed with the plan.

"Well, Madam President," Stewart said beaming with pride, "I have to say it is a privilege and an honor to have handed the baton to you as the nation's first woman Chief Justice swore in our country's first woman President. When I asked you to be my running mate back at the convention I had no idea this would all come about this way but I did know one thing – that you were as capable a candidate this country has ever had and I know without hesitation or reservation that you will do an incredible job."

The moment was not lost on the new President either. While she was energized with adrenaline at becoming the most powerful woman, the most powerful person in the world, she was sad that the man she had come to admire was leaving in this way. She had felt all along that her time would come but not like this.

"Stew, Mr. President, thank you for putting your trust in me and if there is anything any of us can do to help you on your journey, anything at all, you or JJ here just need to ask."

Everything was on schedule, and perhaps ahead of schedule due to the brevity of Stewart's speech. It would be Williams' turn next, to stand before the cameras and tape her first address to the nation and to the world. The White House Press Office would release the videos in one hour and it was Stewart's intention to be far from Washington when the news hit.

"Thank you, Joan, I meant to say, Madam President," Stewart responded. He could hear the sound of Marine One as it landed on the South Lawn. Gone were the massive high walls that the plague of terrorism had forced to be raised. The guard towers were reduced as well. Drone operators and security teams now oversaw remotely controlled weapons, single sniper shots that could knock a bee off of a flower, lasers, sound generators, or massive ones capable of destroying a glider or a 747 stood atop light posts and on rooftops surrounding the White House.

"And now it's time for me to start that journey." As the former President left the Oval Office for the last time, Jackson following closely behind, they stopped in the doorway for one look back.

"You'll be back," Stewart whispered to Jackson and then, with little fanfare, Stewart left the White House for the last time.

Aboard Marine One as the helicopter rose from the South Lawn and flew over the mall and then the Jefferson Memorial and the bridge that led to Arlington National Cemetery, Stewart leaned forward in his seat and gestured for Jackson to come closer.

"Only a few know this but last night, just after dusk, Hill and I rode up to see Elizabeth one last time," he said and then looked out the window at the view below them. Jackson acknowledged with a nod, a look of sadness registered in his eyes.

"I would have asked you to come but you never have in the past, JJ," Stewart continued. "May I ask why?"

Jackson smiled and then looked out the window for a moment to gather his thoughts.

"I haven't even been to my parents' graves since Dad's funeral. No, you both took me there on that first Memorial Day. That's when you introduced me to the President and he expressed his condolences." He looked back out the window as Stewart sat back in his seat.

"I know where they really are, watching over me from above. Up there with Elizabeth and Matt." Stewart smiled.

"Plus, there are so many heroes at Arlington I feel if I visit anyone I have to visit them all and that would take forever—400,000 graves give or take. It pisses me off how many people walk through those gates, go take a picture at JFK's grave, and don't bother to stop for one moment to visit anyone else's. If it weren't for the fallen, so many of those people, including you and me, would be living in a much different world today."

"Well said, JJ," Stewart said, "Well said."

Emma was sitting across from the men. She never took her eyes from the window and neither of the men noticed the tears that ran down her cheeks as she listened to their every word.

Thirty minutes later, as the helicopter carrying the now former President and the two diversion choppers all landed at Andrews, Stewart, Emma, Jackson, and Hill climbed into a black SUV and headed for Air Force One. As seven other SUVs continued on, the one carrying Stewart slowly pulled from the formation and drove to the BOTM hangar.

"One more God-damned meeting!" Stewart protested jokingly as he climbed from the SUV. "Keep the engine running!"

Jackson walked ahead of him, and Emma followed. Hill

and the driver would wait there as the other agents went ahead to the hangar that housed the President's matching 747s. As was customary, one of those birds would carry the former President wherever in the world he wanted to go only on this last trip it would fly without the designation of Air Force One. Stewart had another means of travel in mind at the moment though.

After greeting their former President, White, Sharif, and Buchanan led him into the room where their next mission, Stewart's second time travel adventure, would begin. Secretary Petty and National Security Director Morrison were already there with the BOTM operational team to show their continued support and witness the departure.

Jackson had prepared Emma for what was to come. At first, she had been exasperated that he had come up with such a ridiculous story while their dear friend was dealing with his incurable diagnosis. But once she heard where they were going, believing in the technology or not, she signed on saying, "I trust you two but if you're playing a game I'll be serving you a last supper when we get back!"

The six operatives formed the circle. Emma looked across at White, who she had met only once before. White gave her a wink and a smile and told her to take a deep breath and let it out. As she did, Jackson counted down 3, 2, 1 and they were gone.

They landed on the outskirts of Edinburgh, Scotland in the family room of his maternal grandparents' home. It was mid-November 2005. As he had expected, Stewart found the night nurse fast asleep in the room next to his mother's. His mother's time on earth was coming to an end and while Stewart had tried his best over the years to move her closer to him where he and Elizabeth could have looked after her, she insisted living out her years in the house she was born in. She had spent the last sixty quietly carrying the heart-breaking belief that her brother had been a coward. It had brought shame to her parents who had been ostracized by the community and they had sent her away to America to start a new life where people wouldn't know her name. As they aged, prematurely because of the mental strain, she had left America and her son, a decorated U.S. Marine, and went home to Scotland to care for them.

"Why she stayed here after her parents died instead of coming home I will never know," Stewart whispered to Emma.

"She was home," she responded.

White took her place outside the nurse's room while Buchanan and Sharif headed for the front door. It was the middle of the night and they weren't expecting any visitors, but theirs was standard operating procedure and they stuck to it. The hardwood floor creaked under Sharif's steps but White gave him a thumbs up to continue, the nurse was fast asleep. As Stewart walked to his mother's bedside he knelt down and smiled as he watched her in peaceful sleep. Emma and Jackson stayed at the doorway, there to support him but giving him the privacy the moment deserved.

"Mother," he whispered. "Mother, it's me, your son Richard."

Slowly her eyes opened slightly. As they adjusted to the little light there was in the room she recognized her son. He looked different, older, but she knew the voice and she saw herself in his eyes. But his appearance, her age, and her weakened mental state left her visibly confused.

"It's me, Mother, it really is," he said as he took her hand. "I've come a long way to tell you something. I was able to find out what I could about Uncle Roy. You remember your brother Roy, don't you?"

Stewart could see the enthusiasm in her eyes at first recognizing him was now dimming.

"Mother, I was able to find out that Roy was not a coward in the war. I found out that he did jump that night; he did jump out of that airplane and was a hero. He was a hero, Mom, he truly was."

He went on to tell her everything they had learned from their trip back in time June 6th, 1944 to that airfield in England. He just didn't tell her, couldn't tell her, how they had found out. He told her of a report from the pilot about Roy Stewart's heroic jump over France that night during Operation Overlord, the D-Day invasion.

"We found notes from the pilot of his plane," he told her. "Do you understand what I am saying? Roy was a hero."

What he didn't tell her was that the plane and crew were shot down and killed on the supply run and there were no notes ever made.

Her hand tightened in his and her eyes seemed to light up now, even more than when she recognized her son was there with her.

"Roy boy," she said with a fondness. "Roy boy and my Richard," she said in an even softer tone. Stewart felt her hand slowly loosen. He had felt that in life many times before, on the battlefield and at Camp David. She was gone.

Jackson looked at Emma and saw the flow of tears streaking her cheeks. It was a beautiful moment, and he felt honored to have been there to be a part of it. As Stewart placed his mother's hand down on her blanket, he brushed her gray hair and then stood up, his eyes never leaving hers.

He remained there quietly for nearly a minute and then made the sign of the cross.

Turning to his friends, he said in a softened tone, "Time to go now." A minute later, their travel circle complete, they were back at Andrews. Tears soon turned to laughter to cut the tension as was customary with this crew. Tears, hugs, and handshakes were the order of the day until Sharif noticed something.

"What the hell's that?" Sharif asked as he pointed to the magazine Emma was holding. She had taken a souvenir and that broke protocol.

"We're going to have to send you back, Emma," Stewart said firmly, tears still fresh in his eyes.

"Yeah, no soup for you!" Sharif said with a laugh.

Petty and Morrison had remained there having been assured the mission would last, should only last, a few hours. They had settled into the briefing room making calls and working emails until they heard a BOTM technician call out, "they're back!"

"Welcome home, Mr. President," Petty exclaimed.

"I'm back to General now, Mr. Secretary," Stewart responded with a wink.

"I have news for you all, big news. Doronin has been found dead in a bath tub at his estate outside of Moscow!" Petty continued.

All eyes turned to Buchanan who quickly said with a smile, "Wasn't me!"

"No, no, it wasn't us," Morrison offered. "Our intel reports that his wife found Doronin in the shower with another woman who was playing with the plumbing. Reports are that both of the bathers slipped and didn't survive the fall."

Stewart and Jackson locked eyes and nodded their approval.

"That's not all, Mr. President – I mean General Stewart," Morrison continued. "The Pope has announced his retirement, effective immediately, citing health reasons. The Cardinals will assemble in two days for a conclave at the Vatican to vote in his successor."

Jackson stepped back from the circle to look at Stewart. Since the inception of the BOTM program many had debated its pros and cons and whether it should have been used at all, for any purpose. Tonight had been a good night, a good trip and aside from Emma's contraband it had been an enriching experience for them all.

"Okay, now what?" Stewart asked. "I guess it's time to get on board one of those big birds out there and figure out where the heck we go next. I'd also like to call Mrs. Doronin and offer my condolences. Her husband was an ass but she has grit. I always enjoyed our conversations. Elizabeth liked her too." Stewart paused. "And I want to speak with His Holiness."

Jackson smiled and asked his team to huddle up in the circle once more.

"Before we do that, Mr. President, we came up with some other suggestions for you. How about we spare us all some jet lag and you choose from the following options?"

It had been a long day and night but recognizing there might not be that many of them left for him, Stewart encouraged Jackson and the team to proceed.

"First choice is A, where we go back to Honolulu in December of 1844 to use sniper rifles on some raiding pirates." Stewart was intrigued.

"Or there's option B. We all think it's finally time for you to see your hero Abe Lincoln up close and personal, maybe a little ride to Gettysburg, Pennsylvania on November 19, 1863. We've got the proper attire right down the hall in the changing room."

"You sure you don't want to take a break and rest up a bit Mr. President?" Petty suggested.

"We'll have plenty of time for that when we're dead," Stewart replied with a smile.

"What have you gotten me into?" Emma said, astonished by the suggestions.

"Then there's option C. The pyramids always fascinated you. Want to go watch a few being built? Some people think the aliens did it so who knows, maybe we'll run into Doc Moretti while we're there," Jackson added.

"You already know the answer, JJ," Stewart responded with a grin. "I choose D, all of the above – but let's do Hawaii last. I hear the beaches are spectacular and I always wanted to spend a Christmas there."

Petty stepped forward and assured the team.

"We'll leave this area staffed and secure until you all return safely. Morrison and I need to get back to Washington but you all enjoy the ride."

Stewart turned and shook Petty's hand.

"Adios, my friend" Stewart said in a softened tone.

Moments later, they were gone.

THE END

Made in the USA
Middletown, DE
19 April 2024

53229821R00148